THE LIFE
OF JOE BEELER,
UPPER MIDWEST TRADER

LAWRENCE DIEDRICH

LITTLE CREEK PRESS
AND BOOK DESIGN
Mineral Point, Wisconsin USA

Copyright © 2018 Lawrence Diedrich

Little Creek Press®
A Division of Kristin Mitchell Design, Inc.
5341 Sunny Ridge Road
Mineral Point, Wisconsin 53565

Book Design and Project Coordination:
Little Creek Press

First Printing
October 2018

All rights reserved

No part of this book may be used or reproduced in any manner whatsoever without written permission from the author.

Printed in Wisconsin, United States of America

For more information or to order books:
or visit www.littlecreekpress.com

Library of Congress Control Number: 2018957898

ISBN-10: 1-942586-49-3
ISBN-13: 978-1-942586-49-4

DEDICATION

To the memory of Annie Diedrich

ACKNOWLEDGEMENTS

Bonnie Trahan-True
Karl Trahan-True
Edward Brandsey
Larry Layne
Rita Layne

ABOUT THE AUTHOR

Larry Diedrich worked as a Manufacturing Engineer for Instrument Company in Middleton, WI and resided in Lodi, WI for 25 years.

In 1999, Larry and his spouse Annie retired to Heber Springs, Arkansas and settled into retirement enjoying the best years of 35 years that they were married.

Both Annie and Larry were pilots living in an airport community, Skypoint Estates and enjoyed the best it had to offer.

With their Aeronca Chief, they toured the Southern fly-ins. Their greatest trip was their two month honeymoon trip to Alaska with the Chief.

Tragedy struck nine years ago with the passing of Annie from cancer.

Larry immersed himself in the reenactment scene, attending many "rendezvous," meeting new people, gathering information which resulted in this book!

TABLE OF CONTENTS

Chapter One: The Early Years 6

Chapter Two: The North West Company of Montréal. 12

Chapter Three: Working for the North West Company 19

Chapter Four: On the Path of Self-Employment. 50

Chapter Five: Clouds of War and Relocation. 64

Chapter Six: The War of 1812. 75

Chapter Seven:
Post War Years and Restructuring of the Fur Trade 100

Chapter Eight: The Arkansas Country. 126

Chapter Nine: Relocation to Sylamore Arkansas Territory 178

Chapter Ten: Loss of Grandparents 202

Chapter Eleven: Tragedy Strikes and the Decline of the Beaver. . . . 214

Chapter Twelve: Rejoining of the Family and the Final Years 228

CHAPTER ONE
THE EARLY YEARS

Joseph Henry Beeler was born in 1780 at Conestoga Town Pennsylvania, the second child of George Peter Beeler and Caroline Frances Salzemann. He had four other siblings: an older brother and three younger sisters.

His father, George Peter Beeler, was a German Lutheran from around Lancaster Pennsylvania, born in 1759. He was well-educated (homeschooled) and had been apprenticed by his father to some of the gunsmiths around Lancaster to learn a trade. He also became an experienced tradesman and storekeeper.

His mother, Caroline Frances Salzemann, was a Swiss Mennonite from Baltimore, Maryland, born in 1761. She was from a well-educated family of teachers who were well-versed in elementary and higher education.

George and Caroline were married at the Salzemann residence in Baltimore in 1778. They then took up residence at Conestoga Town where George owned property inherited from his father.

The Beeler siblings included an older brother George; Joe; and three sisters, Germaine, Mary Elizabeth, and Doris. Unfortunately, tragedy struck when typhoid took George's life at the age of three, and measles took Doris's life at the age of one.

Conestoga Town was located about ten miles south of Lancaster, Pennsylvania, on the Susquehanna River. It was a hamlet of approximately 250 people situated on the main road from Lancaster to Baltimore pointing south, making a crossroad hub for traffic and trade.

George Beeler's property of approximately forty acres consisted of woods, pastures, and hayfields. He owned two horses, two cows, a two-story house of 1,200 square feet, a barn, and a shed structure where he had his gun shop and store business. His tax assessment was approximately 2,200 pounds.

George and Caroline's political views were with the patriots, not with the king. George was a member of the local state militia and was one of the many businessmen that supported Anthony Wayne and his light infantry regiment with supplies, thereby furthering the cause of the revolution.

These were tough times to be living in the Pennsylvania area with the revolution going on (i.e., loyalists, redcoats and Indian raids by the Delaware, Iroquois, and Shawnee). The war came close to them in 1779–1781 with raids on American settlements along the Susquehanna River by Mohawk leader Joseph Brant and Tory John Butler, notably the Cherry Valley and Wyoming Valley raids. But then again, these were tough times living up and down the entire Atlantic seaboard during the revolution.

With the revolution over in 1783 and the loss of little George to typhoid in the same year, the Beelers continued to struggle to make a living and repay the debts incurred during the war, mainly for supplies, to the Continental Army. (The script received from the Continental Congress was worthless.) With the loss of their youngest, little Doris, to measles in 1786, the Beelers decided it was time for a move to points west.

After selling their property in Conestoga Town and partially paying off their debts, they had enough money reserved to outfit themselves with a good team of mules and a good wagon to transport their household goods and other family belongings.

In the spring of 1787, traveling north and just west of Lancaster, Pennsylvania, they picked up the old John Forbes Road, which carried them all the way to the town of Fort Ligonier. (This road was constructed by Brigadier General John Forbes in 1758 for the second attempt to capture Fort Duquesne in the French and Indian War. The first attempt to capture Fort Duquesne was in 1755, which resulted in the defeat of General Braddock by the French and their Indian allies.)

After spending a month at Fort Ligonier utilizing business contacts from his gunsmith days in Conestoga Town, George was advised that the small town of Franklin, approximately sixty miles north of Pittsburgh up the Allegheny River to its confluence with French Creek, (the terminus of the old Venango Trace) was a good location providing opportunities to establish a trading and gunsmith business. He was advised by these contacts that there were Indian tribes to the west (Seneca, Cuyahoga, and Delaware) that were eager for trade. His gunsmith and blacksmith skills would provide a valuable service and repair of their tools. Also, there was an increasing settler population of Scot-Irish and German coming into the area.

Upon arriving at Pittsburgh, selling their mule team and Conestoga wagon, George contracted with a keelboat operator to transport the Beeler family and their belongings upriver to Franklin arriving there in July 1787.

Getting established in the trading and gunsmith business took about two years. The integrity and honesty of George and Caroline Beeler stood them well. Locally they were known as honest people with whom to do business. Also, Caroline, being educated and a good teacher and homeschooling her own kids, soon found herself taking in children of families from the surrounding area. George's honesty and fairness in dealing with his Indian customers also put him in good stead. Their family and business did well.

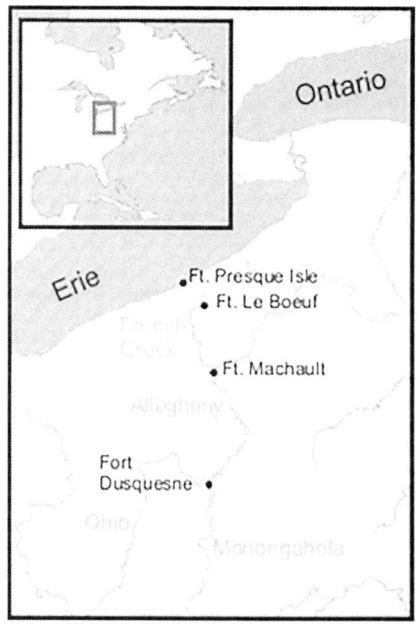

The Venango Trace

But there was trouble brewing on the horizon. In western Pennsylvania, a lot of the settlers were small farmers who grew grain, corn, alfalfa, and vegetable gardens along with livestock, which provided them substance. Having a couple of good years of weather provided crop surpluses, which were sold to provide other necessities the family needed for survival. Converting the surplus grain crops to alcohol cut down on transportation expenses to get this commodity to market. In essence, every farmer ran a still to produce the alcohol and was indirectly classified as a distiller.

This put George Beeler in a conundrum. The settler farmers who purchased the necessities they needed used the alcohol product as a medium of exchange. He didn't want to turn them away and hurt the business, so reluctantly, he took the alcohol product. His in-house inventory continued to increase. His Indian customers got wind of George's inventories, and some pushed George for alcohol. Caroline strongly insisted that George not do it. Being a good Christian man, he didn't!

The few Indian customers that pushed George for alcohol and were refused, being the bad apples that they were, started to sully George's reputation with rumors and lies about them being cheated in their dealings with him.

To reduce his inventory of alcohol, George contracted with his keelboat operator and a whiskey buyer in Pittsburgh to transport and buy his alcohol. After covering expenses, he was lucky to break even and at the most made about two to three cents per gallon.

In the spring of 1790 rumors were coming from the East. The new administration, under newly elected president George Washington's secretary of the treasury, Alexander Hamilton, was strongly pushing for a new tax of two to three cents per gallon on whiskey. This was justified because of the war debt of fifty-five million dollars the new government had assumed. The western farmers and distillers objected strongly because this put them in unfair competition with the big eastern distillers due to their transportation costs. In addition, with Spain now in control of the Mississippi River and New Orleans, which they closed (this was ceded to Spain by France at the end of the French and Indian War in 1763), the western farmers/distillers couldn't ship their products down the Ohio and Mississippi Rivers to New Orleans.

George saw this all coming. Concerned for his family and business, he informed Caroline it was time for another move, to which she agreed.

George had gotten to know some of the operatives including Thomas Frobisher and Duncan McGillivray of the North West Company of Montréal through the sale of fur obtained from his trading deals with his Indian customers. The company, northwesterners as they were known, had a port and trading base fifty miles north of Franklin at Presque Isle on Lake Erie. They liked George and offered him a job as a trader clerk, which he accepted.

The Franklin property was sold, and the move was made to Presque Isle. In September, the family and their belongings boarded the Northwest vessel The Beaver and were transported via Detroit to Mackinac Island in 1791. And a new chapter was opened.

Typical Great Lakes Schooner Used in the Fur Trade 1790 to 1820

CHAPTER TWO
THE NORTH WEST COMPANY
OF MONTRÉAL

The North West Company of Montréal was a fur trade consortium, formally established between 1778 and 1780. Its biggest competitor was the Hudson Bay Company, established in 1680 by the royal charter of King James II. His brother Prince Rupert was, so to speak, the CEO. The territory controlled by the Hudson Bay Company consisted primarily of factories located on the James Bay and Hudson Bay shorelines. The company was very conservative in its methods of field operation. That is, they encouraged the Indian tribes to bring their furs to the factory locations to conduct their trade. The Indian tribes were not happy with this arrangement because of the long yearly trips involved, but they put up with it until competing traders and companies entered their territories. This all changed with the conclusion of the French and Indian War, the French leaving, and the vacuum being filled by the British traders in 1763.

Initially, the British traders were stopped by Pontiac's War in 1763. The Indians, left out as usual by the Paris Treaty of 1763, attempted to redress their grievances by Pontiac's Rebellion. They did pretty well considering they took all of their objectives except for Detroit and Niagara. They did get the attention of the British military and politicos in London which resulted in the Treaty of Fort Stanwix brokered by Sir William Johnson, the chief British Indian agent in North America, in 1768. It essentially drew a north-south line west of the Alleghenies to preserve all Indian lands west of this line from colonial settlement and expansion. As usual, this treaty was full of potholes and raised more issues than it solved.

The list of British traders that entered the fur trade of the old Northwest and Upper Canada after 1768 was remarkable in that a decade later most were principal players in the North West Company. Some of those names were Alexander Henry; Joseph, Benjamin, and Thomas Frobisher; Simon McTavish; and Peter Pond. Most were Scottish Highlanders, except for Peter Pond, who was a Connecticut Yankee.

The traders pretty much followed the old French trails and streams, settling their trading posts on or around the old French trading sites including Detroit, Mackinaw, and Grand Portage, and by the time of the American Revolution in 1775, the fur trade was putting approximately 200,000 pounds per year through Montréal and New York.

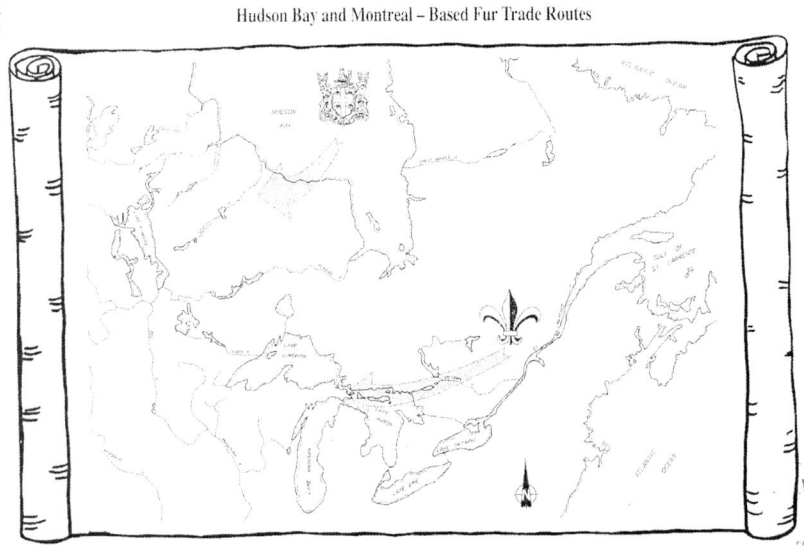

The traders also learned, some the hard way and some the easy way, what it took to have a good trade relationship with the Indian tribes, such as the giving of gifts, the joining of the feast, and marriage into the tribe. As with any good human relationship, being a part of the family has its advantages, which usually far outweigh the disadvantages.

The American Revolution caused some disruptions in the fur trade, such as the military control of the Great Lakes and an embargo on buying goods from the colonies, forcing all goods to be imported from the mother country. Sharp businessmen, however, always found ways around these obstacles. Mainly, the groundwork was laid by the original traders. Most of the business was funneled through Montréal, thereby making it the center of commerce in the fur trade.

The broker/buyers in Montréal put in yearly orders for trade goods to manufacturers in England where the orders were filled and delivered by ship to Montréal the following spring. The goods were broken down and loaded aboard thirty-six-foot Montréal canoes manned by contract voyageurs (French/Canadian farm boys) for delivery to Mackinac Island and Grand Portage on the north shore of Lake Superior. Here the goods were repackaged into ninety-pound packs, loaded in the twenty-five-foot Northern canoes for delivery to the outposts located in the tribal territories. The winterers or hibernators would do the trading with the tribes for the furs. In the spring, the traded pelts would be bailed and packaged into ninety-pound packs and returned to Mackinac or primarily Grand Portage for the exchange of new trade goods that were returned to Montréal for eventual shipment for sale in New York or London. Then the cycle repeated itself for another year.

Being centrally located, Grand Portage became the main hub in this yearly cycle. In about 1782, the North West Company's first general meeting and grand rendezvous was held in the great hall at Grand Portage and continued until 1802.

From 1778 to 1780, the competition was fierce and costly between the competing companies. It was decided that it would be in the best interests of all concerned to join forces, and the North West Company was the result. A total of twenty shares were divided between the investors. The major shareholders were the Simon McTavish and Frobisher Companies of Montréal. The principals of these companies were Simon McTavish and Joseph, Benjamin and Thomas Frobisher with eleven shares. All had earned their spurs in the business during the early years following 1768.

In 1787, Benjamin Frobisher died. He was the Montréal business head for Frobisher Company, and Joe was the fieldsman with Thomas, a competent trader. Smelling opportunity, the "marquis" Simon McTavish approached Joe Frobisher and proposed a partnership between the two companies. Joe accepted. The McTavish, Frobisher and Company was born. With their eleven shares in the North West Company, McTavish and Frobisher became the company's sole Montréal agent. To control the London end of the trade, he formed a partnership with John Frazier (a family member) known as McTavish, Frazier and Company. He also recruited an up-and-coming businessman named John Jacob Astor to import North West Company furs to New York. The structure of the company was broken down as follows: The Montréal brokers at the top were full partners who controlled the majority of the shares. Next, the winterers or hibernators who were full partners held one or two shares at the most. Then the trader clerks with no shares were not partners. Clerk interpreters were under the trader clerks, and the contract voyageurs and laborers were at the bottom. The trader clerks could expect an income of 100 to 300 pounds per year and the remote possibility of becoming a full partner. The clerk interpreters could expect an income of 50 to 100 pounds per year. And the voyageurs could break even or expect 20 to 30 pounds per year. In most cases, after paying back their debts to the company for goods consumed over the year, most of them were still in debt or, if lucky, broke even.

The company also had an apprentice program for young gentlemen clerks and training that ran for seven years which paid, in total, the princely sum of 100 pounds. Some of the employees considered this outright servitude or slavery. Either way, there were a lot of takers for this program.

The gentleman clerks in training were young literate boys of fifteen to twenty years old, first time away from home, free from the discipline of parents, and left to their own devices to pick up the "yin and yang" foibles of being an adult. Some of them made it, to carry their own water so to speak, and some of them didn't. The ones that made it usually spent their lives working for the company or other companies, having families (taking an Indian or Métis wife), and spending twenty-five to thirty years in the field as a hibernator. Some even became partners in the company with one share. The ones that didn't make the cut usually ended up back home with their families or ended up somewhere on the outside of the law.

From a business sense, the organization was an unmitigated disaster, but it worked! And the North West Company gave the Hudson Bay Company a run for its money.

A short note on the political situation in the year 1792. After the Treaty of Paris in 1783, there were many unsettled issues and differences. In the old Northwest Territory, the British garrisons never left Forts Oswego, New York, Niagara, Detroit, Mackinac, Prairie du Chien, and Vincennes. Unofficially, the justification for this was the unpaid debts (Tory properties confiscated and destroyed by patriots) incurred during the war. Thin you might say, but it worked because the young American nation had problems east of the Alleghenies to resolve and minimum resources to do it with. The fur trade was open-ended to British and American Yankees and the tribes involved, but the truth was the British fur men were taking furs from American soil and getting away with it. The international border wasn't even defined at this time.

This all changed with Jay's Treaty of 1796 when two issues were resolved. The first issue was the removal of British garrisons from the above described forts along with free access by citizens of both nations, including the Indian tribes to the old Northwest Territory and Upper/Lower Canada to conduct business and trade. The second issue were the issues of war debts and the undefined international border which was sent to arbitration for resolution. Primarily, the treaty normalized trade relations between the U.S. and Britain and kept the U.S. out of French influence. (The French Revolution was ongoing at this time.) The politics of the ongoing issue in Washington at that time is beyond the scope of this story. The treaty was to be in effect for ten years, terminating in 1805–1806.

Pinckney's Treaty of 1795 with Spain also had an effect on the trade business in the old Northwest Territories because it opened up the Mississippi River and the Port of New Orleans to American trade.

Because of these two treaties, the major issue for the North West Company was what they were going to do about the relocation of their two major centers of operation, namely Grand Portage and Mackinac Island when the international border was defined. In 1792 this was a major concern, but one to be resolved in two or three years.

This was the world George Beeler and his family entered when they arrived at Mackinac Island in September 1791.

CHAPTER THREE
WORKING FOR THE
NORTH WEST COMPANY

The family spent the winter of 1791–1792 getting settled in at Mackinac Island. George's time was spent learning the business operations of the North West Company's Southern District which covered the Michigan, Indiana, and Illinois country. From Mackinac Island south to Fort Dearborn, southwest along the Illinois River to Peoria, straight west to the Des Moines River confluence with the Mississippi, then north past Prairie du Chien to the mouth to the Minnesota (St. Peter) River, then straight east across present-day Wisconsin to Green Bay.

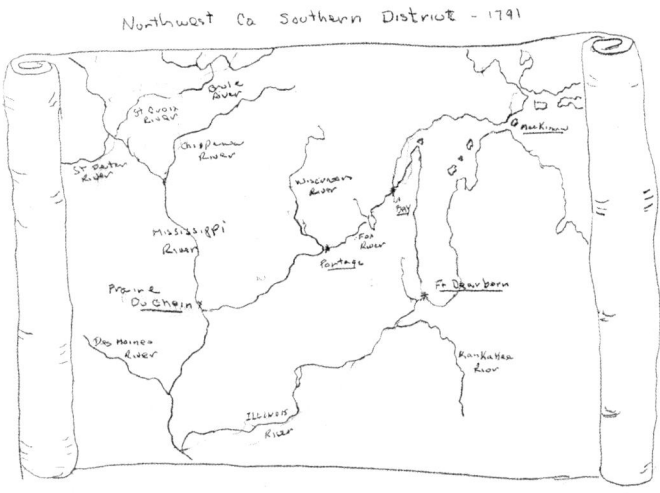

In the spring of 1792, George's first posting was to the company post at La Bay (Green Bay, Wisconsin). It was decided by George and Caroline that young Joe would go with his father, and the two girls, Germaine and Mary Beth, would remain with their mother at Mackinac.

With her background as a teacher, Caroline soon found herself immersed in the job of educating the children of the Mackinac community and the British garrison posted at the fort, which provided the family with a good source of income.

George spent the early spring and summer of 1792 settling the winterer accounts, inventorying pelts, food shipments from Detroit, and setting up trade deals for food and canoes with the Menominee Indians in the vicinity of La Bay (Green Bay) for the coming winter.

Common Trade Goods

This list is derived from a compilation of various fur trade journals and is not exhaustive. Many "trade goods" were also used for non-reciprocal gift giving, an important consideration in any trader's equipment.

Blankets	Axes
Capotes (blanket coats)	Files
Chief's coats (ornamental)	Fishing nets & twine
Chief's shirts	Fire steels
Calico cloth	Vermilion (powder for body paint)
Cloth Leggings	Rum, diluted and mixed
Ribboning	High Wine
Thread	Clay smoking pipes
Sewing supplies	Firearms (flintlock muskets & pistols)
Mirrors	Gun flints
Beads	Gun Worms
Brass and copper ornaments	Priming wire
Trade silver/jewelry	Brass & copper kettles (nested)

By late June, the fur bales had been marked and loaded on the company schooner, the Athabasca, and George and little Joe arrived at Mackinac. Within a week, he and Joe along with Duncan McGillivray, the Mackinac post factor, were on their way to Grand Portage for the North West Company annual meeting and powwow. They met most of the company luminaries, Simon McTavish, the Frobishers, and the Mackenzie cousins Alexander and Roderick. As usual, the internal politics of the company was a major part of the annual meeting, but George, as one of the newbies, kept his involvement to a minimum and observed, a skill at which he was excellent.

Early September found George and Joe back at La Bay (Green Bay). Before leaving Mackinac, George and Caroline again decided it would be best if she and the two girls continue to remain there, for security and their education. Caroline was established in the community as a teacher and had up to a dozen children in her classroom. Joe, as the oldest, went with his father. It provided an opportunity for him to learn about the fur trade business from his father and the skills to survive in it.

Caroline and daughter Mary Elizabeth

Joe Beeler was twelve years old and in the company of his father who was first posted to La Bay in 1792. During the next three years, young Joe learned the ins and outs of doing business with the main customers, the Indians.

Late fall of 1792 found George taking three canoes and twelve men down to a place called "The Portage" located where the Fox River and Wisconsin River are only about a mile apart. He had the crew build wintering quarters on the east bank of the Fox River where the portage trail began. This location was set up roughly in the middle of the Ho-Chunk (Winnebago) people and today is the city of Portage, Wisconsin.

It was a mild winter that year. Trade was brisk and profitable. George earned the respect of the Indians by being fair and consistent. He didn't follow the usual company practice of using rum for trade. Expecting their rum, the Indians were upset at first. Fortunately, the ones with common sense won out over the knuckleheads that didn't. It was fair, consistent, and firm practices that prevailed in dealing with them, and George was respected for it. In fact, it was his men that he had the hardest time keeping in line and disciplining when they got too far into their cups. He had to physically bang a few heads together, but eventually even the "thickest" came to realize that life under George's management wasn't too bad.

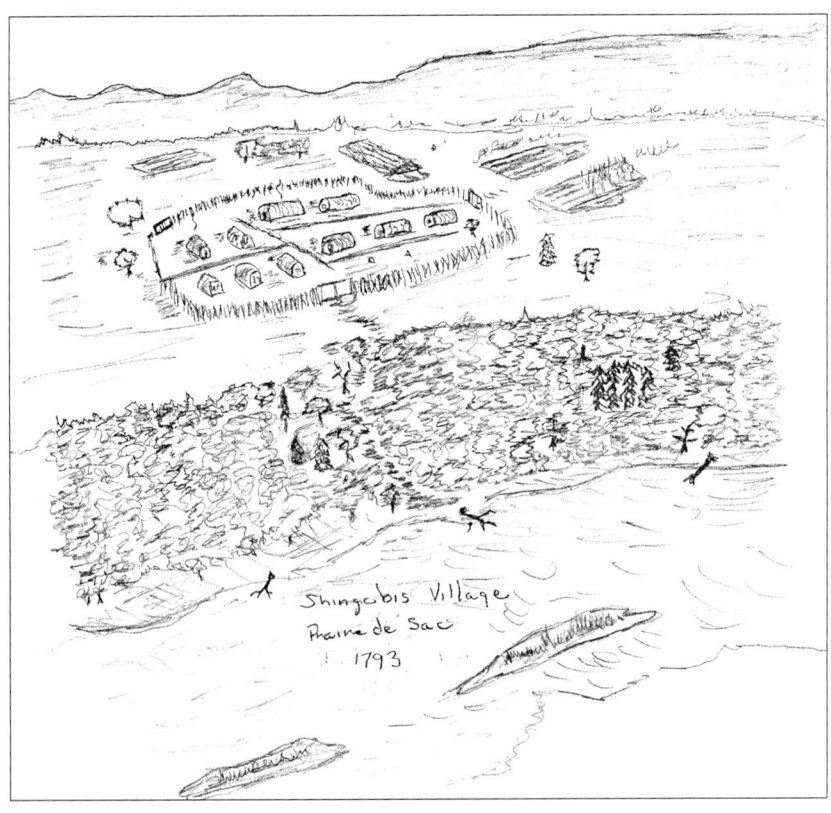

The mild winter allowed George to take a canoe and five men along with young Joe to make some local side trips to get to know the country and the people. About twenty miles southwest down the Wisconsin River they found a Sauk village of ten longhouses (approximately 120 people) situated on the high west bank of the river. Today the village is the city of Prairie du Sac, Wisconsin. This was the village of Shingabis, and it became an important part of young Joe's life.

Sauk Chief Shingabis

It was here that he met and got to know a little eleven-year-old Métis girl that went by the name Magpie. Her Christian name was Anita, the same as her mother. Her stepfather was Shingabis, and she had two stepbrothers who were also her first cousins. Let's explain the connection.

Anita, the mother of Annie, or Magpie as she was commonly known, and her twin sister, Celeste, were born in 1764 of a French father and Fox mother. Anita met a Sicilian trader in 1780 by the name of Francisco Alberti whom she married. They settled in the village of Ste. Genevieve located in the old Spanish Missouri Territory on the west side of the Mississippi River approximately fifty miles south of St. Louis. They had one daughter, little Anita/Annie/Magpie born August 1, 1781. Two years later in 1783, Francisco passed away of typhoid, leaving Anita and little Annie to fend for themselves. Adding to Anita's daily troubles, she and her twin sister Celeste were strikingly good-looking women. Anita had her hands full keeping the "tomcats" at bay and away from herself and little Annie.

Anita's twin sister, Celeste, met and married Shingabis the head man/

civil chief of the Sauk village at Prairie du Sac in 1779. This union produced two sons, Stone Hawk in 1781 and Porcupine in 1783. Celeste, upon hearing of the death of her sister's husband, Francisco Alberti, and knowing they had no one to provide for them, prevailed upon her husband Shingabis to bring them back home to Prairie du Sac, which he did in the fall and winter of 1783–1784.

Tragedy struck again when in the winter of 1785, Celeste passed away due to complications of malaria and pneumonia leaving a grieving and fractured family, a widow with a daughter, and a widower with two young sons. So, in 1787, Anita married Shingabis, and the family was joined together once again.

Mother Anita and Little Magpie/Annie

The Sauk people were from a territory on the south side of the St. Lawrence River and Lake Ontario in western New York State. Due to the pressures from the Iroquois and the Wyandot tribes during the beaver wars of the mid-seventeenth century, they migrated to northern Illinois/southern Wisconsin areas where we find them in the latter years of the eighteenth century.

The Sauk had a patrilineal clan system, that is descent was traced through the father. The families were formed into different clans, (i.e., fish, thunder, bear, deer, snow, wolf, etc.) The tribe was governed by a council of sacred clan chiefs, a war chief, the head of the families, and the warriors. These fell into three categories: civil, war, and ceremonial. Only the civil chief was hereditary. The other two chiefs were determined by demonstrating their ability for war and their ability with spiritual power.

The Sauk were closely allied with the Fox who were noted for their hostility toward the French, having fought two wars against them in the early eighteenth century. After the second war, the Fox took shelter with the Sauk having been decimated by the French.

By the end of the eighteenth century in the 1790s, the main bodies of the two tribes had relocated to western Illinois at the confluence of the Rock and Mississippi Rivers in a village called Saukenuk. Shingabis's band, which was of the Snow/Wolf clan, was one of the few large bands left in Wisconsin.

The Sauk were farmers and hunters. The women cultivated corn, pumpkins, melons, chili peppers, and onions. As hunters, they made yearly forays onto the plains of Kansas, Nebraska, southwestern Minnesota, western Iowa, and western Missouri to hunt buffalo. Naturally, through the New Mexican/Spanish trade connection, they obtained horses and the necessary equipment, including saddles, bridles, lariats, and other necessaries required in the use of horses and became very proficient in the use thereof.

Passing west through Osage, Pawnee, and Lakota lands did not endear them to these tribes. But the Sauk warriors were proficient horsemen and quickly gained the upper hand in a clash with these tribes in the use of firearms. They eventually made peace with the Lakota and soundly trounced the Pawnee in almost every conflict. The Sauk had firearms, but the Pawnee didn't, so the Pawnee avoided them at all costs. The Osage were not ones to back down from a good fight, and neither were the Sauk. So, the two tribes were continually at war with each other, like the Ojibwa and the Lakota.

George and his men spent about two weeks at Shingabis's village. Accompanied by one of Shingabis's relatives as a guide, and owing to the mild weather, they proceeded down the Wisconsin River to Prairie du Chien. They spent a couple of days there and then proceeded down the Mississippi to Rock Island, Illinois, and spent about one week there with the Sauk, with the benefit of a good introduction by Shingabis's relatives. His party then proceeded up the Rock River, through Kickapoo lands to the Yahara River, which confluences with the Rock River near present-day Edgerton, Wisconsin. Proceeding up the Yahara brought them to a region of four lakes known today as Madison, Wisconsin. Following the Yahara north from this area brought them to a flat prairie-like savannah. Passing through this area for about twenty-five miles brought them back home to The Portage.

Sauk Warrior

The winter of 1792–1793 passed quickly. Because of the mild weather, the Ho-Chunk, Kickapoo, Menominee, and Sauk/Fox came to The Portage to trade. Business was very good. George's consistent, firm style of management coupled with fairness earned him the respect of his Indian customers and his crew. His crew came to depend on him, and he came to depend on them—a win-win for everybody.

Young Joe, with the consent of his father, began to spend more and more of his free time at Shingabis's lodge at Prairie du Sac. He soon became a favorite with the family and was taken under their wing. He became well-versed in their culture. This was to stand Joe in good stead in the years ahead of him. But the significant part of these visits was the "spark" between Joe and little Magpie.

By the spring of 1793, the yearly business cycle of the company continued on into the new year. Pelts were cleaned, inventoried, and packed in ninety-pound packs. George got a jump on the paperwork, all required inventories were done, and all the accounts of his men were up-to-date. At the end of May, the entire crew headed up the Fox River to La Bay. Details of the business were taken care of, and the fur packs were loaded on the company schooner, the Athabasca, and shipped to Mackinac Island.

George and Joe were reunited with Caroline, Germaine, and Mary Elizabeth. They had roughly a month together until George and Joe accompanied Duncan McGillivray, the Mackinac factor, to the Grand Portage for the North West Company yearly meeting.

A short note on the "Dish of Grand Portage politicks" that summer of 1793.

Young Roderick McKenzie showed up leading the brigades from the Athabasca country. His news was that the chief factor, Alexander Mackenzie, with a handful of voyageurs and two Indian guides had set out up the Peace River with the intent of reaching the Pacific. The marquis was not happy at this news. In 1789, when Alexander had led a party up the Grand River (McKenzie River) to the Arctic Ocean, the marquis had snubbed him by sending him a severe letter of reprimand. He should be tending to the company business and not running off exploring on his own.

At the same time, the Montréal partners were consolidating their power in the company and were dictating terms of policy and implementation of such to the hibernators (the wintering partners). One of the minor gripes of this ongoing power struggle was that McTavish, Frobisher and Company (who had eleven shares and controlling majority of the North West Company) had the policy of filling the top positions with family and relatives, including nephews William and Duncan McGillivray and brother-in-law Charles Chaboillez that had married into the family. This nepotism was the start of a brouhaha that would play out over the next decade. The next two years were typical for those times for anyone involved in the fur trade in the old Northwest Territories. George found himself covering the Southern District by operating out of La Bay and The Portage. He consolidated his business and friendship with Shingabis's band and, by doing so, set up the trade coming out of Prairie du Chien, Rock Island, and the Northwest Illinois country. He took a couple of trips down to the portage of the wild onions via the Chicago River, Des Plaines, and Illinois River on down the Mississippi and then up to Rock Island, returning to the portage via the Rock and Yahara Rivers. These trips brought him and the North West Company back in contact with the Pottawatomie, Miami, and Kickapoo tribes resulting in moderate but steady trade.

Also, a couple of trips up the Wisconsin River to the rapids at Wausau and the Wolf River brought him into contact with Simon Chaurette (Northwest factor of the Lac du Flambeau district) and the Ojibwa tribe, Chakauchokama (Old King) and the Menominee tribes.

These trips with his father seasoned Joe and rounded out his education as a young man. He learned how to deal with the Indian tribes and learned the operation, business, and politics of the North West Company. So, upon his fifteenth birthday in 1795, with his father's approval, he signed up with the apprenticeship/clerk program of the North West Company for a period of seven years for a princely sum of 100 pounds. Joe was now a young gentleman. Also, the spark between Joe and little Magpie had developed into a full-blown romance with the approval of both families.

Shingabis and Anita decided that Magpie should be sent to Caroline at Mackinac to further her education and be taught how to behave like a proper young lady. Her parents knew, because of conversations with George and Caroline, this would be good for her. Being in the company of Germaine and Mary Elizabeth would be a good thing also! So, in late spring or early summer, Magpie, accompanied by her parents, George, and Joe, arrived at Mackinac.

Thus, a major event in the lives of Joe and Magpie/Annie began.

Joe, along with his father, was at Grand Portage in July for the annual company business meeting. The discontent of the previous year, 1794, erupted again as the winterers were angry with the Montréal partners (especially Simon McTavish) who were consolidating their control of the company by setting terms of policy, which dictated to the winterers how business was to be conducted. Simon McTavish didn't even show up for the meeting that year, instead sending his nephew William McGillivray as his representative. William was being groomed by his uncle Simon to take over the company upon his retirement.

The winterers responded by choosing Alexander Mackenzie to represent them. They succeeded in rolling back some of the dictates of policy of operation and maintained their autonomy in conducting the business operations of their field posts.

Simon McTavish responded in his usual fashion, through negotiation and absorption of his opposition, by hiring Alexander to an inside position with McTavish, Frobisher and Company. The next year, Alexander showed up at Grand Portage as McTavish's representative.

Fort St. Louis, Fond du Lac District

Joe's life as a young gentleman began with his assignment to the Fond du Lac department in Duluth, Minnesota under John Sayer, the chief factor. Mr. Sayer assigned him as a clerk to J.B. Cadotte out at the White Oaks Lake Post at Deer River, Minnesota. The party of ten men and three canoes left Fond du Lac in late August or early September up the St. Louis River to the savanna portage.

The savanna portage was seven miles of slough, wetlands, and bog consisting of thirteen pauses about half a mile apart. It took them two days to cross the portage. An experience that Joe never forgot. This placed them on big Sandy Lake adjacent to the Mississippi River. Following the river north, passing through present-day Grand Rapids, Minnesota, for approximately 125 miles brought them to White Oaks Lake. On the north shore of the lake they constructed their post and set up for trade with the surrounding Ojibwa.

It was a typical winter with cold, snow, and ice. Joe did well with his boss Mr. Cadotte and fellow workers. Because of the skills and experience he learned under the firm hand of his father and Shingabis, he did well in dealing with the Ojibwa. The only area that Joe had trouble with was in the use of rum. He didn't drink, and despite his boss's orders to use rum in dealing with the Indians, he did so reluctantly.

His skills as a hunter and fisherman were put to good use in supplying the food larder. The Indians, the ones in the know, quickly picked up on Joe's skills and invited him along on many hunts. He skillfully navigated through the social side of the Indians' culture and avoided taking a wife when it was offered, but still joined in the feast and giving of gifts when necessary.

Early May found the party back at Fond du Lac via the savanna portage with about thirty-five packs of fur. This was average for the big Sand Lake District, and John Sayer (the factor) was satisfied with the year's performance. As usual, July found Joe with the Fond du Lac principals back at Grand Portage for the annual meeting.

The topic of concern that year in 1796 was the ratification of the Jay and Pinckney Treaties by the U.S. Congress with the approval of the Washington administration. This treaty placed the international boundary on the Pigeon River and its flowage to Rainy Lake and Lake of the Woods, placing Grand Portage on American soil. Also, the Oswego New York, Niagara, Detroit, Vincennes, Prairie du Chien, and Mackinac forts were being turned over to the American military. The British garrisons had to vacate to be replaced by American garrisons. Even though Jay's Treaty allowed free access by American and British citizens as well as Indian tribes to the territories on both sides of the border, this put the fur trade business in an uproar because the lines of communication, supply, and physical location were totally disrupted. Take Mackinac Island as an example. The British presence was ingrained in the social culture of the island and the surrounding area. This necessitated the British locating forty miles northeast to St. Joseph Island and the construction of a new fort, village, and trade center. With the incoming American military came the government bureaucrats, including custom services, etc.

Discussions that year were on the eventual relocation of the company from Grand Portage to the Kamistaka River at present-day Thunder Bay, Ontario. This river had originally been used by the French in the late seventeenth century, but was abandoned in favor of Pigeon River and a nine-mile portage at Grand Portage. It was a chance conversation between Roderick McKenzie and an Ojibwa that this route was rediscovered and checked out by Roderick. Another factor that moved the discussion about relocation forward was Simon McTavish never really was that happy with Grand Portage.

Joe's next assignment for the 1796–1797 winter was to the lower Red River Post under Charles Chaboillez (Simon McTavish's brother-in-law) located near the city of Pembina, North Dakota. This was a good year for Joe because he was rubbing shoulders with some of the insiders of the company, including Alexander Henry the elder. This post located on the Red River flowage and plains country of western Minnesota and the Dakotas was where the bulk of the food staple pemmican was obtained from the Indian tribes, (i.e., Mandan, Lakota, Hidatsa, and Assiniboine).

Pemmican was a mixture of ground buffalo meat and berries over which melted buffalo fat was poured and allowed to cool. The company had found that this staple, when provided to their crews, provided most of the nourishment needed to get to the winterer's post and survive the following winter. In fact, without this staple, the company's northwestern operations could never happen.

To procure a yearly supply of pemmican, the party of ten men, led by Francis Coleret, proceeded west up the Pembina River via canoe and portaged over to the Souris River following this river upstream for approximately 150 miles to the present-day Minot, North Dakota. This placed them about fifty miles straight north of the Mandan villages located on the Missouri River confluence with the Knife River, about forty miles north of present-day Bismarck, North Dakota.

This route or the route following the Assiniboine River west out of Winnipeg House to the Souris confluence was the path that brought the British traders to the Mandan villages a decade before the arrival of Lewis and Clark.

Mandan Villages Knife River Dakota

These Mandan villages were high traffic crossroads in the fur trade. British traders came from the North and East, from Big Stone Lake via the St. Peter's River (The Minnesota River). New Mexican/Spanish traders came from the Southwest, and some, not many, American traders were coming up the Missouri from St. Louis. The Spanish traders had been crisscrossing the plains for the last seventy-five years, bringing horses, horse equipment, foodstuffs, and Spanish silver in the form of pieces of eight or rials. In return, they were looking for firearms, powder, bullets, and assorted hides such as tanned buffalo robes, deer hides, etc. It was because of the Spanish traders' activities and influence that the plains Indian tribes from Texas to the plains of western Canada developed their horse centered cultures.

Mandan Village on the Missouri River

The winter the party spent at the Mandan villages was a new experience for Joe, and he picked up a lot. He made some local acquaintances that would help him in the future. Early April found the party and the load of pemmican back at the lower Red River Post. By mid-May everything they needed to do had been done, and the hibernators were underway back to Grand Portage for the yearly (1798) get-together.

Again, the main topics continued from the previous year included the effects of Jay's Treaty and the location of the new international border and the effects on the business because of the removal of the British garrisons with replacement by the American garrisons and customs agents. Of lesser note, but of equal importance, was the hiring of David Thompson, formerly of the Hudson Bay Company. Mr. Thompson had an excellent surveyor's background. The company assigned him the job of surveying the new international boundary and determining exactly where it was. He was given free latitude in picking his own crew to do this task, and one of his choices was Joe Beeler.

Joe was pleased and completely surprised by the appearance of Annie/Magpie accompanying his father, George at Grand Portage. Annie, under the firm hand and guidance of Caroline, had blossomed into a beautiful young woman of seventeen, and she had plenty to say to Joe. The short version was that they would be married that year, or else. It might be said that Annie made quite a social splash at Grand Portage that year. At the dances, her dance card was full, but any potential suitors quickly found her heart belonged to Joe. That's not to say that when she became miffed with Joe's behavior she played him off against some of the suitors, but like the good one she was, she took care of his bumps, abrasions, and lumps. Of course, it must be said that Joe usually came out on top in the scuffles being six feet four inches, weighing 220 pounds and having skills with the knife, tomahawk, pistol, and fists.

Young Annie Grand Portage Social Affair

Wedding plans were made and set in motion. Everyone at Grand Portage was aware of the upcoming wedding, an Joe knew he had better be there, or else.

David Thompson and his party set off up the Pigeon River in mid-July on the boundary survey job. Their route took them to Rainy Lake, Lake of the Woods, up the Winnipeg River to Lake Winnipeg and then down to the lower Red River post, then up the Pembina portage to the Souris. They traveled upstream to present-day Minot, North Dakota, then south fifty miles to the Mandan villages on the Missouri River. After trading for horses, they left the Mandan villages and paralleled the Missouri River down to present-day Yankton, South Dakota,

(James River confluence) where a big trade rendezvous was occurring that year. A majority of the traders present were the New Mexican/Spanish, for they only appeared at this location about every third year. It was heavily attended by the Indian tribes, including Lakota, Crow, Cheyenne, Kiowa, Arapaho, Pawnee, Osage, Ponca, Hidatsa, Arikaree, Sauk-Fox, Assiniboine, Minateree, and even some Cree and Ojibway.

As stated previously, the major items of trade were Spanish horses, mules, silver for English trade guns, powder, ball, baskets of produce, meat products, furs, blankets, dressed and painted buffalo hides. Naturally, alcohol was a major part of the trade haggling.

Leaving the rendezvous, Thompson's party struck off in an easterly direction reaching the St. Peter's (Minnesota River) about 100 miles west by south of present-day Mankato, Minnesota. Exchanging their horses for canoes with the local Lakota, they proceeded up the St. Peter's confluence with the Mississippi (at present-day St. Paul). At this point, Mr. Thompson turned to Joe and said, "Take two men in a canoe, go find your Annie, and get married. And the best to both of you."

Mr. Thompson turned north up the Mississippi toward its headwaters and by early fall of that year, after traversing the country south of Lake Superior, found himself at Sault Ste. Marie in late November. He met with Mr. Alexander Mackenzie and reported on the preliminary findings of his trip, which he had completed in about five months.

Joe and his party arrived at Shingabis's village around October 15. He and Annie got married, and what a wedding it was. Both families, friends, and relatives were there to give Annie and Joe a big sendoff. They were fortunate in that George used his influence and got Joe assigned to him as his clerk, allowing them to spend the winter at Mackinac.

The annual meeting of the year 1799 was as rambunctious and eventful as any other year, but two events occurred that had a profound effect on the events of the next four or five years. The separation from the North West Company by the following Montréal partners: Forsyth, Richardson, and Company; Parker, Gerard, and Ogilvy Company; and John Mure of Québec. The rub here was the disagreement with McTavish policies and divisions of company shares. These principals joined together and formed the New North West Company, better known as the XY Company, which became, along with the Hudson Bay Company, rivals to the northwesterners. Needless to say, McTavish, Frobisher, and Company were upset with these results.

The second event that caused its share of disruption and bad feelings revolved around Alexander Mackenzie. Even though Alexander was working for McTavish, Frobisher and Company he knew, because he wasn't a part of the McTavish family, he would never be one of the insiders, so he made plans to change this. At the meeting, he announced his pending retirement. This caused a major stir among his patronizing/supporting winterers. He said he would reconsider his retirement if he could negotiate some major changes in company operation policies. His goal was to force the retirement of Simon McTavish. So, with letters and petitions from his supporting winterers, he and William McGillivray headed back to Montréal for the confrontation with Simon McTavish. Simon McTavish, being upset about the new XY Company and then being hit with the Mackenzie situation, was backed into the corner of non-negotiation and direct confrontation. So, instead of following his usual pattern of negotiation and absorption, McTavish fired young Alexander Mackenzie, putting him out on the street of unemployment, but as a very rich man!

Mackenzie ended up in London during the winter of 1799–1800. He became a social celebrity, wrote a book on his explorations and discoveries, and became popular because of it. Plus, the king knighted him for it.

The principals of the XY Company approached Mackenzie and offered him a majority share which he accepted. Mackenzie's motivation was to get back in the fur trade, which he knew and was good at, but more so, the idea of revenge against Simon McTavish was really pushing him into this partnership. So, for the next four to five years, the XY Company gave the northwesterners a real run for their money. The downside of it was that the XY Company lost their assets, and the northwesterners made profit or often barely broke even. The old saw that "revenge never makes a profit" is still valid. Suffice to say, where there was a North West Company post, you would find an XY Company post nearby.

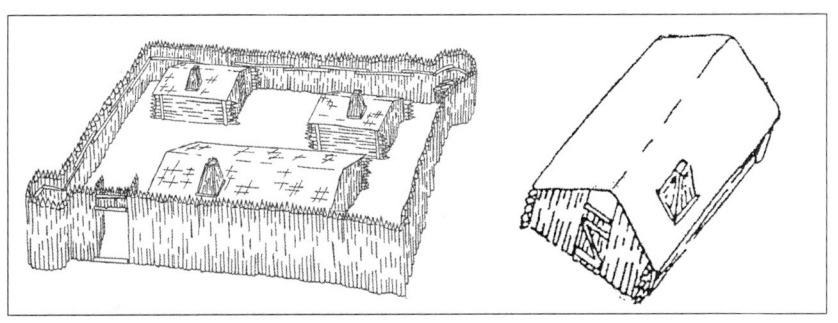

NWC Post with Adjacent XYC Post

During this time, Annie traveled with Joe wherever he was stationed. In the spring of 1800, while stationed at Fort Francis on Rainy Lake, they had their firstborn daughter, whom they named Linda. Having his family with him on station and being an apprentice clerk put quite a burden on Joe, but that was okay. What Annie wanted, Joe gave her. This also strained Joe's relationship with his boss, the post factor. Annie usually won the boss over with her personality, social graces, and hard work. The fact that Joe was still an apprentice clerk created some pecking order problems for them regarding housing accommodations. Usually, unmarried young clerks were housed in the same quarters, and some factors' policies frowned upon marriage until they completed their apprenticeship. In Joe and Annie's case, their notoriety and reputations preceded them. For example, during their year at Ft. Francis, Joe and Annie fixed up an old lodge and moved in for the winter. With their skills and background, they made it a very comfortable home. In fact, there was a constant file of visitors, both white and Indians, to their home. It became the second social center of the post. Linda was born in this old lodge with the help of Métis midwives. The factor was impressed by the young couple and offered them quarters in the post, but they declined.

Left: Annie/Little Magpie. Right: Old Lodge Annie and Joe Occupied at Rainy Lake

The year 1802 found the Beelers back at Grand Portage for the annual meeting with two happenings. The first was the birth of their second child, a boy whom they named Jim, in April at Fond du Lac. The second was Joe's completion of his seven-year clerk apprenticeship and the promotion to the status of full clerk. Joe also made the acquaintance of a seventeen-year-old apprentice clerk by the name of Robert Stuart. In the upcoming years, this acquaintance would have an impact on Joe and Annie Beeler.

George Beeler was voted a half company share for his years of service in the southern district and was made factor of the post at La Bay (Green Bay, Wisconsin). George was 43 years of age.

This was the last annual North West Company meeting at Grand Portage. The move to Port Arthur/Thunder Bay, at the mouth of the Kamistaka River, had been started the previous year because of the international boundary, which had been determined to be the Pigeon River. The new headquarters was named Fort William (after McTavish's nephew William McGillivray).

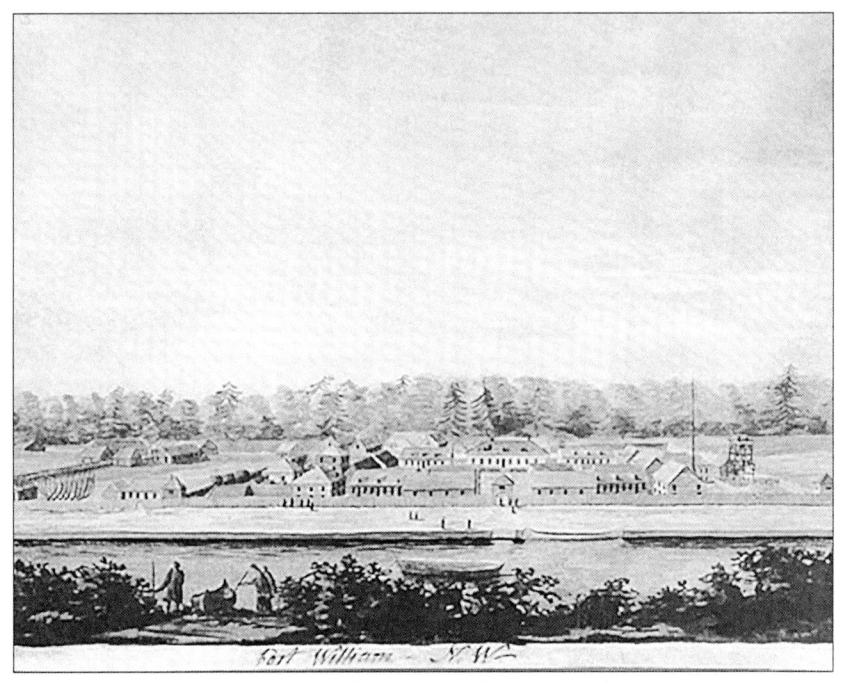

Fort William, the New NWC Headquarters Replacing Grand Portage

The XY Company continued to operate out of Grand Portage. In fact, it was in 1802 that Sir Alexander had the company build a grand fort and depot on the hill about three quarters of a mile back from the bay. The hurly-burly of competition continued as usual.

Joe and Annie's son, little Jim/Little Big Head, was having health problems. He had been a sickly child since his birth in April and had not outgrown his ailments. It was decided that Annie and the two kids would accompany George back to Mackinac, enabling grandmothers Caroline and Anita to support Annie in caring for Jim. Anita was a proficient herb healer, a holy medicine woman in Shingabis's Snow/Wolf clan.

Though it was a no-brainer decision for Joe or Annie—be away from her husband and tend the children or be with her husband and neglect the children—this was a tough decision for Annie to accept. With the grandmothers' caring support and the family surrounding them, Annie knew in her heart what had to be done. They kept in contact by writing letters while understanding that the delivery system was slow and at times undependable. But what choice did they have? Things only moved as fast as a horse or the paddle-power of a voyager manned canoe.

For next two years (1802–1804) Joe was posted as chief clerk to Sandy Lake of the Fond du Lac District. His boss and factor was Charles Bousquet, who was experienced in the trade and not a bad man to work for. Joe did well at his clerking job. He was good at ciphering and keeping the accounts—skills learned under the firm hand of his father and mother. Dealing with the Ojibway in giving credit, collecting accounts due, and keeping the dispensing of high wine to a minimum as needed kept Joe on the right side with his boss and his Indian customers. It was a tricky path to tread, but Joe did okay.

The highlight of Joe's two years at Sandy Lake was the occasional letter from Annie that reached him. Joe discerned from her letters that her patience in tolerating their separation was wearing thin. Little Jim under the care of his maternal grandmother's herbal medicine had outgrown his sickly ailments. He was growing into a typical spoiled hell-raising Indian kid. His grandfather Shingabis was mainly responsible for this. Linda/Sparrow was at Mackinac with her paternal grandmother, Caroline, being tutored and instructed in reading, writing, ciphering, and the finer points of conducting herself as a proper little girl. But Sparrow had a mind of her own like her mother, with a stubborn streak to match.

The year 1804 was pivotal for the Beelers and the company. Annie had decided with Joe's reluctant consent to join her husband at Fort William and left the kids in the care of the grandparents. Joe agreed to Annie's decision knowing that the kids were in good hands.

In July, Simon McTavish passed away, and his nephew William McGillivray took over. His first effort was to resolve the competition with the XY Company by negotiating a merger of the two companies. This resulted in a massive reduction of the workforce, putting many men out of work. The most prominent person forced out was Sir Alexander. McGillivray made it a part of the merger that McKenzie was bought out and was no longer a part of the company. McKenzie retired a rich man back to Montréal, was elected to the Lower Canada parliament, and eventually retired back to Scotland where he remarried and died sometime around 1820.

On the political side, there were rumors that the American government had purchased the Upper and Lower Louisiana Territories last year (1803) and were on the move to consolidate this. This brought more American competition and problems in the form of custom agents, military garrisons, and fur traders. Life never gets easier!

Joe slipped past this unemployment problem and was assigned to the lower Red River post under Charles Chaboillez arriving here in September 1804 with the rest of the wintering hibernators and Annie in tow.

As usual, the primary job for the season was procuring the yearly supply of pemmican from the plains tribes located in the vicinity of the Mandan villages on the Missouri River. The man picked to lead this party was Francis Antoine Larocque. Joe was the clerk of the party and was accompanied by Annie. The party arrived at the villages around

October 1 and set up to do business as usual. About the fifteenth of the month things changed when, to everyone's surprise, the American expedition of Lewis and Clark arrived. Things weren't the same from that day on.

Lewis and Clark Arrival at Mandan Villages 1804 at Fort Mandan

Captains Lewis and Clark immediately let it be known to the northwesterners that they were on American soil and that American sovereignty and law was the rule of the day. Not being happy about the whole situation, the northwesterners vented their frustrations to Lewis and Clark. Lewis, being a straight-laced stiff professional military type, didn't allow much leeway to the northwesterners. Clark, on the other hand, was more of a realist. Understanding the gravity of the situation, he allowed more leeway and softened Lewis's attitude, resulting in negotiations that were acceptable to both parties.

The northwesterners were allowed to stay until spring and complete their trading for pemmican and furs with the surrounding tribes. Lewis and Clark completed their wintering post, Fort Mandan, and set about establishing peace between the Mandan, Arikaree, and the Sioux.

Joe and Annie were fascinated by the presence of the Americans that winter and spent much of their free time amongst them. In fact, Captain Clark took a personal interest in the young couple and spent many hours of conversation over a good pipe and a fire discussing personal interest in politics of the day. Captain Clark told Joe and Annie that if they were ever in St. Louis to look him up, and he would see what he could do for them, which he backed up by giving them a letter of introduction.

The time spent with the Americans did not settle well with Mr. Larocque, and this caused a strain between Joe and him. This rift would cause problems for Joe and the company in the near future.

An incident took place in late October/early November when a small party of Bloods and Piegan (Blackfeet) came in to trade. One of the party, a young warrior who was the owner of the sacred "bear knife bundle," took notice of that pretty little Métis woman who lodged with the northwesterners. He told his fellow warriors that he had plans for him and Annie.

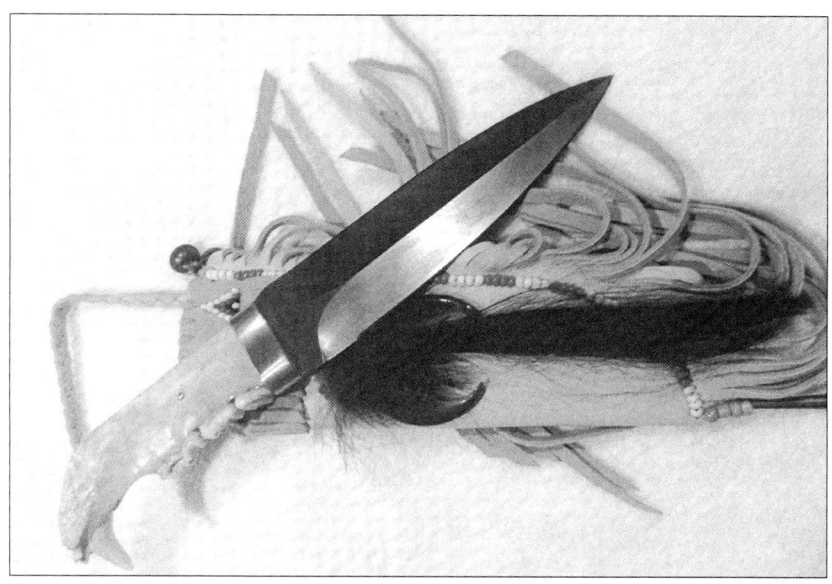

Sacred Bear Jaw Knife

Once his party departed after completing their trading, he hung back and waited for the right time to abduct Annie. It was in the early evening when Annie, as usual, went to get water from the river for the evening meal. The Blood sprang upon her, bound and gagged her, threw her on his pony, and departed. Annie knew the further she got from the village the greater the risk that she would never see Joe and her family again. She managed to slip off the pony, hitting the ground and faking unconsciousness. Fortunately, the Blood had bound her hands together in front of her. Also, she had her knife in the folds of her capote. When the Blood stooped down and rolled her over, she deftly slipped the blade past his ribs into his heart.

When Annie didn't appear back at their lodge in a timely manner, Joe was concerned. He knew she went for water and knew how much time it took. He found her two brass kettles laying in the sand by the river and read the sign of the scuffle that occurred. Immediately, he got his pony and picked up the trail. After going less than two miles, to his surprise, he saw his Annie coming toward him on an Indian pony.

Upon meeting, he saw she had a bear knife and a fresh scalp. After hearing Annie's version of what happened, Joe told Annie they must go back and finish what this young Blood buck started to make sure it never happens again.

After reaching the scene of the incident, Joe told Annie to find and open the bear knife bundle. Meanwhile, he took the Indian's body, hung it upside down in a nearby oak and disemboweled it. He had Annie bring him the two bear jaws from the bundle and insert one in the body cavity and the other in the mouth. He then took some of the paint from the bundle and painted bear claw prints on the throat and chest of the body. Joe hoped to show any Indian coming upon the scene that this poor soul's bear medicine had failed him and turned back against him. This was sure to guarantee nightmares for any Indian that would see this.

Returning to the village and back to their own lodge that night, Joe cleaned up the scalp and attached it to the bear knife scabbard. He then had Annie, over her objections, wear the knife whenever she was outside their lodge. Joe wanted to make the point that Annie's spirit medicine was strong, so strong that it turned the bear bundle medicine against the young Blood warrior and killed him. The story of the young Blood hanging in the tree down the river spread like wildfire. Also, the fact that the Blood's pony was tied up outside the Beeler's lodge gave credibility to the strength of the pretty little Métis spirit medicine, and she was not to be trifled with.

Come breakup in late March found the Americans continuing up the Missouri. Half of the northwesterners, led by McCracken, were back at the lower Red River post. Larocque, with ten men and a pack train, went with the Crow back to Powder River/Big Horn country to ascertain beaver potential and develop plans of opening a trade post for the Crow/Cheyenne the following year. July found the hibernators back at Fort William for the annual company meeting.

The years of 1805–1806 politically were a taffy pull for the company. The absorption of the XY Company the previous year had only solved one of the many problems facing the company. It left the major competition of the Hudson Bay Company to be dealt with: the expansion of the Americans via the Lewis and Clark expedition up the Missouri and on to the West Coast; the Zebulon Pike expedition to the headwaters of the Mississippi during which he shot down the British flag at the Leach Lake post claiming American sovereignty over the area; and Jay's treaty of 1796 had expired and was not renewed. The bitterest pill came on August 26, 1805, when General James Wilkinson, governor of Upper Louisiana, issued an edict that barred foreigners from doing business on American soil, thereby negating the years of business efforts the British traders had done in pioneering commercial routes across Iowa, Minnesota, and the Dakotas.

The American government with custom tariffs, President Jefferson's non-importation decrees, and the building of a handful of trading factories along the frontier, were trying to undermine the long-established friendship of the British fur men with the Indians of the old Northwest Territory. Additionally, the growing unrest among the Indians because of Tecumseh's Confederation kept many of them from their hunting grounds (no beaver, no furs).

On the international scene, the Napoleonic Wars were raging on the European continent of which Great Britain was one of the major belligerents. This further depressed the fur trade market, driving prices down, and driving prices of trade goods and transportation up.

In trying to wiggle out of this economic mess south of the border and try to restore some order to the trade, Montréal merchants who were also members of the North West Company in 1806, along with some American partners, formed the Michilimackinac Company.

The major player in this company was John Jacob Astor. He had been dealing with the northwesterners for the past twelve to fifteen years and in creating partnerships with Simon McTavish had become the New York outlet for Canadian furs. Additionally, Astor was in the import/export business, owning or having part interest in five or six ships, which allowed him to have dealings in Europe, the Far East (bypassing the British East India Company) and the West Indies. Unfortunately, this business was brought to a halt by Jefferson's Embargo Act of 1807, which was the result of the British frigate HMS Leopard firing on the USS Chesapeake killing three, wounding eighteen, boarding and taking five crewmen for impressment on June 22, 1807. This act effectively shut down all American ports and prevented the shipment and receipt of trade goods from England, slamming the door on Canadian companies involved in the fur trade south of the border. It hurt American business more than the French and English. This gave Astor an incentive to pursue his idea of eventually gaining control of the fur trade south of the border, an idea that he had been nurturing for at least ten years.

In early 1808, Astor made an offer to the Montréalers to buy the troublesome Michilimackinac Company, which was refused. Later that year two of the four Montréal firms sold out their interests to the other two remaining partners Forsyth, Richardson Company and McTavish, McGillivray Company. Beset by the 1807 embargo that was extended in 1809 by the Macon's Bill Number 2, the Montréalers finally yielded to Astor in 1811. They partnered with him and formed a company called the South West Company. Its sphere of operations south of the border would extend from the Great Lakes westward past the Mississippi, but would be excluded specifically from a territory beyond the Missouri River. Astor always kept a couple of cards up his sleeve for future business deals.

The agreement was finalized and signed January 1811.

The new organization followed a pattern of operations similar to Canada where field traders were not partners in the company. The traders traded entirely on their own risk, bound only by the supply contracts and debts. Buy goods in the fall on credit and settle the accounts in the spring with fur.

CHAPTER FOUR
ON THE PATH OF
SELF-EMPLOYMENT

What did this all mean for Joe and Annie? At the annual company meeting in July 1806, Joe was informed that his services were no longer needed. He and Annie were not surprised, knowing that Mr. Larocque's report back to Charles Chaboillez was not in their favor and knew it was only a matter of time. Also, they knew that it was time after two years to get back with their kids and family. They were actually looking forward to rejoining them at Mackinac.

That same year George Beeler sold his half share in the company and announced his retirement. George joined Caroline back at Mackinac and settled into semiretirement by dabbling in gun sales and repair, selling his services as a free trade agent at the yearly fur rendezvous and becoming a wholesaler in the fishery business. He was forty-six.

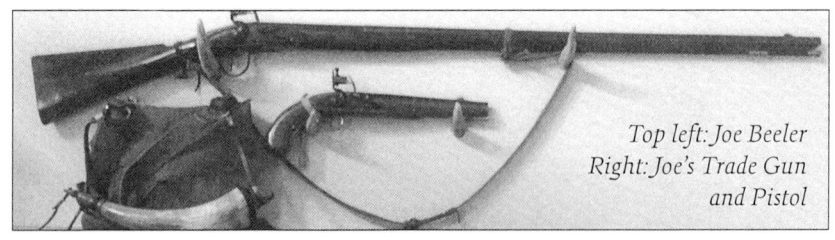

Top left: Joe Beeler
Right: Joe's Trade Gun and Pistol

A short note on Joe's two sisters. In 1799, Germaine met and married a young British officer (Ensign Townsend), and they were residing at Fort St. Joseph, located on St. Joseph island approximately forty miles northeast of Mackinac. Mary Elizabeth met and married a young Lutheran preacher (Bruce Loudenhagen) from Detroit, and they settled about 130 miles south of Mackinac in a place called the Kilbourn District located on the Milwaukee River flowage, part of the Indiana territory.

Joe and Annie hitched a ride back to Sault Ste. Marie on the North West Company schooner, the Otter. They bought a canoe and supplies then headed south to Mackinac with a stopover in St. Joseph to visit with Joe's sister Germaine and her husband, Ensign Townsend. Arriving at Mackinac, they spent time reuniting with George, Caroline, and their daughter, Linda the Little Sparrow.

Conversations centered on the topic of what to do about unemployment. Rather than working for another company, George suggested a partnership with Shingabis and other tribes in the Portage area. Convince them to bring their fur harvest to Joe, who then would be their agent in selling the furs at St. Louis and returning with the trade goods. The advantage of doing this would bring them top prices for their furs, and with Joe's connection with Captains Lewis and Clark, it would lead to sources providing the best quality at the lowest cost for the trade goods. In other words, the Indians would be working with themselves bypassing the middleman, the white trader.

With this idea in mind, Joe and Annie with little Sparrow headed south arriving at Shingabis's village in early September 1806.

After listening to Joe's idea, Shingabis considered it sound, but convincing the tribal members and any other tribes that would want to participate was the real problem. Typically, the tribes were used to trapping the furs, trading them for goods needed, and then the deal was done. This approach was backwards from what they were accustomed to. That is, trap the furs, consign them to a white man, depend upon him to get the best return on their furs, and then wait an indeterminate time for the trade goods. It was going to be a tough sell. But what the heck, "nothing ventured, nothing gained"!

Invitations were sent to the neighboring Fox, Kickapoo, and Winnebago tribes to come to Shingabis's village at Prairie du Sac for a Trade Council. Shingabis managed to convince a majority of his tribe of Sauk to accept the premise of the idea. Of course, Joe being a part of Shingabis's family and having lots of relatives in the tribe carried a lot of weight.

Over 100 Indians attended the Council. Why not! It never hurt to listen and talk. Besides, any Indian worth his salt never passed up a good feast and a chance to talk with his peers. Upon the completion of the Council, over a third of the participants liked the idea and would consider it, getting back to Joe and Shingabis the following spring of 1807. Shingabis and Joe's reputation is mainly what carried the most import of convincing the participants to consider the idea, and Joe declared up front that there would be no alcohol involved whatsoever. Plus, the tribes were well aware of the politics ensnaring the trade companies and the cutthroat competition amongst the traders, with the Indians receiving the brunt of it in the field. Also, the influence of Tecumseh's Confederation was spreading throughout the old Northwest country, primarily driven by Tecumseh and his brother The Prophet, causing further disruption amongst the tribes and the fur trade. Dicey times!

That winter Joe and his two brothers-in-law, Stone Hawk and Porcupine, ran a trapline in the bluffs north of Prairie du Sac along the Baraboo River bottomlands almost back to the Portage. With the women's help they produced two 90-pound packs of mixed furs (bobcat, martin, fisher, fox, deer, and beaver skins).

It was a good winter for the family because Annie and her kids were back in the home nest with Anita and Shingabis. Little Big Head/Jim was a hellion Indian kid. The Sparrow, after being under the influence of her grandmother Caroline, schooled in the etiquette of being a proper little girl, coupled with a stubborn streak like her mother, had some rough adjustments to make getting along with her mother and grandmother. But being spoiled by a doting grandfather allowed her to make the cut.

Come April 1807, 35 Indians from the Fox, Kickapoo, and Winnebago showed up at Prairie du Sac with about twenty 90-pound packs of furs. The idea had taken hold. The Sac's had 10 packs to add to the totals. A council was convened that resulted in three Fox, five Kickapoo, three Winnebago, and four Sauk chosen to man three 25-foot northern canoes to haul the 30 fur packs. A fourth 18-foot canoe containing the baggage and foodstuffs would be manned by Joe, Stone Hawk and Porcupine (his two brothers-in-law), and Little Big Head/Jim. The party was heavily armed, and the warriors chosen were the most experienced.

St. Louis 1807

Selecting a secure and hidden camp 10 miles above St. Louis on the Illinois shore, Joe, Stone Hawk, and little Jim proceeded on to St. Louis to reconnoiter and get the lay of the land. Finding that Captains Lewis and Clark were not in town (away on business in Washington and Virginia), Joe looked up acting Governor Bates and presented his letter of introduction. Governor Bates directed him to Mr. Auguste (Rene) Chouteau with Governor Bates's letter of introduction.

Joe and Mr. Chouteau got right down to business. The furs were brought in, prices were haggled over, and within five days all business was completed. Joe wanted to get his party out of town as quickly as possible because even though St. Louis only had a population of around 1,200, it was a rough and tough frontier river town. Even though the party was made up of 18 seasoned well-armed men with four canoes loaded with an abundance of trade goods, it was a tempting target for the town's gutter scum and river rats.

Joe was approached by four Canadian voyageurs looking for work in passage back to Mackinac. After a discussion amongst the complete party and knowing the extra paddle power could be used, they were hired with the understanding that they would be under tight scrutiny. If they didn't carry their workload or if they got into a ruckus with any of the party, they would be left on their own maybe minus their hair. They got the message and fit in very well.

Fourteen days later the party was back at Prairie du Sac, and a grand feast was held with the distribution of the goods. All parties were more than satisfied, and Joe and Shingabis gained a couple more notches in trust and their reputations.

Three of the Canadian voyageurs bought a canoe and supplies with their earnings and continued on their journey to Mackinac. The fellow named Pierre Paquette who stayed behind was a young stoutly built man with a likable, easygoing personality. He was kind of like a wart—he grows on you—and Annie took a liking to him.

In the spring of 1808, only three canoes filled with twelve packs of furs headed to St. Louis. The party consisted of all Sauk warriors (ten in number) plus Joe, Annie, the two kids (Sparrow and little Jim) and Paquette, the Canadian.

What happened to the rest of the tribes? One must be an Indian to ask an Indian that question. Another way to answer the question is to say "old habits don't die." Upon arriving in St. Louis, Joe and his party were happy to find that Captains Lewis and Clark had arrived back in town. Captain Clark was especially thrilled to see Joe and Annie with the kids and introduce them to his new wife, Julia, whom he had married the previous year. In fact, the Beeler family was invited by Mrs. Clark to stay with them while they were in St. Louis. The Beelers graciously declined but accepted a couple of invitations from the Clarks to attend some social events.

With help from Captain Clark and Pierre Chouteau (Auguste's half-brother) the entire Beeler party was put up in secure, comfortable accommodations, and even though the trade business was completed within five days, the Beeler party stayed another five days for the social activity before departing for home.

Even though the Beelers and the Sauk had made out okay with the trips to St. Louis, the political events of the day were pressing in and causing change—for the worse. With the unrest coming from the influence of Tecumseh's Confederation, the continuing expansion of American settlements into the old Northwest Territory, the continuing embargoes and changes in custom tariffs, and the free-for-all competition resulting from the opening of the Upper Missouri River trade, it was becoming clear that the security of the St. Louis trips was in question.

That fall the Beelers decided to establish a home and a trading post on Devil's Lake located in the bluffs ten miles north of Prairie du Sac. Joe hired Mr. Paquette and four French-Canadians, one who went by the name of Jacques Deserve, from La Bay to build the home, trading store, auxiliary buildings, and corrals for livestock, which were all completed by the end of 1808.

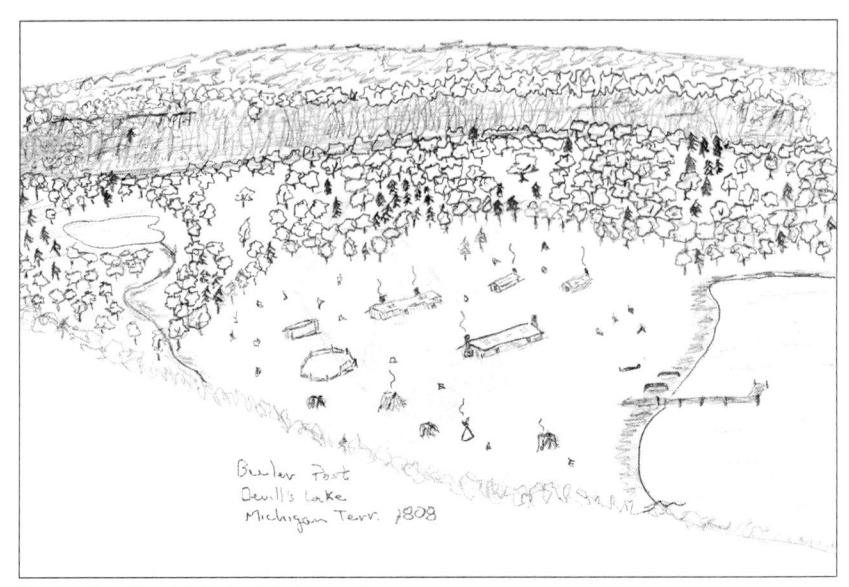

Beeler Post Devil's Lake Michigan Territory

This location put the Beelers in a central area relative to the Winnebago, Menominee, Kickapoo, and the Sauk at Prairie Du Sac. Business was slow in the beginning because of the Beeler's reluctance to trade in alcohol. But Joe's reputation and Annie's hospitality carried the day, which was extended to all customers, that is until they crossed the line of good behavior. As usual, there were few of these and Annie's rules were backed up by Joe's enforcement methods.

At Joe's insistence, Annie hung the bear jaw knife adorned with the Blood's scalp on the wall directly behind the counter in the trading store, and occasionally she wore the knife as she went about her daily business. Naturally, the story of Annie's strong spirit medicine spread amongst the tribes, and this directly affected their behavior when around the Beeler's post. When Annie said, "Jump!" the Indian asked how high!

As Joe said to Annie, "We're using the Indians' faith/religion to promote their best behavior. Works every time."

In the spring of 1810, Joe made his customary trip to La Bay to sell his winter's take of furs and restock his trade goods. This was accomplished by Joe's father, George, acting as his agent at Mackinac in dealing with Michilimackinac Company or other Montréal companies in getting the best quality and prices for his goods. He was also able to keep shipping costs down by either contracting with the northwesterners for shipment by schooner or more often by hiring Canadian voyageurs to "paddle power" via canoe to get the goods to La Bay. Because Joe had managed to create a nice nest egg of trade goods from the two St. Louis trips, he was able to deal in cash with the Montréal companies, thereby owning his inventory paid for upfront.

A violent disagreement erupted on this trip between Jacques Deserve, one of Joe's Canadians, and a gutter scum by the name of Ron Otto. Jacques was in a game of cards run by Otto, and after losing quite a sum, he figured out the game was rigged. Being of short temper, Jacques tore into Otto which resulted in the tavern being busted up.

Jacques Deserve

Jacques and Otto spent the night, courtesy of the local constable, in the La Bay calaboose with a court date in about a month to appear before Judge Reaume to answer the charges.

Joe, not wanting to lose Jacques since he was a good worker and Joe liked him, intervened with the judge and got the court date moved to the following day. Judge Reaume was a fair, practical man and ran a good court. He listened to the particulars of each side of the story and ruled that twenty dollars from each defendant would settle the matter of damages and court costs. Joe paid Jacques' costs and said he would cover Otto's bill with the proviso that he be handed over to the northwesterners as an indentured consignee deckhand for two years on the company's schooners. Judge Reaume ruled in favor thereof. Case settled!

Otto objected violently, but the judge said, "Pay the twenty dollars or be a deckhand." All knew Otto couldn't come up with the fine, and all knew having Otto out of La Bay would be a good thing. Plus, the judge and Joe both knew the northwesterners were always looking for warm bodies on their ships, and a little gratuity would also be forthcoming. Joe agreed with the judge that it would cover any additional court costs incurred delivering Otto to the northwesterners.

Ron Otto

George and Caroline had hitched a ride on the Athabasca to La Bay and accompanied Joe, Mr. Paquette, and the crew of four French-Canadians back to Prairie du Sac and the Beeler's home at Devil's Lake.

Northwestern Schooner Athabasca

In 1810, Astor established the Pacific Fur Company. Some of his partners in this company were Canadians that he enticed away from the North West Company. Three of the individuals were Robert Stuart and his uncle David Stuart and Ramsey Crooks, a Scot who first arrived at Mackinaw in 1805 at the age of twenty.

The business model of the company was patterned after the North West Company, and the intent was to establish a headquarters on the Columbia River in Oregon Territory. One of the goals was to cut down on transportation costs by shipping trade goods from Boston/New York around Cape Horn and then up to the Columbia River. The year's catch of furs was then shipped directly to the Chinese market, sold or bartered for spices, ceramics, silks, etc., which were then shipped to London or New York, and the cycle was completed.

To put this plan in place, the ship Tonquin under Captain Thorn left New York in April 1810 and arrived at the mouth of the Columbia River in March 1811. Leaving supplies, equipment, and personnel to build the outpost headquarters on the river (Fort Astoria), the ship proceeded to Nootka Sound of Vancouver Island to trade for otter pelts. Due to incompetence and lack of good manners, Captain Thorn insulted a local chief who then attacked the ship, which was blown up, killing the whole crew and many Indian attackers. This happened in June 1811.

The Tonquin

At the same time, an overland party of sixty men led by Wilson P. Hunt of Trenton, New Jersey, left Mackinac in early April 1811 for the Columbia River. After a long and troublesome journey, the party arrived at Fort Astoria late February 1812. About this time, news of the Tonquin disaster had reached Fort

Astoria. It was decided that Robert Stuart, Ramsey Crooks, Joe Miller, and Robert McClellan, with a party of seven men, would return to St. Louis to report the bad news. After leaving Fort Astoria in June 1812 and crossing the Bitterroot Mountains, the party turned southeast to avoid the troublesome Blackfoot tribes and crossed through South Pass, picked up the Platte River and reached St. Louis in April 1813.

This was a poor start for Astor's plans of dominating the West Coast for trade. The only two good points of this venture were the establishment of Fort Astoria, giving the United States a claim to the Oregon Territory, and two months after the arrival of the Tonquin and the building of Fort Astoria, northwesterner David Thompson arrived, having navigated the entire length of the Columbia River.

Fort Astoria on the Columbia

In 1813, the Pacific Fur Company officials wanted to abandon the fort and sold it to the North West Company. Despite this sale, because of the War of 1812 hostilities, the British sloop HMS Raccoon, with Captain William Black commanding, went through the motions of seizing the fort, renaming it Fort George. Ah! The military must always have their day.

The post soon became the center of the North West Company operations in the region and had no direct competition in the fur trade for the next ten years. The best laid plans of men and mice. John Jacob Astor got no cheese for this expenditure of men and money.

One of the cards that Astor kept up his sleeve was the chartering, but nonactivation of the American Fur Company in 1810. This kept his Canadian partners in the South West and Pacific Fur Companies from exercising any claims on this nonactive quiescent company.

Did these events affect the Beeler family? Not in the least, although the Wilson P. Hunt party did stop at Prairie du Sac to confer with Joe and Shingabis. Mr. Hunt even went so far as to offer Joe a job with him to journey to the Columbia. Joe thanked him, but refused the offer.

Joe and Annie were more focused on the political situation of April 1811 with regard to the tribes' ill attitudes toward Americans because of settler encroachments, the influence of Tecumseh's Confederation, and the ongoing Non-Intercourse Acts imposed by the Madison administration jeopardizing the yearly delivery of trade goods on which the tribes came to depend.

The Beeler's policy of the minimum use of alcohol in trading with the tribes was successful for the most part, but as usual, there were always situations when their policy was circumvented.

In late December/early January 1810–1811, a party of six Menominee came in for trade. Because two or three of the party were already partially in their cups, the Beelers knew they were in for a spot of trouble. It began in the trade store when one of the bucks demanded rum and Annie refused. He started to get physical with her, so she pulled her bear jaw knife and cut him. Joe and Mr. Paquette heard the commotion and promptly tossed him not so gently out the door. He groused and complained some then crawled off to his party's lodge set up outside the Beeler compound.

Joe conferred with Annie and Paquette and said, "We've got to put an end to this crap." He instructed Paquette and his two brothers-in-law Porcupine and Stone Hawk to go to a bear den he knew of on the bluffs and drag that critter out, bind him, and bring him home. The men knew this was possible because of the hibernation phase the bear was in.

It was nightfall by the time the men brought the critter in. Proceeding to the Menominee's lodge where they were all soused and fast asleep, they tied the critter by one leg to the end of a twenty-five-foot rope tied to a tree right next to the lodge. Joe then set a medicine pole about ten feet from the entrance to the lodge and hung Annie's bear jaw knife on it. Just below it he hung a scrotum bag of a bull buffalo that he had been saving.

By this time, the young bear (he was about two years old) had come out of his hibernation stupor and was not happy with the situation. With Mr. Paquette, Stone Hawk, and Porcupine sitting on and holding him down, Joe quickly removed his scrotum bag with its contents. They turned him loose and got out of the way. Needless to say, all hell broke loose. Being tied to the tree and only having one direction to go, the critter headed straight into the lodge, and six sleeping Menominee bucks had their dreams rudely interrupted.

Come morning, Joe and the men checking the Menominee's camp found complete chaos and ruin. No Indians were to be found. They had departed so quickly, their personal effects were still scattered around camp. All that remained of the young bear was the broken tether rope with a few tufts of fur stuck to it. The only thing left standing and untouched was the medicine pole with the bear jaw knife and buffalo scrotum bag hanging from it.

This event made Joe realize that the attitude of the tribes was becoming a real problem due to the incitement of Tecumseh's Confederacy plus the uncertainty of the trade business because of the embargoes on goods.

He decided, with Annie's approval, that playing on the natives' religious beliefs as they had been doing would give them some security from the natives' bad behavior, commonly induced by rum, when they came to trade at the Beeler's post.

He set a post in the ground in the center of the compound, wrapped it with a large bear hide, took an old Arkansas toothpick blade and replaced its handle with a bear jaw. This he then stuck in the head of the hide and hung from it the large dried bull buffalo scrotum bag. It didn't take the moccasin telegraph long to spread the word, pushed by the six Menominee's experience, of the power of Mrs. Beeler's bear medicine. The totem of the bear protection of the Beeler's post was not to be trifled with, especially when under the influence of rum.

CHAPTER FIVE
CLOUDS OF WAR
AND RELOCATION

In February 1811, Tecumseh paid a visit to Prairie du Sac on his travels through Wisconsin to visit Chief Tomah's Menominee and Chief Red Wing's Winnebago. Joe, Annie, and the entire family were there to take in what he had to say. Due to his family relations with Shingabis and his reputation as a fair trader, plus being well liked by the Sac and Fox, his presence wasn't questioned.

The theme of Tecumseh's epiphany was a return to the culture of the old ways. A total repudiation of the white man's culture and the benefits it provided. Also, he promoted the creation of an Indian nation comprised of all the tribes of the old Northwest territories and tribes from lower Louisiana. His main concern was stopping the encroachment of American settlers into tribal lands. Another grievance was the disruption of the fur trade because of American embargoes, tariffs, and custom fees on English trade goods. He also pushed the theme that the British fur traders and military better understood the plight of the tribes and from

Tecumseh

long experience understood the ins and outs of the fur business relative to the Indian tribes. He urged all who were capable to go to Amherstburg across the river from Detroit, where the British Indian superintendent Matthew Elliott would provide them with blankets, food, guns and powder free of charge. He believed that war with the Americans was inevitable and would happen soon.

Joe and Annie came away from the council feeling the chilblains of uncertainty of the days ahead. They did agree with Tecumseh when he said that war was inevitable soon. After Tecumseh's departure, they decided to let events percolate for a couple of days before sitting down with Shingabis, Anita, and the rest of the family to discuss what happened. Shingabis and Anita were very disheartened at the fact that three quarters of the village agreed with Tecumseh's Epiphany. In fact, over a dozen young warriors were making preparations to travel to Amherstburg. The families, come spring, would prepare to depart Prairie du Sac for Saukenuk to join the warriors who would be there upon their return from Amherstburg. This would reduce the population of Prairie du Sac from about 120 to less than 20. As Shingabis sadly remarked, "This is the end of Prairie du Sac as we have known it." Joe and Annie outlined their plan of safety for the family to Shingabis in that after everyone was joined, the family would travel and settle in St. Louis for the security and connections with local businessmen, Captain Clark, and the authorities for the duration of the war. Shingabis said, "No! I have spent almost sixty winters on this land, and I will not leave it." Anita said, "Where my husband goes, I go." It was decided after much discussion in a council with the remaining twenty or so people that all would settle on the Beeler post at Devil's Lake. Joe would also consign over to Shingabis and Porcupine the remaining inventory of goods.

Joe then wrote two letters, one to his father, George, and one to his brother-in-law and sister, Bruce Loudenhagen and Mary Beth, outlining the results of Tecumseh's visit and what his and Annie's plans were. He proposed that he, Annie, and the family would be at La Bay around May 1 with all bare necessities and the year's catch of furs, sell to Frank Jacobs as usual, and get a letter of credit on the South West Company. This would provide folding money for moving expenses. He urged George and Bruce to dispose of and reduce their assets to the minimum. George and Caroline were then to meet Joe and family at La Bay. They would then proceed via canoe to Kilburn on the Milwaukee River, pick up the Loudenhagens, proceed to Fort Dearborn and down the Illinois to St. Louis, planning arrival there by no later than October. He then sent Jacques Deserve with two men to deliver one of the letters to George and Stone Hawk with two men to deliver the other letter to the Loudenhagens. They were to wait for their answers and then return.

Both parties returned to Devil's Lake by the end of March with the answers.

The Loudenhagens agreed it was a good plan. Bruce wrote that the Potawatomi were worked up too and many parties of warriors were going to Amherstburg also. They would be able to reduce their assets to the minimum, but would have to take the kids (two girls and one boy) and travel to Fort Dearborn to close and settle some accounts there. They would be ready to meet the family there come early September. Plus, the added security of Fort Dearborn would offer peace of mind.

George had a different response. After twenty years, Caroline had established a home on Mackinac Island and was a part of the culture, both during the British and the American tenure, and was highly reluctant to walk away from it all. As she told George, "We aren't spring chickens anymore." Both being in their fifties, George had to agree. But on the other hand, she was also a realist. She saw the uncertainty that existed among the traders and the tribes.

When news of the imposition of the trade embargo by President Madison on March 2, 1811, reached the island, the traders went wild and dammed Astor and the principals of South West Company to high hell! Being in the know, the Beelers got wind of the smuggling of English trade goods stored at Fort Joseph by Robert Dickson, James and George Aird, Allen Wilmot, Joe Rolette, and Tom Anderson, to name a few—all South West Company traders.

Through their daughter Mrs. Hugh (Germaine) Townsend in St. Joseph, they connected with Dr. David Mitchel (the surgeon of the British Garrison) and his Ottawa wife, Elizabeth. To supplement his meager army pay, he had become a trade supplier of goods outfitting winterers. He and his wife were always looking for opportunities (they had twelve kids). After Elizabeth inspected the Beeler properties (house, two acres, and the wholesale fishery business), a deal was struck and finalized.

With about an eighty percent recovery of their assets by the sale, George and Caroline felt better about the move. They got an open letter of credit from the South West Company and, likewise, got the same for Joe and Annie and told them that they would be at La Bay come the middle of May to meet them.

Fort Mackinac 1811

With the good news, the Beelers set about making preparations for departure by April 15. The remainder of the Sauk of Prairie du Sac relocated to the Beeler post at Devil's Lake with the Shingabis family. Porcupine elected to stay with his folks because he had a wife and three kids of his own. Stone Hawk, being single, would go with the Beelers. Mr. Paquette also elected to stay. The family, in two Northern canoes loaded with essentials and the winter's haul of ten packs of furs, manned by Jacques Deserve and the four Canadian hires, set off for La Bay, arriving about the end of April. Finishing up business with Frank Jacobs and talking with James and George Aird as they were passing through gave Joe a good idea of the lay of the land at that point. Much of the conversation was laid on the actions of Robert Dickson, the trader from Prairie du Chien and one-time J.P. there. Through Joe's business connection with Nicholas Bolivar, the Indian agent at Prairie du Chien, he knew quite a bit of Dickson's reputation, and he didn't care for the man. He was a bounder whose methods were always open to question.

George and Caroline arrived by May 1 with their two canoes and essentials manned by four Canadians. Joe told Jacques and his Canadians that he would pay well for the trip to St Louis. Three accepted the offer, but one decided to stay at La Bay. Jacques told Joe that he was Joe's man, and wages were never an issue. Joe understood and told Jacques that he and Annie considered him part of the family, and if he departed, Little Big Head/Jim would be sorely disappointed because Jim considered Jacques his buddy, and Jacques liked the kid.

The Canadians knew a good thing when they had it, and Joe and Annie had their loyalty. They were very fond of Annie and Little Sparrow. God help anybody that threatened their safety. Besides, they enjoyed it when they were the attention of Annie's orders to get off their lazy arses and do something, to which they responded, "Yes, Annie!" just like Joe.

Finally, about the end of May the family flotilla of four canoes departed La Bay for Fort Dearborn. George was short three Canadians at La Bay, so Jacques picked up three replacements, and all agreed to stick with the party all the way to St. Louis. Other than the typical Midwest spring weather of storms and such, the trip was uneventful with a stop for a week at Kilburn to hook up with the Loudenhagens. The party arrived at Fort Dearborn about the end of June, spending about a month waiting for Bruce and Mary Beth to wrap up their affairs. They then portaged the Chicago River to the Des Plaines and down the Illinois to St. Louis.

Fort Dearborn 1811

While passing through Lake Peoria, the party heard of a Lutheran settlement forty miles to the southeast called Funk's Grove. Bruce made a note of this and remarked that this was of import in the days yet to come and filed it away for future pondering!

The trip was, shall we say, eventful while at the same time uneventful because there were no altercations or life-threatening situations. The mood of the country was tense. Every party of Indians met on the way wanted to parley but on their terms, and on a few occasions, it was Joe and George's reputation and diplomacy that carried the day. After a tough confrontation with Potawatomie near Starved Rock (present-day LaSalle, Illinois), the party reverted to night travel and holed up during the day. Finally, after twelve days of travel, the family arrived in St Louis.

Starved Rock Illinois Territory

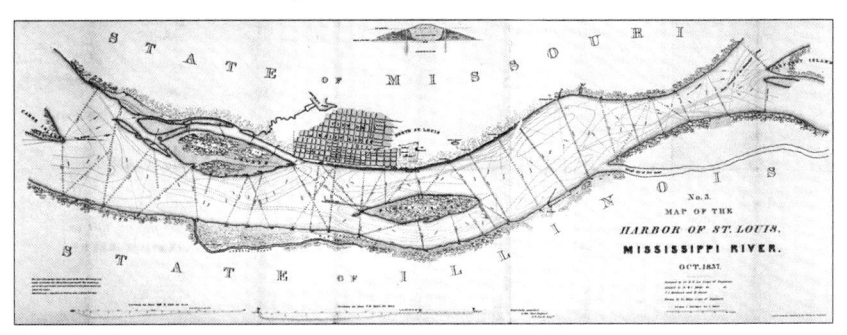

Saint Louis

The family spent well on a month getting settled in and learning the lay of the land. Reconnecting with William Clark, who was now the Indian agent of Upper Louisiana as well as general of the territorial militia, was one of the first orders of business. The general and his wife, Julia, were thrilled to see the Beelers and were most instrumental in bringing the family up to speed socially, business-wise, and politically.

George and Caroline finally settled into a modest-sized store building with living quarters above on Market Street in the business sector on high ground two blocks back from the riverfront warehouses and wharves. Through Pierre Chouteau, George met a young blacksmith/ knife fabricator by the name of Edward Brandsey.

Mr. Brandsey, his wife, Charlene, and two daughters, Michelle and Kathy, had immigrated to St. Louis from Lancaster, Pennsylvania, two years previously and were struggling business-wise to get established. Being from the same area as George and having similar interests in guns and knives struck a spark between the two. and after much discussion, with the families' approval, a partnership was formed and settled in the Beeler building on Market Street, under the name Brandsey-Beeler Essential Stuff Mercantile.

Caroline was happy because not only did she have her children and grandchildren around, she had the Brandsey family to fuss over, too. She was asked by Julia Clark and the Chouteau wives to tutor their kids and found herself teaching a room full of kids three days a week and loving every minute of it! Truth be known, her two grandkids gave her the most happiness and grief, Little Sparrow and Little Big Head. But she was proud of them both. Linda, at eleven, was blossoming into a beauty like her maternal grandmother and mother and loved the genteel surrounding she found herself in. Jim was nine, and it was plain to see that he was destined for the outdoors. He had too much Indian in him, put there by his grandfather Shingabis.

Loudenhagens Home
St. Louis 1811

The Loudenhagens bought a small house just west of the Clarks, and Bruce got a job as a clerk in the main Chouteau warehouse down on the wharves. Mary Beth was kept busy taking care of her family and husband in addition to time spent with activities in the social circle she found herself and mother drawn into. They spent some time in fellowship with a local Presbyterian group led by Charles Gratiot Sr., William C. Carr, and Stephen Hempstead.

Through this fellowship, the family became socially and business-wise connected with the Charles Gratiot family who was related to the Chouteau family (founders of St. Louis in 1764). Charles had a daughter named Isabelle who married Jules de Mun in 1812, one of two brothers of old French aristocracy. It might be said that the de Muns, along with Stephen Hempstead, were influential in causing the Beelers later to relocate and settle in Arkansas.

"Life was good to them," Bruce told Mary Beth, but he had hoped to join the Lutheran settlement at Funk's Grove in Illinois when it was possible to do so.

After meeting many times with William Clark and half-brothers and founders of St Louis, Auguste (Rene) and Pierre Chouteau, Joe and Annie Beeler were offered a limited partnership in Chouteau and Company, with Joe becoming the chief factor of the Chouteau warehouse operations twenty-five miles up the Missouri River at St. Charles.

Chouteau Post St Charles Missouri Terr. 1811

Settling in with Stone Hawk and Jacques Deserve as his facility's segundos, Joe had the place running like a clock and making money for Chouteau Company within six months. Location is a big part of success, and with all traffic going and coming on the Missouri River to St. Louis, passing right in front of the place was a good thing. Joe and Annie made the most of it.

Their unofficial motto was, "Bring in the furs. We got the victuals you need at the right price." Plus, Annie had set up a good eatery right in the warehouse, and there wasn't a boat crew or trader/trapper bunch on the river that could pass it up.

By the spring of 1812, the Beeler family was well ensconced in St. Louis for the duration.

During the winter of 1811–1812, three earthquakes shook parts of Missouri. The first earthquake occurred on December 16, 1811, down in the Missouri Bootheel in the village of New Madrid. The second earthquake occurred on January 23, 1812, in the same general area as the December event. The last and more severe quake was on February 7, 1812, with an estimated magnitude of 7.0. The effects of this last quake reached far upriver past St. Louis. In St. Louis, many homes were damaged by toppling chimneys resulting in house fires. Down on the wharves, the river level dropped and rose as much as ten feet resulting in massive damage to the wharves and riverbanks. Some say that was the morning when the river reversed its flow.

The stories from the tribes trying to explain the cause, though different, all had a common thread; the bear spirit had been awakened from his winter's sleep and attacked by a giant serpent from the underworld. The bear spirit had prevailed in the struggle with the serpent and drove it back to its underworld lair. He had then resumed his winter's sleep but was still highly agitated and did not sleep well. This explained the aftershocks felt after the major quakes and all the unusual happenings, such as the river flowing backward upstream. As Joe said to Annie and Stone Hawk, "Makes sense to me!"

New Madrid Earthquake 1811

On April 30, 1812, soon after the earthquakes, Louisiana joined the Union. It was a contentious process that had its start back in 1803 with the Louisiana Purchase. Article III of that purchase stated, "The inhabitants of the ceded territory shall be incorporated into the Union of the United States and admitted as soon as possible according to the principles of the federal constitution." Rejection of statehood for Louisiana would have been tantamount to rejecting the Louisiana Purchase, and that wasn't about to happen.

After being volleyed more than seven times between both Houses, it was finally passed. A state convention was convened per the Ordinance of 1787, a state constitution was written and returned to Washington, both Houses passed the bill, and President Madison signed it into law.

Louisiana became the eighteenth state and first west of the Mississippi River carved from territory not part of the original lands ceded by Great Britain after the Revolutionary War. The western border of the state wasn't formalized until 1819 by the Adams-Onis Treaty with Spain. Western Florida was finally included at this time with the Pearl River becoming the state line with the Florida Territory.

CHAPTER SIX
THE WAR OF 1812

Like any conflict between multiple parties, there are many aspects to it. Every aggrieved participant sees it from their point of view, and, in most cases, it doesn't match up to reality. That said, this narrative will only cover the aspects of this conflict relative to the Beeler family and parties they were in contact with primarily in the territories of the Old Northwest.

The American side was expanding the nation by settlement in the territories, displacing the Indian tribes in the process. The British side was hanging on to the economic benefits through the fur trade with the tribes and trying to keep the young American nation's sphere of political and economic power in check. The Indians wanted to hang on to their tribal lands and culture (way of life), but they handicapped themselves by adopting the tools that the European culture had to offer and more, so their way of life came to depend on it.

The Sauk were relatives of the Beelers; they were family! The Fox were like family but had to be reminded of it constantly. What about the Winnebago? Joe and Annie thought they were primitive brutes. Don't turn your back on them. The Menomonee were drunks that couldn't even get along with themselves. The Potawatomi and Kickapoo were okay, but the years of bad traders plying them with bad booze for trade had left them weary. The Sioux/Lakota were wily and not to be trusted. Their longstanding war with the Ojibwa had really scrambled their basic character as human beings. The same can be said for the Ojibwa.

Annie and Joe's whole life was tied to the Indian culture and fur trade. When it came to politics, they understood the negative effect it had on the human psyche and had little use for it. In short, they lived in reality and sided with the Indian viewpoint of it. That's not to say they were unpatriotic, because they considered themselves American through and through. If not, they would never have hooked up with and befriended Captain Clark back on the Missouri River at the Mandan's village in 1804.

Focusing on the Sauk in this conflict, their background and tribal culture was centered around their main village of Saukenuk at Rock Island. The civil chief was Quashquame, the ceremonial chief was Pahshepaho, and the principal war chief was Black Sparrow Hawk.

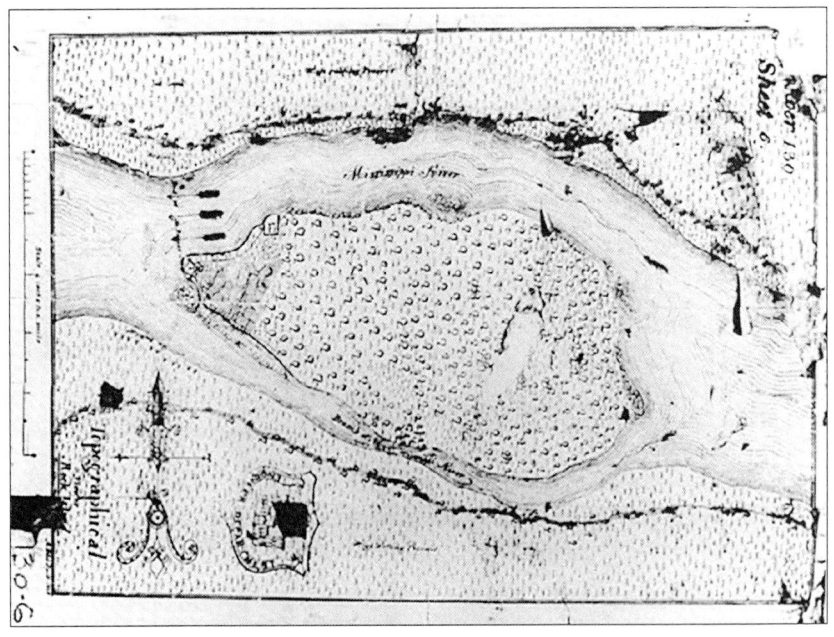

Saukenuk at Rock Island Illinois Territory

The Sauk had a problem with the Treaty of 1804, negotiated by the wily William Henry Harrison, governor of the Indiana Territory at that time. Black Hawk refused to make his mark and flat out refused to abide by it. Truth be known, it was the primary cause of the Black Hawk War of 1832.

Back to the spring of 1812. William Clark, as main Indian agent of Upper Louisiana, took a delegation of Sauk, Fox, Osage, Potawatomi, Miami, and Winnebago to Washington to engender their respect for The United States and to ensure their neutrality.

William Clark's Indian Delegation to Washington D.C.

After meeting President Madison and Secretary of War Eustis, who promised all matter of goods to meet their needs, the delegation returned home to find their relatives preparing for war, which had been declared against Great Britain. To add salt to the wound, Black Hawk had not been asked to be a part of this delegation. Instead, he and a group of warriors headed to Mackinaw to meet with Robert Dickson who equipped them with firearms, powder and shot, and everything else they might need.

The British had captured Mackinaw in July 1812. Dickson induced Black Hawk and his warriors to travel to Detroit to capture same, but arrived too late because General William Hull had already surrendered. After laying over for about a month or so, the British Commander, Lieutenant Colonel St. George, finally attacked the American reinforcements coming to retake Detroit under William Henry Harrison at River Raisin. When Black Hawk and his warriors arrived to join in the battle, it was over with the Americans in full retreat, so no scalps or plunder for them. In disgust, Black Hawk and his warriors packed up and returned home in the fall of 1813.

While he was gone, a number of events occurred.

Nicolas Bolivar, agent to the Sauk, knew there was a neutral element among the tribe that favored the Americans. He and Fox interpreter Maurice Blondeau were trying to get them to relocate at the mouth of the Des Moines River. They almost had their efforts derailed when, in December 1812, a party of Missouri rangers captured two Sauk men on the banks of the Mississippi River. They released the old man but murdered and scalped the younger man on general principles. The murdered man was the brother of Quashquame civil chief of the neutral faction who also signed the 1804 treaty. When the family appealed to the commander of Fort Madison for a present to "cover the dead," they were rebuffed and sent away exacerbating the incident. When William Clark learned what had happened, he was chagrined and directed Blondeau to give $125 worth of presents to the offended family to conciliate them.

In April 1813, Bolivar lead the neutral Sauk and Fox to the mouth of the Des Moines River. Some of the chiefs then visited Governor Howard and offered to fight against the British, which Howard flatly refused. He apparently trusted no armed Indians roaming the countryside, regardless of their allegiance. One chief replied that they could not restrain the young men when war was all around them. And, as the

Americans would not suffer the Indians to join them in that war, they must go and join the British who had invited them to do so.

Despite the bad decisions and defeats, some good news for the Americans developed in the West. A long-standing feud between the Fox and Winnebago came to blows, creating a schism in the British and Indian alliance, which the British seemed unable to quell. Since the Winnebago were staunch allies of the British, the Fox could only turn to the U.S. for aid in their fight. This situation ensured that the majority of Fox remained neutral toward the Americans during the rest of the war. However, the Sauk were now placed in an extremely awkward position. Other tribes aligned with Britain threatened the Sauk if they tried to intervene on behalf of the Fox. The Sauk, therefore, had to decline the pleas for assistance from their old comrades.

In July, Howard sent a request to Secretary of War Armstrong to lead a force to Prairie du Chien and build a fort there. Before he could get a reply to his request, a strong party of Potawatomie and Sauk attacked Fort Madison. Howard changed targets and in September led a force of 1,300 militiamen to Peoria Lake in the heart of Potawatomie country and began construction of Fort Clark. He then sent a reconnaissance force under Major Nathan Boone toward Rock River and Saukenuk.

Convinced that they were about to be attacked, the Sauk convened an emergency council but were filled with indecision and despair because Black Hawk and the other war chiefs were still back in the East. As the council was breaking up, a young man asked permission to speak even though he had not met the necessary requirements to do so. According to custom, one must have killed an enemy in battle. However, the young man was articulate and well liked. Given permission to speak, he immediately proceeded to berate the council for their defeatism and offered to lead the defense of Saukenuk. The oratory of Keokuk, or The Watchful Fox, so stirred the tribe that he was made nominal leader of the Sauk.

Boone's "recon in force" came only within forty-five miles of Saukenuk before returning to Fort Clark at Peoria Lake. Among the Sauk, however, Keokuk leadership was thought to have turned back the American long knives, further consolidating his influence in the tribe.

Black Hawk, returning home, was stunned to find a man who was not even a warrior competing for his leadership of the tribe. This started a bitter rivalry of lasting consequence to the Sac and Fox Nation. While Black Hawk excelled as a military leader, he lacked vital diplomatic and oratorical skills, thus limiting his influence in civil and political matters. Keokuk, on the other hand, possessed the diplomatic skills Black Hawk lacked. Keokuk in time became a good friend of William Clark, and his long leadership of the tribe after the war made him one of the important leaders to emerge in the Sauk Nation.

After being appointed governor of the Missouri Territory in the late summer of 1813, William Clark joined with Nicolas Bolivar and Maurice Blondeau to separate the neutral Sauk from British influence and make amends for Governor Howard's earlier rejection of their offer of assistance. At the September 28 council meeting at Portage Des Sioux, Quashquame and Keokuk agreed to move their people to Moniteau Creek, about fifteen miles northeast of Boonville, Missouri. Their village and new factory under John Johnson were established here and consisted of approximately 1,500 people. Negotiations were also held so that they and their old enemy, the Osage, would not be at each other's throats.

Black Hawk scornfully said Keokuk's band were nothing more than a bunch of old women and men not fit to be called Sauk and if met in battle would be treated the same as their old enemies the Osage. To vent his frustration and rage, he and a large party of warriors attacked and sieged Fort Madison for a month. After the Sauk departed, the garrison abandoned and burned the fort and returned to St. Louis. Black Hawk was satisfied that the detestable Fort Madison was finally gone. It was hated by the Sauk since the day it was built, and the factory was managed by the detestable John Johnson, a typical government bureaucrat.

Fort Madison 1808

For the balance of 1813 and into 1814, Black Hawk was no longer tied to the formal British command and began to fight in traditional Sauk style using hit-and-run raids on the outlying American settlements with ambush their main tool of war. This activity was enough to keep the Missouri frontier highly unsettled and served as an outlet for Sauk frustrations.

Going into 1814, the course of the war was mixed. For the U.S. in the East it was a mess. But in the West things were a little better. Harrison had recaptured Detroit. Oliver Hazard Perry had defeated the British fleet on Lake Erie. At the Battle of the Thames, the British were defeated by Harrison, and Tecumseh was killed, thereby removing the influence of Tecumseh's Confederation, leaving the tribes adrift relative to the pursuit of the war. This news was received by the citizens of St. Louis as a real possibility that the war would soon be over. Sad to say the events of 1814 proved them wrong.

Battle of Lake Erie

Battle of the Thames

Relative to the sporadic hit-and-run raids by the Sauk and Fox along the Missouri and Illinois frontiers, the marauding bands at times found themselves in tight situations being pursued by the local militia or regular troops. Consequently, the warriors would retreat and blend in with family members with Keokuk's band at Moniteau Creek. This caused severe tensions between Keokuk's people and their factor John Johnson. At the same time, the American settlements and militia who were in the know, and out of deference to Governor Clark, Nicholas Bolivar, and Maurice Blondeau, in some cases tried to hold their retaliatory actions in check.

John Johnson, at the end of his rope and being the bumbling bureaucrat that he was, tried to shut down the factory to the Sauk. All this did was inflame the young warriors who wanted to put him on the burning stake. But through the intervention of Nicholas Bolivar and the warriors' relatives, a bad incident was prevented, and John Johnson, tucking his tail, retreated to St. Louis.

How did the Beelers do during this time of turmoil during the war?

Joe said to Annie, "As life seems to get a little easier, it gets more complicated and turns to sour milk more quickly!" Both realized their good fortune in having a partnership in the Chouteau Company and having charge of the St. Charles operations. Plus, the immediate family was secure in the St. Louis area, and all were in good health considering the times in which they lived.

Word had come to them that Shingabis was ailing and having a hard winter.

Business was good because Joe had the exclusive benefit of having all the fur trade of the Missouri, Sauk, and Fox, and at any time there was a goodly number of them camped just outside the St. Charles post. The resulting altercations between the Indians and the Americans continually coming and going kept everybody on edge. Joe and Annie's reputations and goodwill kept the situation from falling apart. It was their segundos, Stone Hawk and Jacques Deserve, and the workforce that were the "oil on the water" that helped them make it work. The men and women were loyal to Annie and Joe and respected them, which Annie and Joe returned in spades.

As stated previously, the location on the river at St. Charles provided an advantage of having all the traffic, coming and going, pass by their establishment. Annie's eatery in the warehouse was like a magnet, drawing a steady stream of customers off the river into the place.

Supplying Annie's eatery was not a problem because her workforce and the Indian encampments had extensive gardens on which to draw. Stone Hawk and Jacques kept two or three hunters busy supplying the meat, and the stocks taken in trade were utilized.

In April 1813, a ragged travel-worn party came off the river to partake of a good meal. It consisted of Robert Stuart, Ramsey Crooks, Joe Miller, Robert McCallum, and a young Cheyenne squaw with her nine-year-old daughter. This was the returning party of Astorians bringing the news of Astor's failed Pacific Fur Company venture. They had left Astoria, Oregon, in June 1812. The tale of their long hard journey is beyond the scope of this narrative, but suffice to say, their arrival in St. Louis was surreal to them, like they had entered another world.

Coming down the North Platte through Wyoming, they had come upon a northern Cheyenne squaw and her daughter. She had lost her husband, an English trader from the North West Company, earlier in the year to malaria. She and her daughter were trying to rejoin her family band of Cheyenne when the Astorians chanced upon her. Being pretty, and knowing some English, the party asked her to join them, which she did, thereby gaining security for herself and her daughter. Plus, the party gained an interpreter because of her skills in sign language and Cheyenne and Pawnee tongues. As time went on, they grew to like her and looked out for her and her daughter. Her name was Fox That Purrs, and the daughter's name was Silly One/Sara, the Christian name given to her by her father.

Stuart and Crooks were surprised upon meeting the Beelers and decided to layover one more day to catch up on current events before heading on down the St. Louis. They were surprised by the relative calm and peacefulness of the Lakota/Sioux on the upper river. Joe opined that this was probably due to the crafty Manuel Lisa of the Missouri Fur Company playing the Lakota off against their longtime enemy, the Ojibwa, who were under British influence.

Passing Fort Osage and all the way down to St. Charles, the countryside was deserted with American settlers forted up at the larger settlements. After Joe explained the war and its repercussions and current status, everything began to make sense to the Astorians, but was still very surreal.

Fox That Purrs

After meeting Fox That Purrs and Sara, Annie liked what she saw, and her woman's intuition was telling her to take a chance. After talking it over with Joe, Annie offered Fox a job with Chouteau and Company, which she accepted. Joe commented, "Annie draws people like lint and dust, and who am I to argue with her. I am just a mere mortal man—nothing more, nothing less." Fox was shy and reclusive at first. Typical of one who had to live and survive by her wits alone and, at the same time, take care of one's child. But after a time living and working in the Beeler establishment, which provided personal security and stability in her and her daughter's lives, she began to open up and became a person most everyone liked. Stone Hawk, the confirmed bachelor, took a shine to her.

Sara/Silly One was a happy and silly ten-year-old child that had to be looked after. She was too naive and trusting, as the name which her father had bestowed upon her suggested. After a couple of months of watching Sara, Annie suggested to Joe that maybe it would be helpful to send her to Caroline for tutoring and refinement in the social graces. Joe had no problem with that idea because if the child could read, write, and cipher, she would have an advantage in handling problems life would throw at her. But he advised Annie that it would be solely up to her mother, Fox. Annie said, "No problem, I'll start working on her!" which she did by taking Fox and Sara to St. Louis and introducing them to Caroline, Char Brandsey, Julia Clark, Mary Beth, and the rest of the social circle. Sara was enrolled into Caroline's class and would be living with George and Caroline while attending school.

Sara, being the new kid in the class, was initially open to childish curiosity, and the other kids took advantage of her, from which Caroline did her best to protect her. But her greatest hero and protector turned out to be Little Big Head/Jim. He, in short, drew the lines of behavior for the other kids relative to little Sara, and if those lines were crossed, the culprit paid the price. In fact, Caroline had to discipline Jim a couple of times when he was a little too rough. "Jim," she would say, "remember these are town kids, not an Indian boy like you, and besides, you should never hit the girls. Your mother and father taught you that!" Poor Jim. But he managed and in the process won the affection of Sara. This relationship followed the same path as it had with his mother and father when they had first met as kids. As 1813 rolled into 1814, the turmoil of the war continued with the frontier unsettled like a teapot just short of boiling over. The altercations between settlers and Indians at St. Charles was a daily occurrence with the Chouteau and Company workforce running interference constantly. One method that Joe and his segundos, Stone Hawk and Jacques, used was a quick toss of the offending parties, white and Indian alike, into the river for a cool off. It worked most of the time, but there were always a few that had to cool off in the St. Charles calaboose. In fact, Joe had an open agreement with the justice of the peace and the town marshal in supplying miscreants to them to cover court and boarding costs. Maybe upon close scrutiny it wasn't above board, but in most cases the problems were solved. Plus, word spread that when in St. Charles, and especially at Chouteau and Company, behave yourself and you won't have any trouble. For the Indians, the thought of one night in the calaboose terrified them, and they also knew if they were the instigator of the problem, Joe himself would deliver them to the marshal. Upon hearing from one of their relatives from Devil's Lake that Shingabis was failing, Joe, Annie, and Stone Hawk set about laying plans to get to Devil's Lake and do whatever was necessary for Shingabis, Anita, and family.

In the spring of 1814, rumors were running amok that a force of 1,000-plus warriors were about to descend the Mississippi toward St. Louis. Governor Clark consulted with Joe, Nick Bolivar, and Maurice Blondeau regarding the rumor. He came away with the conviction that even if it were true, he would take the initiative and launch a force to take Prairie du Chien thereby disrupting the British influence and support for the tribes and build a fort at the prairie like Governor Howard had planned the year before.

Coming to Joe, Governor Howard requested his help on this expedition. "Joe," he said, "I know your solid in with the Sauk, and I know your help in this matter will help in reducing hostilities to a minimum and save lives!" Joe knew that his balance sheet with Governor Clark was tipped in the governor's favor, and this helped with working out an arrangement with Annie.

"Fine," she said, "but I go where you go!"

But for the second time in their marriage Joe said no! His argument was sound, and Annie knew it. Someone needed to keep the business running, and with Jacques' help, that was doable. Plus, the emotional ties needed to be kept with the kids and family while Joe was gone. Annie's heart argued with her mind, but in the end her head prevailed. She said to Joe, "Alright, go. But you will bring my mama home to me!"

In early May, Clark, with 200 men, embarked up the river aboard a gunboat bearing his name. Joe, Stone Hawk, and Nick Bolivar were the designated interpreters. Approaching Saukenuk at the Rock River, canoe loads of Indians approached the gunboat. A warning cannon shot was fired, and upon seeing Joe and Stone Hawk aboard, the Indians signaled for a parley. Joe and Stone Hawk accompanied the Indians to the village. After an hour of parley they agreed to meet with Governor Clark on the beach and work out a truce, which they did mainly because of Joe and Stone Hawk telling them Clark meant business and had the means to enforce it.

Continuing up the river, word of Clark's force reached Prairie du Chien. The Indians there refused to support the British garrison who promptly fled the area. It was a "cake walk" for Clark entering the Prairie. He immediately set the troops under Lieutenant Perkins to the construction of Fort Shelby. Leaving the Governor Clark anchored at the Prairie for support, he took a small party in a bateau and returned to St Louis. He released Joe and Stone Hawk who proceeded up the Wisconsin River in a small canoe to Devil's Lake and Shingabis.

Fort Shelby/McKay, Prairie du Chien

Unfortunately, Clark's efforts were for naught because on July 20, British and Indian forces under Colonel William McKay returned and attacked Fort Shelby. Due to the excellent gunnery skills of his artillery, Sergeant Keating, with a 3-pounder, severely damaged the Governor Clark, forcing its anchor cable to be cut and then floating on the current out of range of the 3-pounder. The 3-pounder was turned on the fort and within two days intimidated the American garrison to surrender. The fort was renamed Fort McKay in honor of their commanding officer.

Joe and Stone Hawk proceeded toward Devil's Lake anxiously because it had been some time since they had received news about Shingabis's illness. They traveled at night and put up at secure secret camps during the day because of the war and the tribal unrest throughout the territory.

As ill luck would have it, they had put in well before dawn, somewhere around present-day Blue River, Wisconsin, and secured their camp. Stone Hawk mentioned to Joe, "I think we are being followed!"

"I agree. How many?"

"Three!" Stone Hawk replied. "Young bucks, Winnebago, looking to put some notches and hair on their poles!"

"Right you are, Brother. We'll just have to accommodate them and introduce them to Annie's bear medicine!"

They covered the canoe. Then they set one bedroll to look like a person laid out under a blanket sleeping and set the other bedroll up against the canoe under a hat and rolled in a blanket with a trade gun across its lap looking for all the world like a person on guard fast asleep! Then Joe and Stone Hawk concealed themselves in the underbrush across from one another and began the wait.

About two hours after dawn, the three young bucks had crept within forty yards of the camp. Three shots rang out, and three balls impacted the dummy bedrolls. Ten minutes later the three Winnebago entered the camp with drawn knives and stood surveying their work. Two pistol shots rang out followed by the thud of a hatchet impacting into the skull of one the Indians followed immediately by three bodies hitting the ground.

Looking over their work, Joe said to Stone Hawk, "You're right on all points, and they will never see old age! I've been thinking, Brother. If we introduce them to Annie's bear medicine, it might raise a flag that we are back in the area!"

"No!" said Stone Hawk. "They're damn Winnebago and the tribe needs to have its memory reinforced again about the power of the bear spirit, and besides, it's for our father Shingabis and Annie."

They scalped the three and hung the bodies upside down, disemboweling each and painting bear tracks and claw prints on the throats and chests. Joe then took a bear jaw and buffalo scrotum bag that he always carried in his medicine pouch, attached it to an old camp knife, and stuck it and the scalps on a post which Stone Hawk had mounted in front of the hanging corpses. They left the possibles of the Indians scattered around and broke the stocks of their fusels. Joe and Stone Hawk put back out on the river and, hugging the south shoreline, put in about a dozen miles from the scene of the incident. They secured another camp for the day trusting to luck that they hadn't been spotted.

Reminiscing afterwards about what happened, Joe remarked, "Hawk, you know five years ago I wouldn't have hesitated in the least about doing what needed to be done, but now I think twice before doing it! What's the matter with me?"

"Brother, not a thing," said Stone Hawk. "I think it shows your wisdom in life and your spiritual beliefs are maturing. Like our father Shingabis has taught us, 'Judgement comes from experience and experience comes from bad judgement!' " "Thanks!" said Joe. "That's why I thank the Great Spirit that he has given me you as my brother!"

"Right back at you, Joe. And, with luck, tomorrow night we should be at our father's home!"

As Stone Hawk predicted, the following evening found them arriving at Devil's Lake. They found the people in a somber mood, and Anita, overjoyed that her two sons had arrived, gave them the synopsis on Shingabis's condition; he was rapidly declining. As Anita said, "My herbs and ministrations no longer have an effect on my husband. He's worn out, and spiritually he's ready to move on!" Shingabis did revive somewhat for a day or so upon knowing that Joe and Stone Hawk were present. He conversed with the family during this time and made known his wishes that he be laid with Celeste, his first wife, in the rock crypt in the small valley coming off the bluffs, known today as Parfrey's Glen.

Shingabis hung on for another ten days before he passed quietly in his sleep surrounded by the family. He was interred as requested, and all traces of the crypt were removed and hidden. The family convened on the future with Porcupine and his family remaining at Devil's Lake with two other families. He said as his father said, "This is my home, and this is where I will remain!"

Joe, Stone Hawk, and Anita began planning the trip back to St. Louis. As it was already June and the summer was almost upon them, the weather was expected to be tolerable. Joe and Stone Hawk were more concerned for Anita's health being that she turned fifty that year. She would respond, "Don't you tell me what to do. I was cleaning your boy's backside from way back, and besides, my herb bag can cover most of what might harm us!" "Yes, Ma!" they replied, and the subject was not brought up to her again.

They decided to head southeast to the four lakes area of Madison, Wisconsin, pick up a canoe and proceed down the Yahara to the Rock River. Then follow that down to present-day Janesville, Wisconsin, cut across the prairie to another Chain O'Lakes region in Fox Lake, Illinois, and pick up the Fox River down to its confluence with the Illinois River at Ottawa, Illinois. Then down to Fort Clark at Peoria Lake, Illinois.

They decided it was more expedient to travois the canoe that they had come upriver with by horse to the Yahara River at the four lakes. Accompanied by Porcupine, his son, and another warrior to return with the horse, the party reached the four lakes without incident. For security reasons, Stone Hawk and Joe decided to resort to night travel and hole up for the day.

Porcupine told Joe and Stone Hawk that if they were up to a two-and-a-half-mile portage, he knew of a water route that wasn't out of the way but would allow them to utilize the canoe for the whole trip. "Not a problem if Mother Anita agrees!"

To which she quipped, "What did I tell you boys?"

"Yes, Ma! Porcupine, what's your plan?" "Proceed down the Rock to the Turtle Creek confluence, (present-day Beloit, Wisconsin). Turn up Turtle Creek, and follow it to its headwaters at a medium-sized lake (present-day Lake Delavan). Portage southeast two-and-a-half miles across prairie savanna to a large, deep lake (present-day Lake Geneva). Follow the river outlet (present-day White River) at the northeast corner to its confluence with the Fox River, (present-day Burlington) and you're on your way! Plus, the water should still be high because of the wet spring/summer we've had!" "Yah!" said Joe. "I remember that route from the winter of 1792–93 coming through here with Paw (George), and it's doable!" Following that route of travel by night, weather permitting, the party successfully passed through. While holed up for the day, near present-day St. Charles, Illinois, a large party of Potawatomi passed by going upriver. Unbeknownst to Joe and Stone Hawk, that party was on their way to join Robert Dickson's call to arms to retake Fort Shelby at Prairie du Chien, which was done on July 20. Because of Stone Hawk and Joe's precautions, they were not detected. On the lighter side, Joe complimented Anita on her ability to remain silent. Unfortunately, she didn't appreciate the humor in his remark, and for two days those "ungrateful boys" who showed no respect for their dear mother bore the wrath of her tongue! But in between the upbraiding, she said, "I love you boys anyway!"

After two weeks of travel they reached Fort Clark at Peoria Lake.

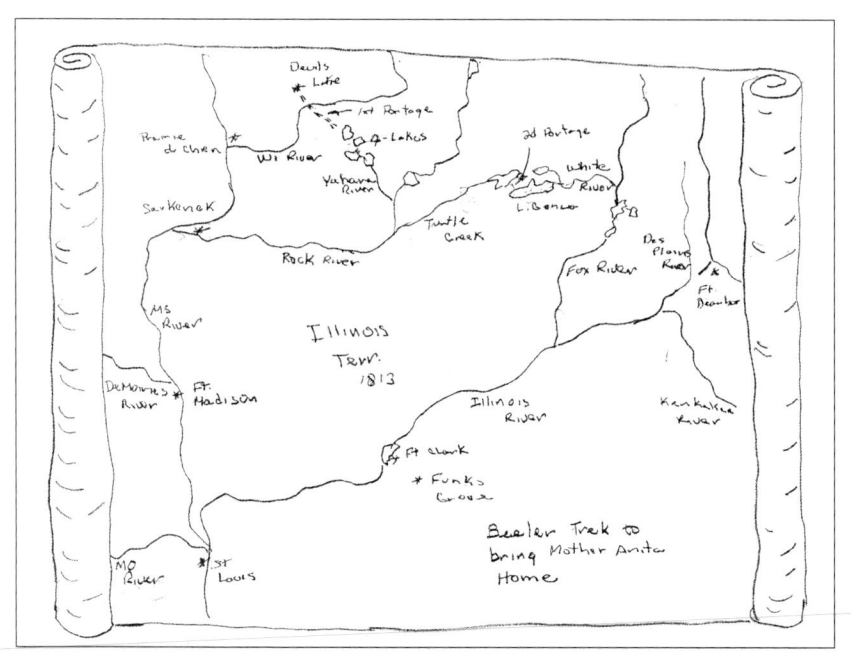

Sometimes circumstances in life step in the way, and one must decide whether to deal with it or step aside and be left wondering if walking away was the right choice.

It was one of these circumstances that Anita, Stone Hawk, and Joe found themselves facing upon arriving at Fort Clark. They found four men from the little settlement of Funk's Grove forty miles to the southeast. They were there to purchase needed supplies and catch up on the war situation. Upon further conversation, Joe mentioned that his brother-in-law Bruce Loudenhagen was an ordained Lutheran minister and had talked a lot about their settlement and aspirations for it. Upon hearing this, the men immediately asked Joe, Anita, and Stone Hawk to accompany them back to Funk's Grove and meet the rest of the people. The congregation was looking for a preacher, and if the preacher was an ordained Lutheran, they would consider that God was putting the best apple in their spiritual pie.

Talking it over amongst themselves, Anita remarked, "Boys, it's the right thing to do and shouldn't add any more than another two weeks for our arrival at St. Louis. But, it's my daughter Magpie I'm thinking about. You boys know her as well as I. And since you boys left two months ago, she has probably torn your home apart, and it is not fit to be lived with by anyone!"

"Yes, you're right, Ma. I will get a message to her via the packet boat leaving tomorrow with dispatches for St. Louis outlining our plans and estimated time of arrival. And I would ask you for a P.S. 'Daughter, your mother loves you, and I am telling you to be Christian!' Also, I will ask Julia Clark if she would personally see that the letter is delivered to Annie! That should keep some 'oil on the water' and relieve my bride's anxiety somewhat," replied Joe.

The party formed up and arrived by horseback at Funk's Grove without any incident. The settlement was overjoyed at the possible prospect of getting a Lutheran preacher. Anita, Stone Hawk, and Joe spent two days with the congregation gathering background for Bruce and being fed and fussed over. Before departure, Joe asked for a bill for the horses, but was told, "No Charge!" Three of the men offered to accompany them to St. Louis, but Joe and Stone Hawk declined saying the men were needed more by their families. Plus, Joe diplomatically told them that a small party could move through hostile country better than a larger party. Joe and Stone Hawk's survival skills wouldn't be compromised by inexperience. Stone Hawk and Joe were proud of Mother Anita because she kept quiet the during the whole conversation!

Five days later, the party reached St. Louis and overnighted with George and Caroline. They sent word immediately to Annie at St. Charles. At 11:00 p.m. that evening, there was a ruckus at Beeler's door, and Annie came bursting in with Jacques close behind followed by Little Sparrow and Little Big Head. Annie embraced Joe so hard that they went sprawling on the floor, smothering him with kisses and scolding him at the same time about how this will never happen again. Anita was next for Annie's embrace and scolding, and then she turned on Stone Hawk with the same. It was quite a rambunctious, emotional half hour with the kids, parents, grandparents, and friends getting reacquainted.

The party spent three days in St. Louis debriefing the Loudenhagens and Governor Clark on what they had seen and experienced. Bruce was especially excited and sent a letter stating his intentions to the Funk's Grove Congregation via the Fort Clark packet boat. They could expect to see him and his family when the war was over and that he would accept their call!

Joe, Annie, Anita, Stone Hawk, Jacques, and the kids arrived back home at St. Charles.

In August, General Howard, enraged by the fall of Fort Shelby and the repulse of his relief force of 130 men on five boats at Saukenuk by the British, Sauk, and Fox forces, sent Colonel Zachary Taylor upriver to destroy all Indian villages and defeat any British forces encountered. But the fickle finger of fate was not in their favor. The expert gunnery of Lieutenant Graham and Sergeant Keating along with the Indians wreaked havoc on the Taylor forces and turned them back downriver with the loss of one boat and a third of the force wounded and killed. After this debacle, the tribes lost all fear of the American military might, and for the next year and a half, the Missouri and Illinois frontiers suffered the ravages of their hit-and-run raids.

In the East, the war was a give-and-take situation. The Great Lakes were controlled by the Americans because of Perry's victory of September 1813. The war on the sea was of little importance because of British Naval superiority, even though it was a give and take with the USS Essex captured off Valparaiso, Chile, and the HMS Guerriere destroyed by the USS Constitution. The British marched on and burned Washington D.C. in August but were stopped cold at Fort McHenry, Baltimore, in September. That same month, British Lord Provost led an army south to Plattsburgh, New York, but was turned back by Captain Thomas McDonough's defeat of the British fleet on Lake Champlain. (This denied British negotiators leverage at the Treaty of Ghent discussions.)

General Andrew Jackson made his military/political career by leading a force of Kentuckian-Tennessean forces south through Creek and Chickasaw country, defeating them in the process. Then pulling together a mixed force of New Orleanians, Boratian pirates, and Creoles with his force of Kentuckian-Tennesseans, they defeated a British army of 8,000 men led by General Edward Packham in December 1814, January 1815.

It might be said that the Brits, in their arrogance, were preparing to annex the entire Louisiana Territory and divide up the spoils accordingly. They even had civilian agents on board who had paid out good money to the War Department for permits to do the dividing. These pompous clowns were prematurely figuring what their profits were going to be! Ole Stonewall proved them wrong.

Battle of New Orleans

Nonetheless, the Treaty of Ghent was signed on December 24, 1814, ratified by the prince regent on December 30, 1814, and ratified by the U.S. Senate on February 16, 1815. Hostilities continued into early March until official word reached the combatants in the field.

Relative to spreading the end of the war news in the old Northwest Territory, British Captain Butler at Fort McKay in Prairie du Chien received the news on May 10, 1815. He immediately sent word to Lieutenant Graham at Saukenuk to call back all Sauk and Fox war parties, at which he was partially successful, with the proviso that if they didn't, they would lose whatever benefits the British had secured for them in the treaty.

When Captain Butler read the terms of the treaty to 800 Indians at Fort McKay on May 10, Black Hawk held up the war belt he had received from British officials in Canada and said, "I have fought the big knives and will continue to fight them until they are off our lands. Until then, my father, your red children cannot be happy." At the conclusion of his speech. He stormed out of the council room. He followed up by leading a large war party to Missouri and having a number of skirmishes with the militia around St. Charles and Fort Howard.

Governor Clark of Missouri, Governor Edwards of Illinois, and Pierre Chouteau were appointed peace commissioners and sent messengers out to twenty-eight tribes to come to Portage Des Sioux to make peace. Gradually, the tribes gathered at Portage Des Sioux, noting that the majority of the Fox tribe was present, but less than fifty of the Rock River Sauk showed up. Governor Clark followed up by sending a messenger to Saukenuk to bring in Black Hawk and the rest of the Sauk. The messenger was scalped, and the Sauk refused to come.

Governor Clark then called on Joe and Stone Hawk to accompany Nicholas Bolivar to negotiate with Black Hawk and his warriors and accompany them back to Portage Des Sioux for the treaty signing. Governor Clark impressed upon Joe, Stone Hawk, and Bolivar, the critical nature of their trip to get the Sauk to come in. Annie, after conferring with her mother, Anita, suggested to Joe and Governor Clark that they accompany the men. Joe and Stone Hawk were reluctant, but after listening to Annie and her mother's reasoning, they agreed. Governor Clark was so enthusiastic that he said to Bolivar, "Follow these ladies lead, and do what they tell you."

The party arrived at Saukenuk without incident, and the first order of activity was renewing acquaintances with family, relatives, and friends from Prairie du Sac with feasting and celebrations. Joe, Stone Hawk, Annie, Anita, and Bolivar then entered council with Black Hawk and the tribal headmen. Gradually, progress was made in the negotiations, and it can be said the wisdom of Anita, wife of the revered Shingabis, is what carried the day.

Black Hawk and the Sauk agreed to cease hostilities and be at Portage Des Sioux in early spring to sign a treaty with Governor Clark.

They appeared on May 6, 1816, to sign the treaty. All the headmen, including Black Hawk, were directed to touch the goose quill to recognize and reconfirm the validity of the Treaty of 1804. The war of 1812 was finally over on the Missouri, Illinois, and Upper Midwest frontiers.

The war left the Sauk and Fox tribes divided politically in the two factions, one under Keokuk and the other under Black Hawk. Keokuk's leadership grew as did his friendship and subservience to the Americans. Black Hawk remained recalcitrant, insisting the Treaty of 1804 was illegal and invalid. This faction came to be called the British Band because of their belief that somehow, someway, Great Britain would again come to their aid. Ironically, settlers moving into Clark County, Missouri, just north of St. Charles where Black Hawk and his band lived, tended to view Black Hawk as an honorable and trustworthy individual despite his hostile past. He made many friends among the settlers, especially the Beeler family at St. Charles, and never threatened them. On the other hand, the same people viewed Keokuk as a drunkard and held in the low esteem.

Annie said to Joe, "It's hard to believe it's been five years since we left Devil's Lake. I thank the Great Spirit that he has watched over our family and kept us safe through the turbulence and events of the war!" And the family settled into the hopeful peace of the coming years ahead.

CHAPTER SEVEN
POST WAR YEARS AND RESTRUCTURING OF THE FUR TRADE

The Annie and Joe Beeler family was doing very well at the Chouteau, St. Charles operation. Not only were they taking trade off the Missouri River, but they had the entire Sauk-Fox trade coming in also, which was the greater portion of their income. So much so that there was a semi-permanent Indian village just outside the Chouteau trading facilities.

On the property was a large volume flowing spring (smaller in size to modern-day Mammoth Springs, Arkansas) which provided clean, slightly alkaloid water, but good to the taste. Joe had Jacques and Stone Hawk's workforce construct a stockade wall with a spring house at the outlet around the spring to keep critters out, four and two legged. He had water piped to the main warehouse, living quarters, livestock barns, the village center, and corrals. Joe had the privies built downstream in back of the facilities, with the stream carrying the waste away about a mile to where it entered the river. The policy "Do your dirt downstream!" was rigidly enforced.

Because of these efforts, incidents of diseases were minimized. Typhoid, cholera, smallpox, and malaria were some of the common afflictions citizens of the nineteenth century had to endure. Providing good public sanitary practices paid off at St. Charles.

Chouteau Post St. Charles Missouri 1811

It can be said that the herbal practices of Mother Anita aided by Fox's knowledge of same helped immensely in keeping the Beelers and friends healthy. Mother Anita's herbal skills were supplemented by a small pamphlet New Guide to Health published in 1814 by a home educated farmer from New Hampshire by the name of Samuel Thompson.

He was self-educated in the practice of using natural herbs and plant derivatives very similar to what the Indian tribes did, especially the Cherokee who had a rich history in the practice of the same. He espoused the use of digestive tract purgatives like mullein and yellow root and sweat baths to break fevers. Not the usual practices of the day which were bloodletting, ingestion of mercury and opiates. He even picked up on the relation of cowpox and smallpox and the inoculation procedure which was starting to pick up steam among the prominent medicos of the time.

Case in point, malaria was an ongoing scourge of the nineteenth century. Mother Anita, when married to Francisco Alberti back in 1781 living in Ste. Genevieve, had encountered a trader with some reddish bark that he called Jesuit medicine. It had been imported into New Orleans from Mexico and Peru. (It was the bark of the cinchona tree).

During the sixteenth century, Jesuits had observed the Indians using it to relieve fever and inflammation, grinding it to a powder and mixing with fruit juice or wine to relieve the bitter taste. Exporting it to Rome, because of the high incidence of malaria there, it was found to be a highly effective treatment for malaria.

Mother Anita through the years always had "her boys" be on the lookout for it and kept her supplied with an ample quantity to treat her family and friends.

George, Caroline, and the Brandsey family had added on to the living quarters of their mercantile building to accommodate both families. Typical of the times, St. Louis was growing by leaps and bounds, and property was becoming much in demand. Because of limited space, the outdoor privies were not always located far enough from the wells, causing underground cross contamination.

The families during the last couple of winters had suffered from chronic colds and coughs along with bouts of diarrhea. Conversing with Joe and what he had accomplished at St. Charles, Ed and George, with the woman's agreement, figured it had to be contaminated water. Mr. Brandsey did some intensive reading on the subject, little there was at the time. Working with Mr. Jules DuMun, an educated and trained civil engineer, they found a method of water filtration called slow sand filtering that was starting to be used back east in the cities.

George and Ed built a 250-gallon sand filter in the upper insulated back room of their building. The bottom layer was fine gravel, the middle layer was coarse river sand, and the top layer was fine blow sand.

A weatherized trapdoor was built directly above it to allow exposure to the air and sunlight and allow natural growth of a bacterial layer composed of leaves and water grass from the river. Building a windmill over the well they then piped water to the filter. In freezing weather they had to resort to bucketing water by hand through a pulley system. The filtered water was piped internally to the kitchen for drinking and cooking uses only.

But the effort paid off because the colds, coughs, and diarrhea almost completely disappeared. A good side benefit of the effort was all the husbands in the women's social circle were soon busy building water systems for their families.

The Loudenhagens, (Bruce, Mary Beth, two girls and a boy) departed St. Louis for Funk's Grove in July 1816. Three men from the congregation had arrived to help the family in the move. They traveled by packet boat to Fort Clark at Lake Peoria and from there by wagon with household goods to Funk's Grove to take up service for the congregation.

Stone Hawk, the ole bachelor, picked up and continued his courtship of Fox, and she accepted his proposal of marriage. They were married in October 1816. There was a good celebration, so much so that Governor Clark and Julia were present, with Governor Clark giving away the bride. Annie and Mother Anita told Fox in women talk, "Very good deal, my sister."

Fox then asked her husband, "Stone Hawk, will you build us a lodge in the manner of my people?"Hawk replied, "Fox my love, whatever suits you plumb tickles me to death." And he did build a sixteen-foot diameter Cheyenne buffalo hide lodge, which became their home.

Little Big Head/Jim being of fourteen years was, with the recommendation of his grandmother Caroline, finished with his formal education and came back home to St. Charles. He had developed a passion for horses over the previous five years. With help from his uncle Stone Hawk, his skills became very proficient.

The following year Silly Girl/Sara, also with Caroline's recommendation, was finished with her formal education and returned to Mother and family at St. Charles. She and Jim became almost inseparable. Their relationship blossomed.

Always fond of the genteel side of society, Little Sparrow/Linda had developed into a beauty of sixteen years, just like her mother and grandmother. Sparrow was more than not at odds with her mother and grandmother but got along well with her paternal grandmother, Caroline. Her mother and grandmother were totally aligned with the Indian culture as Caroline was with the white culture. Sparrow, being a young and inexperienced youth, hadn't yet mastered the balance needed to live between the two cultures like her parents and both grandparents. But she left a string of broken hearts amongst the young men of St. Louis. Until in the spring of 1817, when her attention was focused on a young artillery sergeant based at Fort Belle Fontaine at one of the many dance activities that were held year-round in the St. Louis area.

She tried to get Sergeant Garner Ray Dearmon's attention at a couple of the events to no avail. He seemed to be totally indifferent to all of her feminine wiles, so much so that in complaining to her mother and grandmothers she said, "I hate that man. He's such a pit. He's not normal!"

"Linda," remarked her mother, "just because he's not falling all over you like these other young sprigs shows me he's worth pursuing. Just like your father, I pursued him to Grand Portage and laid the law down regarding our relationship and he came through. So I'm saying, girl, if he's worth it, stop your whining and go get him!" So, Linda stopped whining and got him. Sergeant Dearmon never had a chance, not that he gave in willingly. But in the fall of 1817, he made Linda his bride.

Left: Ray Dearmon/Sarge. Right: Linda/Little Sparrow

Joe said to his bride, "Annie, I feel a tinge of old age creeping in on us!" "Bull floppers, husband!" and then Annie attacked him! The peace following the war was secure but fractured because many uncertainties existed regarding the fur trade. There were suspicions and distrust between the Canadian and American traders and supply houses and more so by the Indian tribes who understood the Canadians and knew what to expect from them. Not knowing how to deal with the Americans, they distrusted them even more. But due to the political boundaries reestablished during the Jay's Treaty limits of 1796, the Indians were forced to deal with the Americans. Also, the rising national pride of America for Americans and the exclusion of all foreigners from the fur trade on American soil, coupled with the government reestablishing and expanding the factory trade system were fueling the fires of uncertainty.

The awakened bear that came out of the woods at the end of the war was the American Fur Company, established by John Astor back in

1810 and managed by his two able lieutenants, Ramsey Crooks and Robert Stuart. Their goal was to consolidate the company's hold on the fur trade south and west of the Upper Great Lakes.

Both Astor and his Canadian partners Forsyth, Richardson & Company and McTavish, McGillivrays & Company knew that sooner than later Congress would be passing an exclusion act thereby limiting the life of the South West Company. In September 1815, William McGillivray and Astor met in New York, and after haggling over the details, not knowing when the exclusion would happen, but both knowing the temper of the times, they signed the contract renewing the South West Company for another two years. But Astor included a clause that if or when the exclusion happened, the agreement was to end.

During this time, both Crooks and Stuart were in St. Louis planning a trading trip up the Missouri backed by Astor. Astor convinced them to drop this plan and laid out his plan and visions for American Fur focusing on gaining control of the fur trade of the Upper Great Lakes on the American side of the border. As history shows, Ramsey Crooks became the point man with Robert Stuart falling back into the lesser role.

As predicted, the Exclusion Act was passed into law on April 29, 1816, and the South West Company principals were concerned about their trade goods, furs, and bottom line incurred from the 1815–16 season, primarily, what the arriving American customs officials and Indian agents would do. Ramsey Crooks was sent by Astor to Mackinaw to oversee and negotiate these problems and deal with the new Indian agent Major William Henry Puthuff.

Robert Stuart was in St. Louis at this time trying to dispose of the Missouri trade goods, which Astor refused to take back. He gave Stuart a letter of introduction to Charles Gratiot asking for his help in approaching J.P. Cabanne & Company and other principal St. Louis traders in setting up arrangements for Astor to become their main supplier and marketing agent. In return, Astor would not outfit anyone else for opposing them on the Missouri River. He did, and they did, and a tentative deal was struck. Stuart also managed to move his trade goods and make a slight profit.

The focus of Ramsey Crooks was to get the trade goods for the 1816–17 season past American customs, get trading licenses for his winterers, and get them in the field. Because of not having experienced American winterers, he made use of Canadians, which was allowed under the Exclusion Act. That is when the president or his administration could issue the exception licenses through the War Department or territorial governors Cass of Michigan, Edwards of Illinois, and Clark of Missouri.

For the lucrative Fond du lac district he chose three old northwesterners, William Morrison, Eustache Roussain, and Pierre Cote. He persuaded them that if the South West Company did die in 1817, their contracts would shift on advantageous terms to the American Fur Company. Little did they know the buzz saw that they were sailing into.The Hudson Bay Company and the northwesterners were competitors since 1780 with the rivalry getting down and dirty in the last ten years. Lord Douglas, Earl of Selkirk, had become the majority shareholder in the Bay Company (Sir Alex Mackenzie had warned William McGillivray back in 1806 about Lord Douglas).

In May 1811, The Bay Company deeded him approximately 116,000 square miles around the Red River in Southern Manitoba, western Minnesota, and eastern Dakota. He established a colony of Irish-Scottish crofters just north of the border smack dab in the middle of Métis country who primarily supplied the northwesterners with pemmican and vital foodstuffs for the western voyageurs.

The tension and harassment between Métis, crofters, and rival company men finally climaxed on June 17, 1816, with the Métis led by Northwestern winterers killing twenty-two of the crofters including their governor, Robert Semple.

Selkirk Settlement on the Red River

The Seven Oaks Battle

Lord Douglas was moving west through the lakes with 100 mercenaries of the Swiss Regiment de Meuron he had recruited when word reached him of the Red River incident. Vowing revenge, he coasted the north shore and captured Fort William. Then he set about absorbing the trade of the surrounding area for the Bay Company.

Crooks' three Fond du Lac traders were taken prisoner by Selkirk's scouts and moved to Fort William. They protested their innocence, explaining they were employees of the South West Company and working American territory. Selkirk considered them northwesterners and confiscated about $12,000 worth of goods, including seventy kegs of high wine, and was in no mood to be reasonable. He ordered the trio to be sent to Montréal for trial, but at Sault Ste. Marie they managed to escape and made their way back to Fond du Lac by December. Despite finding the district overrun by Bay Company men, they managed to recoup and make a fair trade for the season.

William McGillivray and the northwesterners were at first going to strike back with physical violence but had second thoughts and proceeded to get recompense through the civil courts. They dragged Selkirk through the courts for the remaining years of his life. (He died in 1820.) Relative to Crooks/Astor and the damages to the South West Company for the 1816–17 season, they about broke even. As Astor sensed, Ramsey Crooks was an adroit negotiator.

Robert Stuart was sent to Mackinaw where he became the resident manager and overseer of American Fur operations well into the 1830s when Astor sold out to Ramsey Crooks.

Ramsey Crooks spent the next two years getting outfits going to Indiana, Illinois, Michigan, Green Bay, Prairie du Chien, and St. Peters (Minnesota), consolidating American Fur's hold on the Upper Great Lakes as planned. There were bumps in the road along the way, for instance, the Lieutenant Colonel Talbot Chambers interference affair at Green Bay and Prairie du Chien of which Astor and Crooks put in the hands of the St. Louis lawyer newspaperman Thomas Hart Benton, a prominent name in Missouri history.

In 1817, the South West Company was at the end of its life. After the return of furs from the 1816–17 season and inventory of all assets, the

Canadians asked $100,000, which Astor accepted, and American Fur became publicly active. Astor was 54, Crooks was 30, and Stuart was 32.

A personal note on Crooks. He found time to have a dalliance with a Chippewa girl, which produced a daughter born on May 30, 1817, on Drummond Island. He gave the child his name, educated her, and included her in his family when he married his white wife.

Focusing back on the Beeler Family, how did the American Fur Company impact them?

Joe and Annie had been running the St. Charles Chouteau operations for six years now and had all of the Missouri Sauk and Fox trade up to the Des Moines River. In addition, Joe had been made a full partner in Chouteau and Company by Auguste and Pierre Chouteau and Governor Clark. With the constant ebb and flow of the business and politics of the fur trade, this was a huge stabilizing factor for Annie and Joe.

So, when Ramsey Crooks came through town in the spring of 1817, he had a number of tasks to complete. First, he wanted to finalize the tentative deal made the previous year by Robert Stuart with J.P. Cabanne & Company and other principal St. Louis traders for Astor to become their primary supplier and marketing rep for their furs. Second, he wanted to set up a trader to cover the Sauk and Fox trade out of Illinois, Iowa, and Missouri Territories. This is why he made a beeline straight to St. Charles to see Joe Beeler. Joe had all the background, was a northwesterner, American citizen, and was in solid with the Sauk and Fox, Governor Clark, and the Chouteaus.

He spent a long week with Joe, Annie, and Stone Hawk, haggling, cajoling, pleading, and offering very good terms as an employee of American Fur. After the second day, he realized that when negotiating with Joe he was also negotiating with Annie. They were joined emotionally at the hip, and if he wanted Joe, he also got Annie.

He also focused on Stone Hawk but soon realized Stone Hawk with his bride, Fox, had their sights set on new horizons toward the setting sun.

Jacques was a good man highly capable and competent, but Ramsey couldn't hire him as a trader because he was a Canadian, and the Exclusion Act would cause complications that he didn't want to be burdened with. Lastly, Jacques would never leave the Beelers; he was family.

Joe and Annie were fully in tune with the economic, social, and cultural changes that were sweeping westward as the young American nation expanded, and they went through its growing pains and the politics that resulted because of it. Their sympathies laid with their involvement in the fur trade and the Indian culture. As stated previously, when the settlers came in, the fur trade died on the vine, and the Indians reaped the lumps of this decline. They knew that the Illinois Territory was in the process of attaining statehood (which happened in 1818). The Missouri Territory would follow suit in the near future. And wonders of all was the docking of the first steamboat Zebulon M. Pike at the Chouteau wharf on Aug 2, 1817.

Also, the cut-throat competition that existed on the Missouri River passed and stopped at their St. Charles operations every day, and Joe didn't want any part of it. But more so, Joe liked being his own boss, with Annie's allowance, and that wouldn't be the case working for American Fur. Ramsey told Joe that his second or lesser choice to run the Sauk and Fox trade was the season traveler Astorian Russel Farnham and his chief clerk young Daniel Darling. Unfortunately, they didn't know the Sauk/Fox. Joe told Crooks he should consider the Arid brothers, George and James. Even though they were Canadians, Crooks could get exception licenses for them from Governor Clark with Joe "greasing the rails" with the governor in exchange for Crooks keeping his operations north of the Des Moines River. Crooks accepted. James Arid ran the Sauk/Fox for the next two years while breaking in Farnham and Darling, who took over in 1819. Joe's operation wasn't stepped on too hard. Besides, as far as the Sauk were concerned, Joe and Annie were Sauk!

The next three years were turbulent for the American Fur Company, but due to the diligence and drive of Ramsey Crooks, and to a lesser degree Robert Stuart, plus the massive financial backing of Mr. Astor, the company prevailed. The American Fur Company earned a reputation of being relentless, and if it encountered an obstacle, business or political, it absorbed it, ran over it, or outflanked it out of business.

For example, Mr. Astor was owed money by the government because of loans made to finance the war. Astor and two Philadelphia financiers purchased a large block of loan bonds at eighty cents on the dollar and paid for them with bank notes worth half their face value. Even President James Monroe owed Astor because of personal loans made in previous years. The "spider" had webs set in so many places that at times even the spider was unaware until circumstances of an event brought it back to the light of day.

Another event that happened in 1820 was the buyout of the North West Company by the Hudson Bay Company. This had to happen because of the bloodletting that was dragging both companies into financial ruin. This in itself was a significant problem for American Fur and was one of the obstacles that kept the company out of the Missouri River trade until 1827. Then, in Ramsey Crooks' style, he went after the Missouri River and Rocky Mountain fur trade with no-holds-barred for the competition.

Between the years of 1816 to 1820, the Beeler Family did as well as any other family of the times. They were a close-knit family, strong of character, and in relatively good health.

In 1816, one of Joe's partners Auguste Pierre Chouteau (A.P.), with his cousin Isabelle Gratiot DeMun's husband Jules DeMun, approached Joe about joining them on a trading expedition to Santa Fe, New

Mexico. It was well known along the frontier that the Spanish authorities were not friendly to foreign traders, for example, Zebulon Pike's Colorado expedition of 1806–1807.

Joe declined, as he did with the Astorian William Hunt back in 1811, but he supported the two men's endeavors relative to the Chouteau and Company board of directors.

The expedition arrived near the headwaters of the Arkansas around the Spanish Peaks region and had a successful winter's hunt and trade. But the Spanish found them in the spring of 1817, confiscated the furs and goods, and tossed them in the Santa Fe calaboose. After a contentious trial, Chouteau, DeMun, and their men escaped the Spanish rope, were put on decrepit horses, and sent packing with the warning, "Come back and the noose will be applied next time!" The party returned to St. Louis riding the scrawny horseflesh, full of good stories, and dead broke, incurring a loss of $30,000 or more.

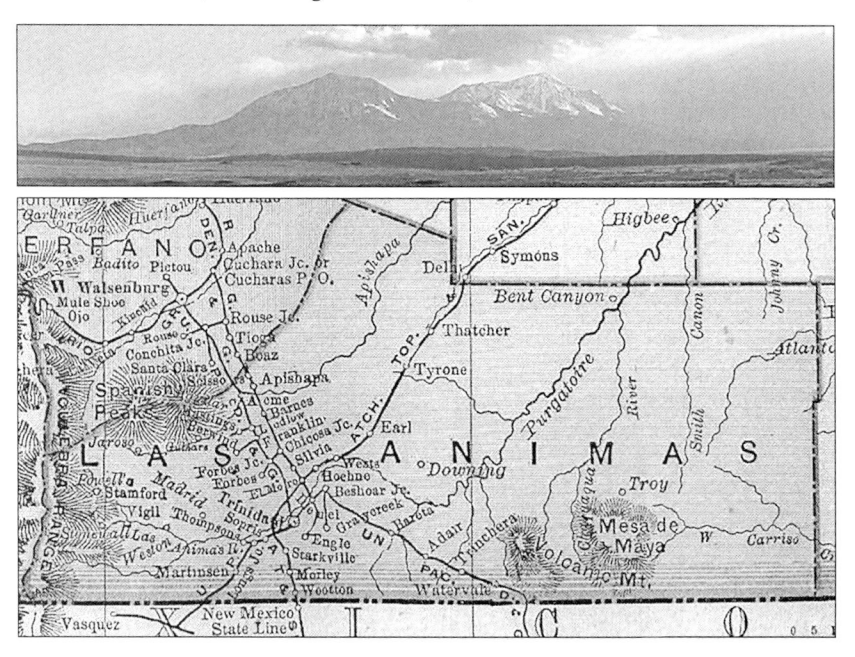

Spanish Peaks Region

Joe held his opinion and prevailed upon his bride to do the same! "Annie," he said, "be Christian!"

Little is known of Jacques' background except he was born of French-Canadian parents in the little town of Lucerne, Lower Canada located about 100 miles northeast of Lake Simcoe. He was from a typical Catholic family of nine siblings. His illiterate parents were poor farmers and trappers.

At age fourteen, he was indentured by his father to Frobisher & Company of Montréal as a laborer/paddle-man for seven years on the yearly Montréal canoe freight flotillas to Mackinaw and Grand Portage. He bounced around the country and the fur trade for a number of years until he met up with the Beelers in the fall of 1809 at The Portage in Wisconsin. The next ten years with the Beelers were good for Jacques because he grew as a person in character and reputation.

Jacques Deserve

In 1818, Chouteau Company had a contract with the government factory at Fort Osage for delivery of two dozen horses. Joe asked Jacques if he would be willing to undertake the delivery. Jacques agreed with the request that Little Big Head/Jim and Sara would accompany him to help with the delivery. Joe had no problem with it, and Annie also agreed after she slept on the idea overnight. Stone Hawk opined that with Jim's skills in horse handling, it was a good idea. With Hawk's working on his bride, Fox, she agreed that Sara could make the trip also. Jacques said "I've got my crew and need no more!"

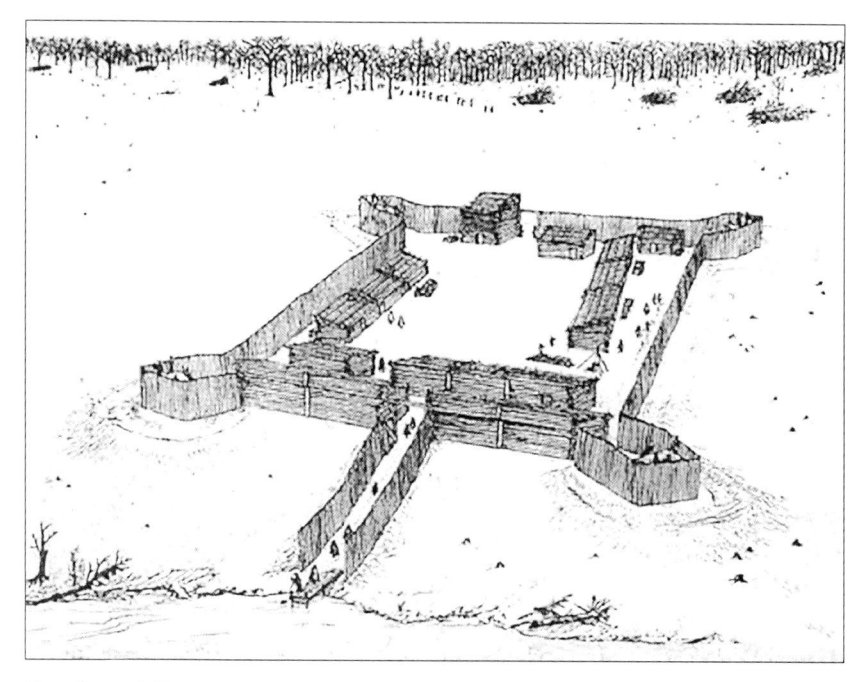

Fort Osage Missouri Terr. 1818

Fort Osage was built in 1808 on a site marked by William Clark in 1805 as part of the Treaty of Fort Clark with the Osage and established a government trading factory there. It was abandoned during the war in 1812 but reoccupied in 1815.

The particulars of import were that the Osage ceded their lands east of the site to the U.S. Government (which was practically all of Missouri east to the Mississippi River). In exchange, the government would garrison the post with troops for the protection of the tribe in typical government bungling with no foresight of what the consequences would be. The policy of the Jefferson administration was the relocation of all eastern tribes west of the Mississippi. This policy would continue for the next eighty years and be part of the reason for settlement and development of Arkansas and Oklahoma during those years. Case in point was the settlement of the Cherokee in these lands and the immediate hostilities with the Osage over hunting lands. This led to the establishment of Fort Smith in 1817 and Fort Gibson in 1824.

Jacques estimated about a two- to three-week trip (about 300 miles) to make the delivery. It was accomplished within this timeframe without the loss of any animals except for a couple of lames along the way, which speaks well for Jacques and Sara and Jim in caring for the lames, keeping the animals on the trail and delivered in good shape.

The deal closure went well because George Sibley, the factor, paid the invoice in full but with twenty dollar gold pieces instead of the letter of credit as initially requested by Chouteau & Company. Jacques was beside himself and tried to keep the transaction details under wraps, but then again he knew how the frontier telegraph worked. He took the kids and established a secure hidden camp five to eight miles back down the river. But his old addiction for the cards caused him to foolishly seek out the games at the post. He told the kids no campfires, stay concealed, and he would be back at first light.

Upon first light the next morning, Jacques hadn't returned. Jim told Sara, "We've got trouble, and we must find Uncle Jacques!" Backtracking carefully toward the post, they found him so badly beaten that he was near death. Carrying him back to their camp, they tended to him but he was too far gone. Jacques managed to whisper to them that two river scum had waylaid him after he left the card games and that they had beaten him for the whereabouts of the gold. He whispered, "I'm sorry kids. I love you," and passed away in their arms.

After getting their grief under control and wits about them, Jim and Sara moved the camp two miles further downriver and buried Jacques in a hidden grave on a knoll about a mile back from the river.

Going back to their camp, they sat up and waited out the day and night for the river scum they knew were coming for the gold. About an hour before dawn they heard voices and paddles in the water approaching.

Half an hour later two men entered the camp and advanced on the two shapes rolled up in the bedrolls. As they were about to strike with their knives, an arrow struck one through the throat and a hatchet embedded itself in the skull of the other. After the thrashing about, quiet and silence ensued. Jim and Sara came out of the bushes and surveyed their handy work.

Jim remarked, "Sara, we have to make Mother's bear medicine for Uncle Jacques. It's what he would have wanted." Scalping both, the bodies were hung upside down on an oak and disemboweled. Bear tracks were painted about their throats, and their knives were jammed into their mouths. A post was set up in front of the bodies, and their scalps were pinned to it with an old knife. Locating the canoe the scum had come downriver with, Jim and Sara broke camp and proceeded downriver toward home.

Traveling at night and putting up at secure hidden camps during the day, Jim and Sara arrived back home at St. Charles in about a week with the sad news of Uncle Jacques. The family took it hard. He was a part of the Beeler family.

Joe, Annie, Stone Hawk, and Fox spent quite some time listening to Jim and Sara tell their story about the trip and its outcome. The parents knew that the kids were emotionally fragile because of it. Joe praised them for their actions and said Mr. Chouteau was proud of them for the safe delivery of the horses and gold payment received. The parents told the kids that Jacques knew the chance he was taking by returning to the card games and wouldn't want them to have any regrets for his mistake. Life was tough on the frontier in the 19th century and you have to face the consequences of the decisions you make.

Joe and Stone Hawk took Jim aside and said it was good medicine making his mother's bear medicine when dealing with the two river scum. Within a week after Jim and Sara's return, the moccasin telegraph was telling of the two bodies hung in a tree downriver from Fort Osage, done in by the bear knife medicine. When any tribesman came into the trading room at St. Charles where Joe had Annie's bear jaw knife hanging, he would approach it and give a slight bow of his head and, if Annie was present, give her the same.

Upriver, the tribes wouldn't go within a mile of the site with the hanging bodies. And amongst the white folk, there was the typical uproar that no one was safe in their beds because of the atrocity committed upon the two poor white men.

George Sibley and the officers and soldiers of the garrison, who were in the know, knew the story of what the two river scum had done to Jacques, and they deserved what they got. The best part was that they were done in by a couple of kids. George sent a party downriver to the site to cut down the bodies and bury them. That was the end of story as far as he and the staff at the fort were concerned.

Governor Clark was visiting the Beelers at St. Charles and asked Joe, Annie, Stone Hawk and Fox if he could meet the kids. He congratulated them on a job well done and said he too dearly missed ole Jacques. He chuckled and told them of a similar incident he remembered happening back in 1805 up at the Mandan villages in the Dakotas. On a later occasion, while visiting George and Caroline and the Brandseys, he told them they should be proud of their kids. They would do well in the years ahead.

In the years following the War of 1812, the American nation was maturing economically and politically, and its impact was being felt on the world scene. In its westward expansion through rampant land speculation, import/export trade with the world's major trading partners of the time, and its breaking into the industrial revolution, it was realized by the political factions, the Madison administration, followed by the Monroe administration that a sound financial policy system needed to be established.

The new Republicans espoused tariff protection, internal financial regulations, and a central bank of the United States (BUS). Their opponents, the Democratic-Republicans in alliance with the old Republicans, espoused a return to Jeffersonian principals of limited government, strict construction of the Constitution, and the rise of southern pre-eminence.

Without getting into details, the result was the Panic of 1819—the first major peacetime financial crisis in the United States followed by the general collapse of the American economy persisting through 1821.

It can be summed up by quoting from historian Harry Ammons' book James Monroe: The Quest for National Identity: "The Panic of 1819 ... was compounded by many factors ... overexpansion of credit during the postwar years, the collapse of the export market after the bumper crops in Europe in 1817, low prices of imports from Europe which forced American manufacturers to close, financial instability resulting from both excessive expansion of state banking after 1811 and the unsound policies of the second Bank of the United States, and widespread unemployment."

The panic started the transition of the nation from a colonial commercial status with Europe toward a dynamic economy driven by a capitalistic business cycle of supply and demand!

Relative to the fur trade, this downturn was some of the pressure that drove the amalgamation of the North West Company with the Hudson Bay Company and the strong emergence and domination of American Fur (aka Astor, Ramsay Crooks).

The panic hit Chouteau & Company like everyone else. Worldwide fur prices were down, and trade goods prices were steadily high despite the relatively low prices of English goods. This was coupled with the lack of good hard currency. Spanish pesos and federal five dollars were the equivalent of twenty gold pieces.

In 1819, young Pierre Jr. Chouteau "Cadet" proposed a trading expedition up the Platte River to its headwaters in the Rocky Mountains (present-day Wyoming) to supplement and expand his brother's, Auguste Pierre (A.P.), trade in present-day Salina, Oklahoma and Kansas to, among other reasons, avoid the restlessness of the upper river tribes, including the Teton Lakota, the Arikaree, Assiniboine, and the fierce competition of the independent traders who worked out of St. Louis.

Stories had abounded since the Lewis and Clark days of the untapped fur wealth in the mountains south of the Missouri with the mountain tribes that Manuel Lisa's expeditions had contact with ten years previously, including Crow, Arapaho, and Cheyenne. The plan was approved by the Chouteau & Company board of directors and set in motion by the recruitment of men, supplies, and financial backing. The plan was unique because even though the Platte River would be followed, the outfit would travel by horse and pack mules because the Platte was too shallow for the draft of a keelboat, even at high water in the spring.

Fox approached her husband, Stone Hawk, with the request. "Husband dearest, would you take me back to the home of my people?" Stone Hawk, being the good husband he was, couldn't say no to his bride when she purred and worked her magic on him.

Truth be known, she had discussed this at length with Annie who said, "Sister, you knew what to do!"

So plans were made by Fox and Stone Hawk along with the kids, Jim and Sara, to join the expedition.

The family had been surprised the previous year when young Jim/Little Big Head had appeared out of the blue at Hawk and Fox's teepee with three ponies, five blankets, and one new northwest trade musket as the "bride price" for Sara/Silly Girl! When asked by Hawk and Fox, "Why do you want her as your bride?"

Jim replied, "I like her and have liked her since the first day we met. Now is the time to do something about it." As said, the family was astonished. Joe told Stone Hawk to let Jim wait a day or so before accepting the price and giving approval. Annie and Fox got wind of the men's little ploy, and it was stopped right then and there. Stone Hawk accepted and gave his approval for the exchange of nuptials for the kids. Annie cornered Joe and berated him for playing around with the kids. Affairs of the heart are not to be trifled with. As Fox told Annie, "Men. The older they get, the more the boy comes out in them!"

The wedding was a typical Beeler family affair with goodwill and best wishes given to the kids. Governor Clark officiated and united the couple as the civil minister. Even the Sauk warrior Black Sparrow Hawk attended.

Left: Sara/Silly Girl. Right: Jim/Little Big Head

The expedition left St. Charles in April 1820 hoping to be in the mountains of Wyoming by late September and set up for trade with the plains and mountain tribes for the 1820–1821 season.

Annie, Joe, and the family were sad to see Stone Hawk, Fox, and the kids leave, but all understood the ever-ebbing cycles of life and what tomorrow brings adds to the richness of memories of the past. Stone Hawk and Fox would find her Cheyenne family, and Jim and Sara would start their family. But this part of the story and adventures thereof would make a complete story in itself.

The year 1820 was a shed-fall year for the Beeler family. The nucleus of the family was intact in the St. Louis area. George and Caroline were sixty-one and fifty-nine years and in reasonable good health considering the times. Mother Anita at fifty-six years old was spry and agile as a willow switch. Joe and Annie were forty and thirty-nine years and in good health. Joe often opined that it was due to Annie's orneriness rubbing off on him.

The family was saddened and troubled by the death of good friend Julia Hancock Clark, wife of Governor William Clark.

As stated previously, Linda and Sergeant Ray Dearmon had exchanged nuptials in September 1817 and had presented the family with a little boy, Matthew Shannon, in June 1818, and a little girl, Shana Marie, in April 1819.

Mother Anita commented to the kids, "Isn't it wonderful to be grandparents at such a young age!"

As Joe mumbled to George and Sarge over a quaff of ale, "It's all relative to mileage on the frame! But I do love the grandkids. Spoil them and then send them to the parents. That's what my father-in-law Shingabis did for me!"

Sergeant Dearmon was discharged from the army in 1818. Being twenty-one years old, he went to work for George and Ed at the mercantile. He had been born near the Pearl River in West Florida, the son of Morris and Margie Dearmon. He was the third son of five siblings, three boys and two girls.

At age sixteen, he had enlisted in the Madison County, Alabama Mounted Riflemen, part of Brigadier General John Coffee's second regiment of mounted riflemen (cavalry) and participated in General Andrew Jackson's campaigns against the Creek Red Stick warriors in the Siege of Pensacola to drive the British out of Forts San Miguel and San Carlos, and the Battle of New Orleans.

At the Battle of New Orleans, young Garner Ray was part of the force that counter-attacked and recaptured the right flank battery of Jackson's defensive line and anchored this spot for the duration of the battle. He and the survivors of the force were decorated. And for Garner Ray, it was a field promotion to sergeant of artillery. He threw himself into the discipline of artillery over the next couple of years, becoming a very proficient cannoneer and a disciple of Henry Knox's writing on theories on the use of artillery in a conflict. Sergeant Dearmon became as skilled with a 3-pounder as British Sergeant Keating of Fort McKay fame (Prairie du Chien).

Left: Sergeant Dearmon. Right: 3-Pounder Field Piece

After the war in February 1815, Garner Ray was part of a force of artillery that was transferred to Fort Belle Fontaine at St. Louis. As the post was less than ten miles downriver from the Beeler Chouteau post at St. Charles, many of the garrison spent time at Annie's eatery and the trade store for resupplying their personal needs and indulging in the daily activities and gossip involved. The only complaint of the soldiers was the lack of whiskey, but all knew the rules of nondrinking and good behavior were rigidly enforced by Joe, his segundos, and the town constable. Plus, they knew Joe had a good informal agreement with the garrison commander, which was more music they would have to face if the line was crossed.

Joe took notice of the young artillery sergeant after hearing Sparrow complaining to her mother about the sergeant's lack of attention to her flirtations. Knowing his daughter, Joe struck up an acquaintance with Garner Ray and, after some time, took a liking to him and was impressed with what he saw. Learning of Ray's skill with the 3-pounder and his intense interest in firearms, Joe introduced him to his father, George, and Mr. Ed Brandsey. The friendship blossomed from there. Quaffing a few ales with Joe, George, and Ed, they told him that Sparrow had him square in her sights, and backed by her mother and grandmothers, his days of bachelorhood were numbered. Unbeknownst to the women, the men put down bets on Garner Ray's remaining days of freedom. And as fate decreed, Garner Ray and Linda "Sarge and Little Sparrow" exchanged nuptials in September 1817. By 1820, they added to the family numbers with a boy Mathew Shannon and a girl Shana Marie.

In late March or early April 1819, a young traveler named Henry Rowe Schoolcraft stopped in at Brandsey-Beeler Essential Stuff Mercantile looking to purchase a new firearm and get an old pistol repaired that he had picked up in previous years. Sergeant Ray took care of him, and it soon became obvious that Henry was inept relative to firearms, but

Ray hung with him and guided him through his selections and even spent some time with Henry on live loading and firing at targets in the back lot.

During this time spent with Henry, Ray learned of Schoolcraft's previous travels with a Levi Pettibone through the Northern Arkansas Southern Missouri Territory. Ray got Henry to spend some time talking with Ed, George, and him about his Arkansas expedition over a few ales. Schoolcraft was so grateful for the help and discounted prices for his firearm purchases and pistol repair that he gave a copy of his book Journal of a Tour into the Interior of Missouri and Arkansaw to Garner Ray.

This journal was passed between Ray, George, Ed, and Joe. Eventually, it found its way through the hands of some of the influential movers and shakers of St. Louis, including Governor Clark, Jules DeMun, Charles Gratiot, Stephen Hempstead, and lawyer/newspaperman Thomas Hart Benton.

Much discussion of the journal and the Arkansas Territory occurred amongst the Beeler family and the principals mentioned above that winter of 1819–1820.

CHAPTER EIGHT
THE ARKANSAS COUNTRY

As background for this discussion, a review of the Arkansas Territory is needed at this point.

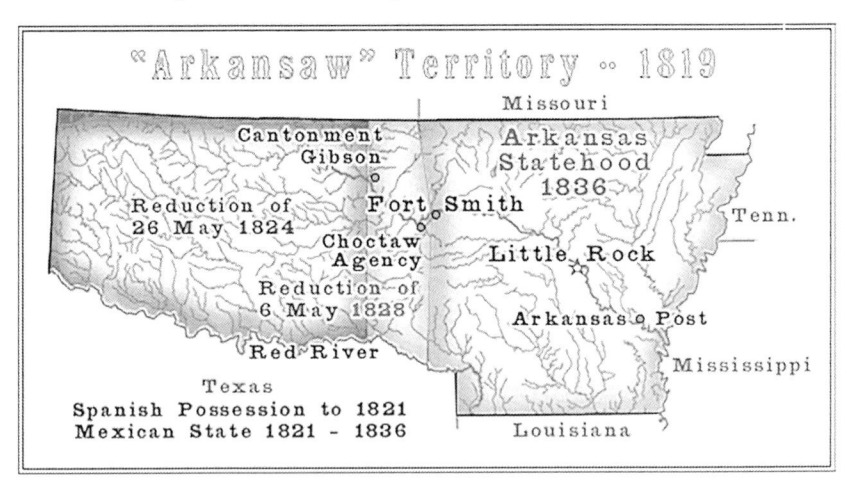

"Arkansaw" Territory ○○ 1819

[Map showing Arkansas Territory 1819 with labels: Missouri, Cantonment Gibson, Arkansas Statehood 1836, Reduction of 26 May 1824, Fort Smith, Choctaw Agency, Little Rock, Tenn., Reduction of 6 May 1828, Arkansas Post, Red River, Mississippi, Texas Spanish Possession to 1821 Mexican State 1821 - 1836, Louisiana]

Arkansas Territory 1819

First, the territory was, relative to when it became part of the United States, part of the Louisiana Purchase in 1803. Congress divided the land into two territories. The land south of the 33 degrees of latitude was named Orleans, and the land north was named Louisiana. In 1812, the Orleans Territory was admitted to the Union as the State of Louisiana, and the Louisiana Territory became the Missouri Territory, with the seat of government moved from the Arkansas Post to St. Louis.

William Clark was elected governor, and a legislative council of nine members and a lower house of thirteen members were elected to Congress. Lawrence County was created by an act of the Missouri Legislature under Governor Clark and divided from New Madrid County on January 15, 1815. The county seat was initially located at OleDavidsonville on the Black River. Lawrence County along with Arkansas County formed in 1813 are known as the two mother counties because they encompassed all the territory of the present-day State of Arkansas.

On March 2, 1819, Congress established the territory of Arkansas separated from the Missouri Territory at the 33 degrees of latitude boundary line. In 1820, Missouri was admitted to the Union under the Missouri Compromise. The politics involved thereof allowed slavery in Arkansas Territory, but Missouri was slave free.

From the Battle of Fallen Timbers and the Treaty of Greenville in 1794–1795 to the passage of the Indian Removal Act of 1830, it was the continuing policy of the U.S. Government to remove the eastern tribes to lands west of the Mississippi River. By 1820, the Arkansas Territory was inhabited by Delaware, Shawnee, Kickapoo, Peoria, and Cherokee to name a few.

Of the original inhabitants of Quapaw, Caddo and Osage, only the Osage was a dominant tribe with which to be reckoned. As previously stated, the Osage and Sauk frequently tangled when contact occurred during hunting excursions. The Osage considered northwest Arkansas, southern Missouri, and eastern Oklahoma their private hunting domain.

The Delaware main town was located near present-day Dew Spring, just downstream from Bull Shoals, cross river from the Flippin Barrens of the upper White River. The chief was known as John Cake.

The Shawnee were located in three towns along the White River. The main camp was located at Norfork tributary. Secondary camps were at Pine Bayou (Moccasin Creek) halfway between Norfork and Calico Rock and Livingston Creek, about nine miles north of Sylamore. The chief was Peter Cornstalk.

Hunting parties of Cherokees had been making forays into Arkansas from 1780 and on. The Spanish authorities welcomed them as a possible buffer from the expansive ambitions of the new American nation. One of the first large groups led by Chief Diwali, known as the Bowl, settled into the Black River and St. Francis River valleys in 1794 after an incident with American settlers known as the Muscle Shoals Massacre.

That same year, after twenty years of sporadic warfare with the English colonies and the American nation, the Cherokee council signed the first of forty treaties that covered the years between 1794 to 1840.

The New Madrid earthquakes of 1811–1812 caused massive disruptions with the rising and sinking of land in the St. Francis River Valley, prompting the Cherokee to migrate to the Arkansas River Valley west of present-day Little Rock, with many settling along the way in the Ozarks between the White and Arkansas Rivers in North Central Arkansas.

Increasing federal and state pressure on the remaining Eastern Cherokee led to the Turkey Town Treaty of 1817 with Andrew Jackson as the chief negotiator. Land in the East was exchanged for land in central and western Arkansas. The boundaries were the White River on the north with the Arkansas River on the south. The eastern boundary was a line from Point Remove Creek, just west of present-day Morrilton to the White River just upstream from Polk Bayou, present-day Batesville. Over the next ten years, as many as 4,000 Cherokees migrated to Arkansas.

They established scattered family farmsteads with cattle, crops, slaves, gristmills, and salt works. The families were organized in traditional towns. Kinship ties were traced through the woman, like the Mohawks of New York. The town centers included a council house and a stick ball court. The Cherokees were moving toward a centralized government with a governing council and principal chief who, after 1817, was John Jolly. In 1820, they invited Protestant missionaries, who founded Dwight Mission on Illinois Bayou, present-day Russellville, to teach their children Anglo-American ways. These towns were spread out on the north side of the Arkansas River at Eau Galle Creek, Illinois Bayou, Piney Creek, Spadra Creek, Horsehead Creek, and Mulberry River as well as Dutch Creek and Spring Creek on the south side of the river.

Thomas Nuttall, on his travels up the Arkansas River in 1819, admired the Cherokees for their holdings, farms, towns, and infrastructure. Even though their dress was a mixture of native and European tastes, they still strove to maintain their Native identity.

After meeting Chief John Jolly and his wife at trader Walt Webber's store at Illinois Bayou on April 9, 1819, Nuttall said, "I should scarcely have distinguished him from an American, except by his language. He was very plain, prudent, and unassuming in his dress and manners. A Franklin amongst his countrymen and affectionately called the Beloved Father by his people!"

Because of the ongoing agitation with the Osage over hunting rights with the Cherokee and intrusions of whites, Secretary of War John C. Calhoun, by military directive dated July 30, 1817, sent Major William Bradford and a company of the rifle regiment to build Fort Smith at Bella Point. Located at the junction of the Poteau and Arkansas Rivers on the present-day boundary of Arkansas and Oklahoma.

This was the lay of the land in the winter of 1819–1820.

After a few months of discussion of the Schoolcraft Journal in parallel with the approval and planning of the Cadet Chouteau expedition up the Platte to Wyoming, Joe made the proposal to the Chouteau and

Company board of an exploratory trip through the Arkansas country via the White River, overland to A.P.'s post on the Neosho River in Oklahoma. They would winter over and return via the Arkansas and Mississippi Rivers to St. Louis and report on the same. Board approval was unanimous.

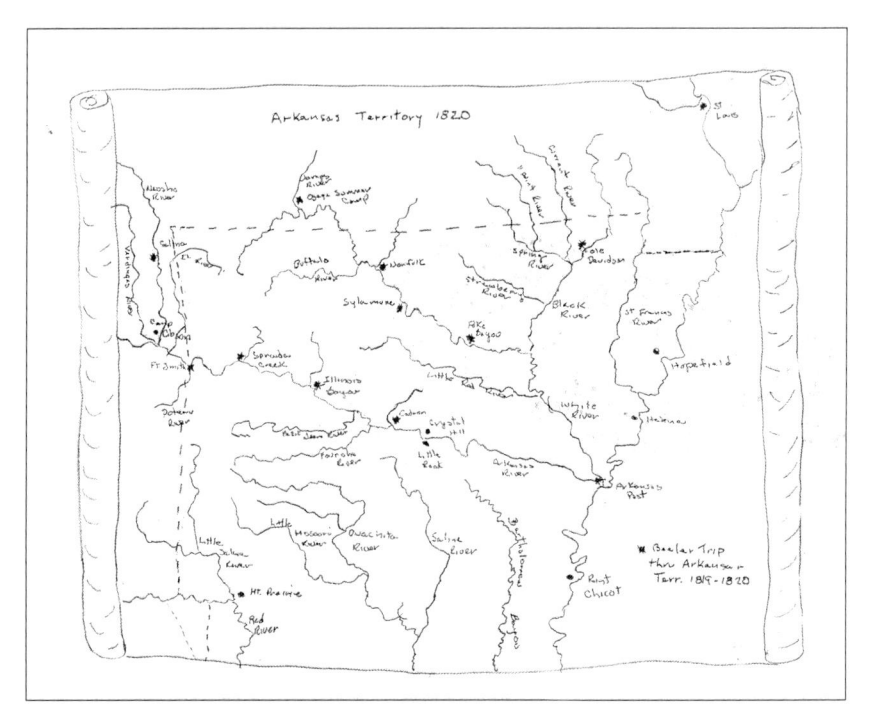

Beeler Trip Through Arkansas Territory 1819-1820

As previously stated, 1820 was a shed-fall year for the Beeler family, with Stone Hawk and Fox with Jim and Sara heading west with the Cadet party and with the intense discussion over the Schoolcraft Journal amongst the movers and shakers of St. Louis. Joe and Annie, after more than ten years in the St. Louis area, agreed it was time for a major move again. George and Caroline, after a good life's run, knew and said they would stay put in St. Louis with the Brandseys.

Shaking out the details of the approved trip, it was decided by the individuals involved, Annie, Mother Anita, and Linda "Little Sparrow" that they would accompany their men.

Annie said, "Joe left me behind twice. A third time will not happen!"

Sparrow said, "My mother is right, and so am I. Besides, since the kids are off the breast and taking nourishment on their own, Grams Caroline and Aunt Charlene have agreed to take care of them, just as Grandma did for Jim and me when Mother joined Paw for two years out on the Dakota prairies."

Mother Anita said, "Someone has to take care of you kids. And I want to hear no sass about Gram's frailty. Right Joe?"

Joe, remembering the trip with Stone Hawk and bringing her back to St. Louis after Shingabis's death, said quietly, "Yes Ma. Not a problem!"

With the women guiding them, Joe and Sarge worked out the logistics of the trip and decided that the party would travel by steamboat to Arkansas Post. Then they would travel by keelboat up the White and Black Rivers to Ole Davidsonville, the Lawrence County seat. Thence by horseback overland to Polk Bayou, present-day Batesville. At which time canoes would be purchased to traverse up the White past Swan Creek, present-day Forsyth, Missouri, to the James River. From there they would travel by horseback west to A.P. Chouteau Post on the Neosho (Grand River) to overwinter there.

Central to this discussion was Joe's concern for the safety of the women. Relative to Schoolcraft's description of the people, the coarseness and rudeness of the white folk was of more concern than the behavior of the Indian people. Annie and Mother Anita immediately understood the basis of Joe's concern and remarked, "We will be squaw wife and mother-in-law to two white traders!"

With that remark, Joe turned to Linda and said, "Well, Linda how are you going to handle that?"

To which she said, "I will be Sparrow, squaw wife to my husband, and leave my cultured ways behind. But I don't like it!"

Joe looked at his daughter. "Linda, that's the only way it can be, and if you can't hack it, you will be left behind. Your good looks are a blessing and a curse, just like your mother and grandmother. And they can tell you from experience what a curse it can be. Plus, your stubborn streak from your mother and grandmother doesn't help you either. So, if you will do this and be a subservient squaw wife to your loving husband, you're going with us. Now turn to your husband and promise him that you will!"

Linda turned to Ray. "Husband dearest, I, Sparrow will be your squaw wife!"

To which Garner Ray said, "Linda come here!" And she did as he folded her into his arms. After which Sparrow was folded into the arms of her mother and grandmother.

Joe gave a sly wink to Sarge and quietly said, "Ray enjoy it, but you know Linda better than most of us, and we must all keep on top of the situation because our lives and safety depend on it."

It was decided that the best time for departure would be late March early April—the same departure time as the Cadet expedition. With the separation of the family, it was a bittersweet time for all. With Stone Hawk, The Fox, Jim, and Sara not knowing when or even if they would see the family again, it was really a tough departure. But they all knew the foibles of life in the nineteenth century, faced it head on, and take the full measure it had to offer.

Joe booked his party on the steamboat Maid of Orleans. It ran a packet round trip between St. Louis and New Orleans about once a month.

It wasn't a luxury boat, but it got the job done and was quicker than the keelboats it competed with at the time. In fact, Joe was able to get his party booked into one of the cabins. He told the ladies, "Enjoy it because there will be no accommodations equal to or better than this for a year or more." He told Sarge, "At least it will give the ladies some security and privacy!"

As Joe was always fond of saying, "When it seems that life is good, it unexpectedly gets complicated and turns to sour milk!" Such was the case when, on March 1, a tall strapping boy of nineteen years showed up on horseback at Brandsey-Beeler Essential Stuff Mercantile and greeted George with, "Hello, Grandfather. I'm your grandson Adam!"

George stepped back, looking him over and asked, "Are you the little boy of Mary Beth and Bruce that I last saw in 1815 before your family's departure to Funk's Grove?"

Adam replied "The one and the same, Grandfather!"

As the boy's story came out, he said his father, Bruce, tried to make a farmer of him, but it just didn't take, which put him at odds with his father. His mother, running interference for him, only kept enough "oil on the water" until the next confrontation erupted.

The short version of his story was that one night he packed his possibles, rifle and such, took one of the family's horses and lit out for St. Louis to learn the fur trade from his grandfather and Uncle Joe.

The family as a whole welcomed young Adam, except Joe had his reservations. He was perplexed on exactly what to do with the lad. With half of the family leaving for the mountains with Cadet's expedition and the other half leaving for the Arkansas Territory, Joe suggested to George that he could take the lad under his wing. George nixed that with the comment, "Joe, the boy wants to learn the fur trade, and that won't happen behind my counter. Remember the opportunities you had with me in the field when you were his age?" Annie and Maw stepped into the discussion and told Joe that he had no spine, and what was the matter with him. The women would take young Adam under their wings. Knowing his bride and mother-in-law, Joe caved immediately and agreed the lad would be going to Arkansas with them.

George sent a letter along with a letter of credit (for the horse young Adam had appropriated) to Bruce and Mary Beth explaining the matter of young Adam and his accompanying the family to Arkansas.

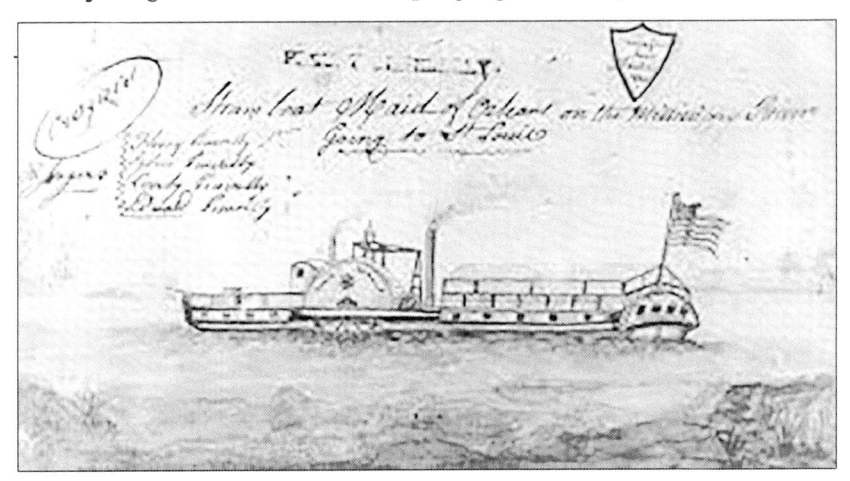

Maid of Orleans

The family departed St. Louis on March 29, 1820, on the Maid of Orleans. After four days of steaming, they arrived and disembarked at Arkansas Post. The voyage was uneventful except for one minor altercation. The women as a whole kept to their cabin and only came on deck during the evening and early morning hours. On the evening of the third day, Annie, Mother Anita, and Sparrow were on deck near the bow enjoying the evening's bug-free breeze. Despite their disheveled Métis squaw appearance, one of the deckhands, who had gotten a bit too deep into his cups, came staggering up to them and reached out for Annie and said he was looking for some squaw time.

Annie pulled her bear jaw knife and cut him on the forearm. Howling in pain he pulled his knife, but before he could move a step, a hatchet came flying from behind and pinned his arm to a wooden stanchion. Before the drunk could respond, Joe removed the hatchet, and he and Sarge picked him up and tossed him overboard.

Later in their cabin, Linda and Adam were visibly shaken by what had happened, but the older folks told them that is how it is, and what Joe had said about their safety was to be taken seriously. Action with serious thought behind it was required to ensure their safety, and the family had everyone's back.

Joe smoothed over the loss of the deckhand with the captain with a few Spanish rials to cover the loss, and the situation was put behind. Plus, the word spread quickly not to fool with the Beeler traders and their squaws.

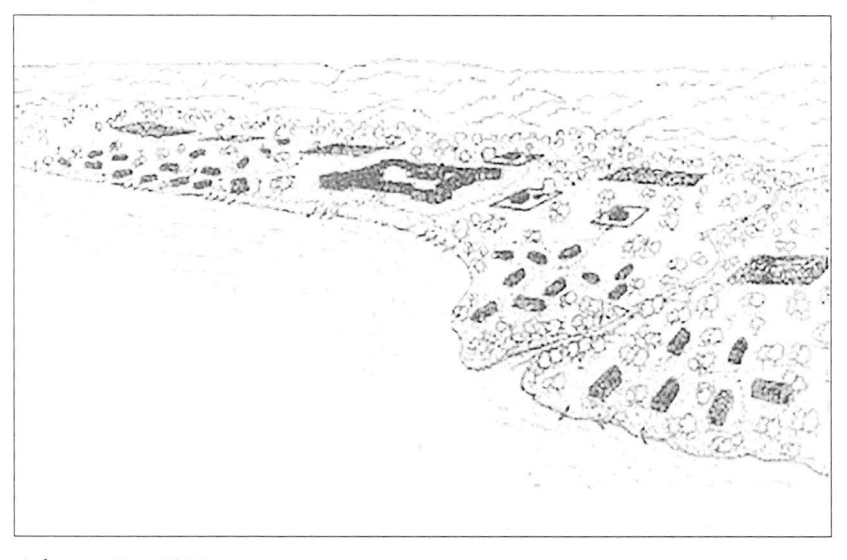

Arkansas Post 1820

The family disembarked at Arkansas Post and was overwhelmed by the hustle and bustle of all the activity in the town. Upon making a few inquiries, Joe informed his party that the heightened activity was due to Arkansas Post becoming the territorial capital last year (1819) upon Arkansas being designated a territory by Congress. Naturally, the town was undulated by lawyers and the territory bureaucrats. Governor James Miller, formerly of New Hampshire, had only arrived in town on December 26, 1819, and was currently involved in getting the territorial legislature to pass a bill relocating the capital from Arkansas Post to Little Rock. This happened in 1820, and Arkansas Post faded back to being the first landing in Arkansas on the way to Little Rock and other points up the Arkansas and White Rivers.

Joe took Adam with him and left Sarge with the women to see what there was regarding board and lodging, and Joe would see to transportation.

It took Annie and Mother Anita about three hours to find lodging and good food at an inn/hostelry run by a gal named Mary John. Being an organized no nonsense woman is what attracted her to Annie and Mother Anita. Mary John cut to the quick and immediately reciprocated in kind and set the Beeler party up for as long as they would be in town.

Fleshing out Mary John's story, Annie found that she was the property of a Mr. James Scull along with the inn/hostelry, but Mr. Scull gave her free rein in managing and running the place. Plus, being an excellent cook, she and Annie were joined at the hip. Mr. Scull, being a lawyer, found his arrangement with Mary John to be beneficial for both of them, and he was a good man.

Annie, being attracted to good people, pulled Joe aside and told him he had to do something for Mary John like buy her freedom from Mr. Scull and let her decide her own destiny. Joe said, "Annie my love, I will approach Mr. Scull with the idea and an offer of $1,000. That would give him a profit of $200, but I think it will be a hard sell."

Joe was right! Mr. Scull wouldn't even consider the offer. He told Joe he had a good thing with Mary John and wasn't about to change it. Plus, he was good to Mary John, and life was good for her.

Mary John had been born a slave in Spanish Louisiana in the early 1790s. She was given the name Marie Jeanne by her master. In 1806, at Arkansas Post, she was sold by Marie Languedoc to Jean Larguier for $600. And in 1811, she was sold to Mr. James Scull for $800.

Over the next 20 years she developed a widespread reputation as a barbecue cook between the post and Little Rock. In 1840, the records show she bought her freedom from Mr. Scull for $800 and the inn/hostelry also. She thrived well in business until her death in 1857.

Joe made inquiries about town, mainly through Mr. Scull, and made contact with Mr. Asa McFletch, an Ohio keelboat operator who traversed the White and Mississippi Rivers all the way down to New Orleans. He had just arrived a day or so ago and was making preparations to proceed up the White and Black Rivers to OleDavidsonville, the county seat for Lawrence County. That was great for Joe because he wanted to stop at the Federal Land Office there. Asa told Joe it would be about five days before he would depart upriver after he was finished with preparations and business. The five days were well spent with the family getting to know the lay of the land. With the post being the territorial capital, a lot was learned socially and economically.

Joe still required that one of the menfolk accompany the women when they went out about town. When the family disembarked from the Maid of Orleans, the incident of the deckhand spread through town like wildfire, and the lower forms of life avoided the Beeler party. But it had to be reinforced one more time when the women, accompanied by young Adam, were coming out of a mercantile and were accosted by a drunk. This time Mother Anita, pulling her stiletto, cut the drunk on the cheek, and young Adam laid him out in the street with a clip of his fusel along the drunk's left ear. There were no more problems while the Beelers were in town.

About April 15, the Asa McFletch keelboat departed the post with the Beeler family on board. It took about twelve to fourteen days to ascend the White River to the small hamlet of Jackson Port and traverse up the Black River to OleDavidsonville.

Asa McFletch keelboat

For Sparrow and Adam, it was a new and enlightening experience relative to the climate and cramped accommodations on the keelboat. The crew and Mr. McFletch were courteous to the women. Annie and Grandma won them over when they took over the cooking duties. With Joe and Sarge going ashore to hunt during the day and bringing back venison, pork, and a bear, everybody ate well. It tasted good because of Annie and Grandma's skills preparing it.

Arriving at Ole Davidsonville on April 29, the family disembarked. The women found accommodations at one of the hostelries. Joe made arrangements with Mr. McFletch to procure two twenty-five-feet or longer Northern canoes for him at Polk Bayou (Batesville). Asa said he would do so and would contact Circuit Court Judge Richard Searcy, a friend of his, to make arrangements with him to hold the canoes and supplies for Joe and the family until their arrival at Polk Bayou.

Ole Davidsonville

Joe and Sarge spent time at the Federal Land Office in Old Davidsonville reviewing surveyed land plats and looking at the requirements and privileges thereof granted by the War of 1812 Bounty Act, which entitled a veteran to claim 160 acres of public lands.

The other part of the act reviewed was "Squatter Rights" which entitled a settler to occupy a parcel of land and purchase it for $1.25 an acre. Also, Joe was interested where the Cherokee Trace laid, the eastern boundary of the Turkey Town Treaty of 1817 land exchange.

Inquiring on where he could purchase some mounts for the families' trek to Polk Bayou, Joe was directed to some settlers living on the Spring River due west of Ole Davidsonville about seven miles. After a conversation amongst the family, it was decided that Joe, Annie, and

Adam would go to Spring River for the horses, while Ray, Linda, and Mother Anita would remain at Ole Davidsonville and pick up what remaining supplies they still needed.

Joe contacted Mr. Solomon Hewitt who lived on the north side of Spring River and owned and operated a ferry across the river. He was able to pick up two horses. Crossing the river to the south bank with Mr. Hewitt, Joe was able to buy five more horses from a Mr. Nevil Wayland and Mr. Mose Robertson. These sales worked because Joe was able to pay in silver Mexican pesos, and Annie's winning ways with the men and their wives paid off as usual. Joe, Annie, and Adam were invited to supper and an overnight stay by Mr. Hewitt and his wife, which they accepted. In fact, the Waylands and Robertsons joined in the supper, and a good evening was spent by all getting to know each other. Joe and Annie picked up much background on that part of Lawrence County, and the settlers were eager for news from where the Beelers had come.

Returning to Ole Davidsonville with the stock the next morning, the family spent two days getting things organized and packed for the seventy-five mile trip to Polk Bayou. Annie and Grandma Anita laid out what went into each pack. Joe and Sarge loaded the horses accordingly. Sparrow and Adam were the gophers.

Finally leaving Ole Davidsonville on May 7, the party reached the Hewitt Ferry crossing on Spring River about mid-morning. The weather was cloudy with the temperature reaching into the low 80s. Joe mentioned to Annie and Garner Ray it was the beginning of the Arkansas heat to come.

Naturally, in crossing over the river on the Hewitt Ferry, all the families came to meet the Beeler party. Introductions and greetings were exchanged, and the Hewitt, Wayland, and Robertson families insisted that the Beeler party stay overnight for supper and lodgings. Joe was slightly annoyed at the delay, but Annie as usual told him to "be Christian" and accepted the invite.

Departing the next morning, Joe got his party on the trail about an hour after sunrise. His intention was to a place on the southwest trail named Dogwood Springs, about ten miles distant. The weather was overcast with intermittent rain showers, and the temperature was in the mid-80s with high humidity. Typical of Arkansas weather in the late spring along with the bugs—mosquitoes, chiggers and ticks to contend with.

Arriving at Dogwood Springs, the party set up their camp. Joe and Sarge looked up Major Haynes who lived nearby and invited him and his family to the Beeler campsite for supper. Mr. Haynes and his wife accepted.

Major Haynes represented Lawrence County at the territorial legislative meeting that convened at the post hosted by Governor Miller the previous year. The Beelers also learned that Mr. Robert Bean, a merchant store owner in Polk Bayou, was the "Ledge" speaker.

It was a very congenial get-together, and the Beelers learned more helpful information. They also received a letter of introduction from Major Haynes, which helped greatly in the days ahead.

Joe, at the women's request, laid over another day at the Springs mainly because of the heavy rains but departed the next day, with sunny but cooler weather, for the small hamlet of Columbia on the south branch of the Strawberry River fifteen miles distant. The party made good time despite the muddy conditions caused by the previous day's heavy rains. The high point of the day was the lack of bugs because of the cool snap; both people and horses appreciated this.

Arriving at the small village of Columbia, which involved a wet crossing of the river, the family set up camp in a grove of sycamore trees for the night. Joe told the women and Sarge that he and Adam would go into town and get a look at things.

Columbia, as described by Schoolcraft, consisted of about fifteen buildings scattered about the west bank of the river, which included a water powered gristmill, a whiskey distillery, a blacksmith shop, and tavern. Joe and Adam stopped at the gristmill, blacksmith shop, and the tavern. Engaging the principals of these establishments in conversation added to Joe's background information somewhat. But after quaffing an ale or two in the tavern, Joe became uneasy about the questions and background conversation he heard about his party camping just outside town in the sycamore grove.

Easing on out of the tavern, Joe told Adam, "Let's get back to camp now, set up a guard rotation with Sarge, and tell the women we will be on the trail before sunup!" Back in camp, Joe explained his concerns. Everyone agreed to camp security and an early morning departure.

As Annie said, "When my husband gets antsy, I pay attention because it's for all of our welfare!"

Joe's concern manifested that night about 2:00 a.m. when Adam, who was on guard at the time, heard a commotion amongst the horses. He awakened Joe and Sarge, and all three moved quietly to where the horses were tied to a common hitch line and found two boys, one twelve and the other fifteen years of age, trying to hide behind a giant sycamore. Collaring both, Sarge said, "Alright you two, back to the campfire and let's straighten this out!"

Annie quickly got a fresh pot of coffee going. The boys sat down and were asked for their story.

They said that they heard the stories circulating in town about the party of traders with their squaws camped out in the sycamore grove. But the rumor that that the squaws were very pretty was why they sneaked out to see for themselves. Some of the older folk said that was nonsense because Indian squaws were typically very ugly and homely looking.

Slightly miffed at this idea, Mother Anita rose to the occasion and said, "Daughter, Granddaughter, shall we pardon ourselves and freshen up a bit for the boys to dispel their idea of ugly, homely looking squaws?" So the women did, and the boys were tongue-tied for the rest of the time they were in camp. In addition, the women stoked up the fire and prepared a scrumptious breakfast for everyone because, as Annie said, "Joe wants an early start, and this will make it happen!"

The boys headed back to town with full bellies and proof that Indian squaws were not ugly or homely. Their experience with the Beeler party set their opinion solid that Indian women were beautiful. And being fussed over and fed by same reinforced this all the more.

As planned, the family was on the trail an hour before sunrise after an eventful night. "Just the way I like it!" remarked Joe.

Leaving Columbia behind on May 12, the party covered the remaining thirty-five miles to Polk Bayou in three days. Because of heavy rains on the second day after departing Columbia, an extra day was spent in camp instead of slugging through mud and getting drenched in the process. Annie remarked to Joe, "You are fortunate to have us women along to provide guidance to you for the decisions you have to make!"

Joe just deadpanned, "Yes, Annie!"

Arriving in Polk Bayou on May 15, the party split with the women and Adam while they looked for accommodations. Joe and Sarge tended to the horses by looking up Mr. Robert Bean, the local merchant, and Judge Richard Searcy.

Checking in with Judge Searcy, Joe found that Mr. McFletch had contacted the judge, who had arranged with Mr. Robert Bean to have two canoes ready for the Beelers. Mr. Bean also bought the horses and made a stable available for the family because the women found no hostelry accommodations in town. At this time, Polk Bayou consisted of about a dozen houses, gristmill, blacksmith shop, tavern, and Mr. Bean's General Mercantile.

While in town, Joe ran into three Kickapoo from a village located on the Flippin Barrens near a Delaware village at Dew Creek, present-day Bull Shoals. Joe picked up their language in his days at Devil's Lake, Michigan Territory, and he was able to get a lay of the land upriver relative to the Indian tribes. He learned that around the middle of June the tribes always held the Green Corn Celebration, which was to be held at the Norfork confluence this year.

He told the family, "This is one event we will be at!"

The family kept socializing to a minimum, and they were able to get on the river within two days and proceeded on their way upriver with Joe, Annie, and Mother Anita in one canoe and Adam, Linda, and Ray in the other.

The weather was rainy and cool, but good time was made despite the high water and fast current. Lafferty Landing was the first stop twenty-three to twenty-four miles upriver from Batesville. Everyone was tired from the strenuous paddling. The Widow Lafferty took pity on the women and offered them accommodations for the night. As usual, the conversation and activities extended long into the night because as Mrs. Lafferty said, "I don't get quality company that often, and I'm taking advantage of it."

Joe laughed and said, "Mrs. Lafferty, don't let these ladies pull your string. I know, being married to Magpie all these years and having a mother-in-law to match. I'm just a mere mortal man. Nothing more. Nothing less!" Joe then ducked and braced himself for the womanly onslaught that followed.

Sarge quietly told Joe, "I thought you knew better!"

"Ray, every once in a while you've got to let a little hang out!"

Mrs. Lafferty extended her hospitality to the Beelers, who stayed another day before proceeding upriver.

Conversation with Mrs. Lafferty revealed that her deceased husband had run a keelboat and had extensive trade with the Indians upriver which proved to be very lucrative. But having their property decimated by the earthquakes of 1811–1812 had set them back. They were recovering their losses adequately when Mr. Lafferty died of pneumonia in 1817.

Annie felt that Mrs. Lafferty was a good, honest woman, so when Joe asked to outline his trade ideas with the Indians with Mrs. Lafferty, Annie consented. Mrs. Lafferty suggested a location twenty-five miles upriver at Sylamore Creek. The one advantage it had was a good flowing spring located on the west bank of the river.

Located about seven miles above Sylamore was a village of Shawnee on Livingston Creek.

Taking Mrs. Lafferty's advice, the family set off for Sylamore. The weather was rainy and cool, which made up for the high water and strong current, but it kept the bugs at bay, somewhat.

When they were about halfway to Sylamore, the family stopped and made camp at Rocky Bayou (present-day Guion, Arkansas) for the night. Continuing on the next morning, they arrived at Sylamore about mid-day on May 20.

Surveying the site on the west bank of the river, it was as Mrs. Lafferty described it. Annie, feeling enchanted by the location and feeling her oats somewhat, told her husband quietly, "Joe dearest, wasn't I right as usual!"

"Yes, Annie, you're right and alright with me for the last twenty-five years and have never disappointed me!" as he swept her up in a tender hug!

The family set up camp near the spring on the west bank of the river and the confluence of Sylamore Creek, settled in, and prepared to survey and explore the surrounding countryside. In conversations after supper each night, the family members each gave their opinion on what they had observed during the day.

As a result, over the next week or so, plans were made as to a site layout for the main cabin, trade store, water power source for a gristmill, blacksmith shop, and other out-buildings.

Crossing the river, Joe and Sarge found a stretch of level ground that ran adjacent to the river for a mile or more with an average width of one-fourth to one-half mile. This land was good river bottomland, and the soil was rich because of the overflooding that occurred now and then in the spring.

It was agreed upon at the family campfire that Sarge would file on 160 acres of this land under the Bounty Act allowed by veterans of the War of 1812.

Joe mentioned that he would like to file for about 100 acres around the spring on the west bank of the river, but because the land was on the west bank of the river, it was Cherokee land. He intended to meet with Chief John Jolly at Illinois Bayou next year on their return to St. Louis and work out a deal for the land.

The ten days spent at Sylamore were pleasant. The weather was not too bad with days in the mid-80s and nights in the 50s–60s. Annie and Mother Anita were kept busy administering to the tick and chigger bites. Sparrow was badly infected with chigger bites when one cool evening she laid down in a patch of green grass. Mother Anita took the poor suffering child down to the creek and bathed her all over with a mixture of yellow root and coal oil and then scrubbed her with lye soap in the creek. Afterwards, she applied a mixture mullein weed and bear oil over the bite areas. Linda was miserable for a day or two, but recovered. Her mother and father told her, "Linda, if you must sit somewhere away from camp, always sit on a rock that has been heated by the sun. Chiggers avoid it like the plague!" Lesson learned.

The other major mishap was with Adam. Joe decided to climb the north bluff just across the creek from their campsite to get a better view of the land thereabout. Adam insisted on taking the lead with Joe warning him about where he was placing his hands on the climb. Snakes you know. And as bad luck would have it, upon grasping one of the ledges with his left hand, Adam found the ledge occupied by a small rattler. The snake quickly struck Adam on the ring finger which caused Adam to lose his grip and fall back on Joe just below.

Adam yelled "Snakebite!" and held up his finger. Joe, wasting no motion, pulled his hatchet and cut the finger off just above the second joint. Taking a leather thong from Adam's legging, Joe put a tourniquet around the finger base and got Adam down the bluff and back to camp. Annie and Mother Anita sized up the situation and immediately stuck a knife into the fire. Upon the knife getting red hot, they applied it to Adam's severed finger with Joe and Sarge holding Adam down.

Over the next five days, the women hovered over Adam, keeping him warm and nourished with squirrel and rabbit broth. They kept the wound covered with bear oil. The healing process was good because there was no infection as a result of cauterizing by the hot knife.

Joe and Sarge kidded Adam that without the ring finger he wouldn't have to worry about getting hitched up with any woman. Of course, the ladies found little humor in this joking, but they held their remarks on the matter and told Adam he would never get along well in a world without good women like themselves to take care of him, as currently was the case! During the ten days at Sylamore, the family had many visitors stopping by off the river— Indians going upstream for the Green Corn Festival at Norfork, white hunters, and a keelboat passing by. In the process of conversations, much background was learned for future reference.

By the first of June, the family was on the river heading for Norfork accompanied by some Kickapoo from Dew Creek and Shawnee from Livingston Creek just upriver about ten miles. Joe was able to work out a trade with the Kickapoo and Shawnee in that the Beeler twenty-foot canoes were exchanged for a 28-foot Northern canoe.

Adam was recovering nicely from his injury.

Joe also noticed the reaction amongst the Kickapoo in that they showed great respect and deference toward Annie. He overheard in conversations between them about the great power of the medicine of the bear spirit dwelling in the bear jaw knife worn by Annie. Querying them, Joe asked them where they came by such knowledge. They replied that every tribe of the great northern waters knew the legend of the bear jaw knife medicine and the woman who possessed it. When Joe talked with the family about what he had learned, Annie remarked that she had observed the same. Annie and Mother Anita both agreed it was an advantage for the family's safety. Joe, turning to Sarge, Sparrow, and Adam remarked, "Follow your mother and granny's lead, and you will do well in the days ahead!"

Arriving at Norfork, the Beelers found the Shawnee village a crowded, busy place. There were a couple of hundred Indians and whites there for the Green Corn Festival. Leaving Adam, Mother Anita, Sarge, and Sparrow at the canoe, Joe and Annie headed into the village to reconnoiter.

Annie and Joe felt at ease amongst the Indians of the village. They asked some of the headmen if they could meet Chief Peter Cornstalk.

Chief Cornstalk gave a gracious welcome to them saying that news of them had proceeded them before they had arrived. The chief said the spirit of bear medicine woman with her husband and family was welcomed in his village, and if he could do anything for them, please ask. Joe asked if the chief or his headmen could point out a campsite for the family, which they did.

Returning to the family and canoe, they refloated and proceeded up the Norfork and beached just at the northern edge of the village. Setting to, all went to work building a cane break hut in the manner of the Sauk and a comfortable campsite. Upon hearing that the spirit of the bear medicine woman was in camp, the village as a whole came to see, and the family had more than enough help and advice. They all made quick work of the camp and hut set up.

Left: The Spirit of the Corn Dance Festival. Right: Spirit of the Corn

The family spent the next week celebrating with the tribesmen, white settlers, and hunters that attended the Green Corn Festival. There were no outstanding altercations or incidents. The weather even cooperated somewhat with temperatures in the mid-80s during the day and mid-60s at night. There were a couple of days of intermittent rain and a thunderstorm or two thrown in. The bugs were kept at bay somewhat by the smoke of the many campfires in the village. But with a tight cane break hut and a good camp setup, the ten days were quite comfortable for the family. Adam was recovered enough from his finger injury that he and Sarge went hunting and brought back some venison and pork.

Many visitors came to the Beeler campsite for conversation and feasting because Annie and Granny always had something on the spit.

On the fifth day, three Osage warriors came into the camp, and the leader introduced himself as Sammy Lambert, brother to Rosalie and Masina Lambert, wives of A.P. Chouteau. He and his men had been sent by A.P. to hook up with the Beelers and guide them to Salina, Oklahoma, on the Neosho (Grand River), site of A.P.'s trading post for the Osage.

Joe and Annie were tickled and surprised at the arrival of Sammy and his men. It would make the journey to Salina much easier being guided by someone who knew the way. Joe, Sammy, and Sarge planned the route to be taken and the time involved to complete it.

Sammy said that proceeding up the White River to the mouth of the James River, just beyond Swan Creek, site of a white hunters camp called Forsythe, would place them at an Osage summer hunting camp. There he had horses waiting for them to carry the party down the Osage Trace to Salina. He also emphasized a departure sooner than later because of the onset of the summer heat and humidity. It would mean early morning and late evening travel with layovers during midday. Joe said, "Fine. Let's pull the women into the conversation and get things moving."

Relative to the family discussion on what was the best way to proceed, it was decided to trade the twenty-eight-foot northern canoe for two twenty-footers. With Adam's injury healed, the loads would be better balanced by having three people in each canoe, and with the continuing high water because of the wet weather, the handling and maneuvering would be better.

Unbeknownst to Mother Anita, with Annie's approval, Sammy would ride with Joe, Annie, and Mother Anita, explaining that it was for Joe and Sammy to have clear communication for planning and decision making. Mother Anita became suspicious and cranky, muttering about these young whippersnappers trying to take care of her when she didn't need or care for it. Annie pulled her mother aside and said, "Mother, the men need their man-talk, and besides, who told Linda that we women needed to be good squaw wives to our trader husbands, huh?"

"Yes, daughter, and you my daughter, are right!" replied Mother Anita.

Joe pulled Annie aside and hugged her. "My little Magpie. You've never disappointed me, and I love you all the more for it!"

With Chief Cornstalk's help, Joe traded the canoes with a couple of the Shawnee warriors.

With everybody pulling together, the combined party was able to depart after the second day, that is, after the feast given by Chief Cornstalk in honoring the spirit of the bear medicine woman and her family for joining with the tribesmen in celebrating the Green Corn Festival.

Splitting the loads between the family canoes and Sammy's canoe, the party was on the river before sunup and, as predicted, the summer heat and humidity descended upon them.

Moving up the river during the early morning hours, holing up during the mid-day, and continuing during the late afternoon hours into evening, the party reached the Delaware village at Dew Springs on the Flippin Barrens (present-day Bull Shoals) in three days.

Because half of the village, with Chief John Cake, were still at the Green Corn Festival at Norfork, Joe and Sammy decided to only spend a day there. They invited the remaining headmen to a feast. Sarge, Adam, and Sammy's two warriors went out and brought back venison, pork, and quail. Joe and Sammy laid to and set up a camp worthy of the feast to be held, while Annie, Sparrow, and Mother Anita in their usual fashion set to and prepared a supper second to none.

All in the village were invited and attended the festivities that continued into the night, but much talk centered around furs, trade, and what the tribesmen needed and wanted. Joe was upfront in saying that Chouteau and Company, namely him, would not allow " liquor to be involved in the trade! It wasn't open for discussion. Period!

In private, Sammy said to Joe, "I don't think A.P. will go along with that!"

Joe cut the conversation off and said, "Sammy, that's between A.P. and me!"

The party reached the James River in eight days of travel without any major incidents other than the rainy, humid weather, heat, and bugs.

At the Delaware village, the women were given some bolts of muslin by the Indian squaws. This was fashioned into mosquito netting for each one of the party and greatly relieved the problem of getting rest at night.

As planned, proceeding up the James River about five miles, the party arrived at the Osage summer hunting camp about July 1. The next phase of their journey was about to begin.

Joe was informed by a courier from St. Louis that A.P. Chouteau was in route with a pack train carrying part of the upcoming season's trade goods. A.P. asked if Joe and his party would wait for his arrival and join him for the remaining trip to his trading post on the Neosho River, (present-day Salina).Joe got the family together to discuss the ramifications of this request to which Annie replied, "Joe, you know this would be an opportunity for you and A.P. to make company plans and decisions and allow us womenfolk to get acquainted with our Osage hosts, if you get my drift!"

Joe shook his head. "Annie, my little Magpie. As usual, you have summed it up nicely. What more can I say!"

Annie winked slyly at Mother Anita and said to Joe, "Husband dearest, life has been and is good to you." To which Joe swept her into his arms with a mighty hug.

Getting acquainted with the villagers was a pleasure for Annie and Mother Anita. Soon they were lost in women-talk and activities with the squaws of the camp. Under the direction of the women, Joe, Sarge, and Adam fell to the construction of a summer shelter for the family in the Osage manner of style—saplings driven into the ground, tied at the top and covered over with bark, hide mats, with a smoke hole at the top, and an entrance facing the east. It was a little on the snug side for the whole family, but it was only temporary until A.P. arrived, and then anyone could sleep outside weather permitting.

Sammy introduced Joe to a resident of the camp who went by the name Bill Williams.

Mr. Williams married into the Osage and had been living with them for the last seven years. He introduced the Beeler family to his Osage wife, A-Cin-Ga (Wind Blossom), and his two daughters, Mary Ann, age six, and Sarah, age four.

Williams originally came from Polk City, North Carolina. He had fought in the War of 1812 and went to the Osage as a Protestant preacher with the Harmony Mission. He had a gift for languages and translated the Bible into the Osage language. In the process, he had assimilated into the Osage as a trapper after marrying Wind Blossom and never looked back.

The two families had a lot in common, and the time spent together was beneficial for all concerned. Adam seemed to hit it off with Mr. Williams during the time spent with him on hunts and other daily tasks. Annie remarked to Joe, "I can see the lad growing straighter every day, and what's rubbing off on him from Mr. Williams is helping the lad on the right path to becoming a man like the man I've been sleeping with the last twenty-two years!"

Joe's comeback was "My little Magpie, you have no shame!"

A.P. arrived with the pack train about the August 5, 1820.

Joe and A.P. set to planning immediately on the days and trading season ahead. A.P. also requested that Annie be a part of these discussions because of his experience working with Annie at the St. Charles operations. He remarked that Annie's insights into business problems and decisions in the past had made the company money. And, he was not a person to pass up a good thing.

Their immediate attention was focused on the trip to the Neosho River post and the time and effort to get there. A distance of approximately 150 miles remained, and following the Osage Trace would take the party through southwest Missouri and northwest Arkansas. Even though the trace was a well-worn trail, it wasn't friendly to mule or ox-driven carts or wagons. Hence, the pack train was made up of thirty-five horses and mules supported by ten drovers and five camp keepers, plus three hunters to keep meat on the spits. Sammy had ten horses already in camp for the Beelers.

Sammy reckoned that with tolerable weather despite the summer heat, which called for before sunup starts, a mid-day break, and late afternoon travel well past sundown, it would take about ten days to reach the Neosho River post.

In discussions with Joe and Annie about the upcoming trade season, A.P. estimated that it would cost the company about 8,500 to 9,000 dollars in trade goods cost for fur and hides. That is 1,575 beaver plews, 2,500 deer and buffalo hides, with the remainder bear, otter, coon, and wildcats.

A.P.'s clerk and segondo, Mr. Robert Dupasquier, a literate French-Canadian, supplied the current (1820) St. Louis prices. Beaver prime: two dollars; Deer: one dollar; Cured/Tanned buffalo hide: twelve to fifteen dollars; Mink/Otter/Wildcats: two to three dollars; and Bear: three dollars.

The Neosho/Verdigris/Arkansas Flowage

Mr. Dupasquier remarked that even though the country's economy was starting to recover from the previous year's recession, the 1820–1821 fur season should show a reasonable return. Relative to the tribal conflict between the Osage and Cherokee overhunting grounds, the building of Fort Smith in 1817 had put some oil on the conflict, but there was still background tension, and this would have an unpredictable outcome on the fur season ahead.

After listening to Joe and Annie's plans for the Sylamore post, he agreed that they should be able to get the majority of trade along the White River from where they were at currently, all the way down to Jacksonport. A.P. remarked, "I know what you folks did for the company at St. Charles, and you have my vote on the issue at the board meeting next spring." He also asked the Beelers if they still intended to overwinter at his post on the Neosho, because they could easily return to St. Louis that fall.

Lawrence Diedrich   155

Joe said, "No, I think we will winter over because there is a lot to be learned!"

"I agree, and I welcome the Beeler family to my home!" replied A.P.

On August 15, the whole pack train departed the Osage hunting camp on the James River and arrived at Salina on the September 2.

It was an uneventful trip other than the heat, humidity, and bugs. A few days of rain and thunderstorms brought some relief.

A.P. ran an efficient operation, and his men knew not to cross the line. The messes each night were the center of evening activities, and it soon became apparent to the men that the Beeler mess had the most pleasant aromas wafting from it during the meals. They also soon figured what it took to get Annie and Mother Anita to cook more than the family needed and end up with the extra in their messes.

The men went out of their way to tend to whatever the Beeler women needed and soon found out the women didn't take advantage of them either. There was only one time when one of the drovers got into his cups more than he should have and made some snide remarks about what he would like to do to the Beeler squaws, and his messmates roughed him up severely. That didn't happen again!

Joe and Annie soon found out that if they needed some detail of operations or activities of the messes they just asked Mr. Dupasquier. He had his eye and ear on everything. A.P. said that's why he had him as his chief clerk and segondo! Annie remarked to Joe that Robert reminded her somewhat of Jacques, and she liked him. Joe filed that remark away for the future.

Setting up housekeeping occupied the family immediately. Annie, with her mother's urging, asked Joe if he would set up a lodge for them in the manner of the Northern Cheyenne, like what Stone Hawk did for his bride, Fox That Purrs. And despite A.P.'s offer of setting up residence in his extensive log lodge, there was plenty of room available to provide privacy. Joe declined the offer and said, "What my bride wants, I provide. I think Annie is remembering our times at the Mandan in 1804 and Fort Francis in 1800 where Linda was born!" "Not a problem!" said A.P. "Just give Robert a list of what you need."

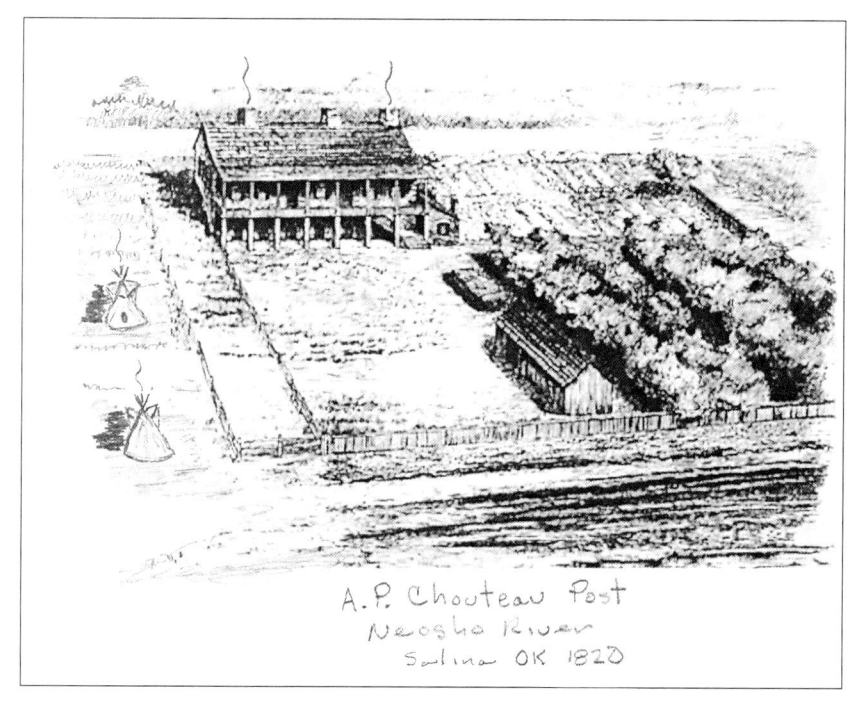

A.P. Chouteau Post Neosho River Salina OK 1820

A.P. had an extensive salt quarry operation about a mile south of his post. This quarry had been worked by the tribes for a least seventy-five years previously and was one of the reasons A.P. had located his post at Salina. He had updated the operation by hauling in cast caldrons from St. Louis to boil the brine that was bucketed out of the salt well. Naturally, there was a scarcity of wood around the mine, and every day the wood cutters had to travel some distance to cut the amount of wood needed for a day's operation.

This caused Joe, Sarge, Adam, and Sammy to travel some distance to obtain the pine poles needed for the two lodges, but find them they did. After setting up the poles as directed by the women, and with an adequate supply of tanned buffalo hides from the post, the two lodges were completed and ready for the season's occupancy.

Annie, Joe, Mother Anita, and Adam took up residence in their lodge. Sarge and Sparrow took up residence in their own smaller lodge.

As the season turned to fall, the routine of daily living settled in. Joe was spending more time with A.P. compared to the business.

Despite the Beeler women frowning on A.P.'s situation of having a white wife, Sophie Labadie, in St. Louis along with cohabiting arrangements with Sammy's two sisters Rosalie and Masina, they grew very fond of the two women and friendships evolved. They were even friendly toward A.P. but considered him a lovable scoundrel for taking advantage of their two friends. As Annie told her mother and daughter, "We have been part of the Chouteau and Company for almost fifteen years, and we will not jeopardize that! It's as my husband says, 'You may not like it, but it's the way everyone's stick floats!'"

A.P. Chouteau

Toward the end of October or first part of November, the Osage were migrating from their summer hunting camps in Missouri and Arkansas back to the Neosho River Valley camp for the winter season. Bill

Williams brought his family to A.P.'s post and set up residence for the season. Adam was overjoyed to see him. Soon after, Bill invited Adam, Sarge, and Joe to join him as partners for the coming trapping season. Adam jumped at the chance, but Joe and Sarge said they would participate as time allowed. For most of the season, Adam spent all his time on the trapline with Bill. He was offered and took up residence in the Williams' lodge.

Annie said to Joe, "That's a win-win situation for Adam, and our privacy!"

"Wife, you are a shameless hussy, and don't forget about my wonderful mother-in-law. I know you women and your women's talk! Nuf said, my sweet!" She attacked him, bowled him over with a hug, and smothered him with kisses!

Joe and Annie spent a lot of their time in the post trading room that season dealing with the tribesman and occasional whites that came through. Picking up the Osage language and some tutoring by Bill Williams was a side benefit. But overall, it gave them a feel for what was ahead of them in setting up the post at Sylamore on the White River. Working closely with Mr. Dupasquier led to another friendship in the days ahead. And as Annie had told Joe, she liked him!

The season passed quickly because the early fall was mild, and the cold of winter didn't set in until the middle of December. Adam was seldom seen, as his time was spent with Mr. Williams getting three traplines in place. Joe, Annie, Sarge, and Linda's time was spent in the post trading store handling the daily business that streamed through the door. A.P. had arranged with Mr. Dupasquier for Annie and Joe to take charge of this part of the operation for the season. Mother Anita took care of the family's domestic needs, which she was content to do!

For all of the family, except Linda, the ups and downs of daily life in the early nineteenth century was handled routinely. Whenever threats to one's safety and life occurred, it was handled decisively with a sound decision based upon one's life experiences and the skills gained from those experiences.

As ole Shingabis was fond of saying to his boys, "Judgement comes from experience, and experience comes from bad judgement!"

Linda had repeatedly been told through the years by her parents and grandparents to not take anything for granted. Think and judge people by what they say and, more importantly, by what they do. Her mother and grandmother had often admonished her, "Don't be a Pollyanna. Learn to trust your instincts, your gut feeling."

They had also told her that the heart of an Indian could be discerned much more easily than a white man's. And "liquor made brutes of them all.

In late December, a couple of Ponca warriors had come to the post to trade, and Annie and Linda had taken care them. They behaved themselves in that they didn't get into their cups too deeply.

The use of high wine (rum) in the trade was one of the bones of contention between Joe and A.P. But as Joe told Annie, it's A.P.'s operation, and he sets the rules.

Anyway, one of the Ponca set his sights on the lovely little squaw that had served him in the post store. He and his companion set to making plans on how and when to snatch her.

They observed that Linda always went down to the river for water to carry back to her grandmother after she finished working at the post store. Garner Ray, Annie, and Joe always asked her

Linda/Little Sparrow

if someone should accompany her, and she always said no. She could handle the chore herself.

The Ponca capitalized on the weak point in Linda's routine. Setting their horses in a camp across the river, they laid in wait for Linda doing her daily water chore. Seizing her when she came up the bank, they quickly gagged and bound her hand and foot, crossed the river and mounted their horses, and headed out west into the twilight of the evening.

After an hour or so had passed and Linda hadn't come to the Beeler lodge, Granny Anita's instincts kicked in, and she hastened to the post store to find out what might have delayed Linda. Quickly realizing something was amiss, Annie looked at Joe and Ray and said, "Please don't let something terrible happen to our Sparrow!" Backtracking on the path to the river, Joe and Ray read the sign of the struggle! Joe looked at Ray and said, "Oh shit! Dammit! This is a repeat of what happened to Annie on the Missouri River in 05! Ray, get the horses ready. Pack enough grub for a week and dress warmly, because if my joints are right, we are in for a winter storm in twenty-four hours. I'm going to get Sammy because he knows the country!" Within an hour, Joe, Ray, and Sammy were on the way, which put them about three to four hours behind the Ponca. The advantage was with the Ponca because they knew that pursuit was inevitable, and they knew the country. They planned to stick to the high ground because they could make better time. Also, they knew the weather would help them because of the impending storm. So, they figured to put as much distance as possible between them and the pursuers by heading west until they hit the Verdigris River and follow it northwest to their country in present-day Kansas.

As predicted, the storm hit late that night and forced Joe, Ray, and Sammy to pull into a willow grove, get a fire started, and tend to their horses, grieved by the fact that the storm was wiping out the trail.

The Ponca, meanwhile, had continued through the storm and hit the east bank of the Verdigris River. They found a cedar grove and set up camp to wait out the worst of the storm. They unpacked their horses and threw Sparrow on the baggage, got a fire going, and prepared something to eat. Feeling pretty good about what they had pulled off, they broke out a jug of high wine and started to celebrate. Linda's ordeal went from bad to worse.

Verdigris River Country

Linda worked at keeping her emotional state stable as she laid bound and gagged on the baggage, cold to the bone, letting her mind work the situation as her mother, father, and husband had continually told her through the years. Size up the problem, figure the pros and cons, make a decision, and follow through with direct action.

She watched the two Ponca as they went through the jug of high wine and start on the second. Remembering what her folks said about the tribesmen in general not being able to handle their "liquor" she knew that it was only a matter of time before they turned their attention to her to work their will upon her.

As she laid there, watching them in their debauchery, the only emotion she had trouble keeping in check was her fury/anger. The audacity of these two buffoons to snatch her away from her family, inflict physical harm on her, and put her through the indignity of being treated like a piece of property. She would bide her time, no matter what the cost to her physically, and make them pay dearly.

As the storm deepened with blowing snow and falling temperatures, the two Ponca got deeper in their cups when one finally remembered their little squaw captive and decided to expand his pleasure. But, as he got to his feet and stumbled two feet, he collapsed and fell flat on his face. The other Ponca watched him and proceeded to pass out where he laid by the fire.

Linda saw her chance and crawled off the baggage, stiff and cold as she was. Reaching the first Ponca, she took his knife from his belt and promptly cut his throat. She cut the binding on her feet and quickly moved over to the other Ponca and slit his throat. She moved to the fire and quickly cut the bindings on her hands. She moved back to the Ponca and drove the knife into their chests to be sure. Remembering her father, grandfather, husband Ray, and her mother's technique, she quickly scalped them both! Even after what she'd done to them, her fury was such that she could have mutilated the bodies, but she didn't because she said to herself, "I'm still a lady!" She built up the fire, she warmed herself, prepared some food and ate, went and checked the horses, then found herself a buffalo robe in the baggage. She wrapped herself in it and fell into a deep slumber.

By the next afternoon, the storm abated enough that Joe, Ray, and Sammy were able to get back on the trail, which the storm had completely obliterated. Sammy said the best bet was to head straight west to the Verdigris River and follow the east bank and hope for the best, because that is what the Ponca would do to get back to their country.

After a couple of hours, they reached the river and proceeded up the east bank. The travel wasn't too bad about a quarter mile or so off the bank because of the drifted snow, and the wind was steady out of the west/northwest. After an hour or so, getting on toward dark, Joe stopped and said, "I smell smoke!"

Sammy and Ray both said, "Time to settle the score!"

They followed the scent that brought them to a small ridge overlooking a cedar grove down on the bank of the river. Leaving the horses, they carefully approached the grove and made their way quietly to survey the situation and form a plan of attack!

To their surprise, they saw Linda preparing a meal over the fire. They quietly approached her, and Joe remarked "Daughter, what's on the spit?"

"Daddy, you've grown particular in your old age, and husband dearest, what took you so long?" She threw herself into Ray's open arms!

Joe surveyed the camp with a quick look around and noted two fresh scalps hanging from a Ponca lance stuck in the ground near the fire and the two Ponca stacked like cordwood thirty feet from the fire. Joe said "Daughter, it looks like you're in charge of this camp!"

"Dad, advice from you, Mother, Ray and Granny and admonishments through the years about using my mind and standing on my two feet is what allowed me to be in charge of this camp!" Hugging him, she whispered to him, "Thank you, Dad!"

The next hour or so Linda related to the men her side of the ordeal. Ray remarked, "Joe, she is from the Beeler gene pool. No doubt about it!" They all dug in and prepared a huge meal and, despite the bitter cold, all slept well with the men rotating on three-hour watch shifts.

Rising early before sunup and packing everything together, Ray asked Joe what should be done with those two Ponca? "Leave 'em for the critters?"No, we'll pack them back to A.P.'s post and string them up in a tree across the river! It's time that the medicine of bear jaw spirit knife be made again. And I will ask Annie to transfer the bear jaw knife to Sparrow. It will protect her as it has her mother." Joe replied.

The post was so overjoyed at the safe return of Sparrow that A.P. declared a feast was to be held celebrating the occasion.

Joe, Sammy, and Ray made the bear jaw knife medicine with the two Ponca dangling upside down in an oak tree with a post impaled with an ole stiletto and bear jaw erected ten feet in from of the carcasses.

Thereafter, whenever Sparrow left her lodge she had the bear jaw knife with the two Ponca scalps attached to the scabbard hanging from her waist. And every night for the duration of the Beeler's stay in Salina, the Ponca's ponies were staked outside of Sparrow and Sarge's lodge.

Annie related to Linda that she was proud of her and that the bear jaw knife medicine would protect Linda as it had protected her for the last twenty years.

And it didn't take the moccasin telegraph long to spread the story of the power of the bear jaw knife medicine protecting the lovely little squaw called Sparrow!

The rest of the season passed in a normal manner, with the typical winter snow and ice storms with warm snaps in between. In addition, the tensions were high between the Osage and Cherokee because of the ongoing horse raids and kidnappings due to the dispute over hunting grounds.

Mr. Williams and Adam kept their traplines going until the first of February when the quality of the fur dropped off because of the impending season change. Ray and Joe helped out whenever activity in the post store slacked off.

Their return was modest in that at the end of the season they had three ninety-pound packs of beaver and two ninety-pound packs of otter, fox, fisher, mink, and muskrat, with some deer hides. Relative to St. Louis prices, A.P. paid them a little over 500 dollars for the lot.

Mr. Williams told Adam that he was a quick learner, a hard worker, and that one-third of the proceeds were his. And if he was interested, Mr. Williams was looking for a partner for the fall season. Adam was overwhelmed! Looking at Joe, he asked, "Uncle Joe, what do you think?"

Joe replied, "Nephew, it's an opportunity I wouldn't pass up!"

So a deal was struck, and Mr. Williams had a trapping partner for the upcoming season. Adam looked at Joe, Annie, and Mother Anita, and said, "That's why I left home, and Dad never understood!"

Joe said, "Adam, I'll send a letter to your folks explaining your decision, and I concur with it! Nuf Said!"

Later in the robes with Joe, Annie said, "Husband dearest, you did right by Adam, and initially you didn't want to take him with us. Besides, Rosalie Lambert was telling me that Adam was showing some romantic interest in her sixteen-year-old niece, and we women think something is about to sprout there!"

Joe replied, "You and your women talk, but I love you all the more, wife. Now you shameless hussy, let's get some sleep!"

Joe was uneasy about the ongoing tension between the Osage and the Western Cherokees and discussed this at length with A.P., asking him what he thought and if there were any long-term solutions to end the rift. A.P. related how he and his brother Pierre had been doing business in the Three Forks area of Arkansas for twenty years with the local tribes, especially the Osage. In his opinion, it was poor government policy and bureaucratic incompetence!

Case in point, A.P. was appointed Western Indian agent back in 1805 by General Wilkinson. Not a problem! Dealing with the local tribes on their grounds and their customs was good for business and Pierre and A.P. "Joe, I don't have to tell you, because your past has shown you the same thing. Plus, you wouldn't be a full partner of Chouteau and Company if it were otherwise!" said A.P.

But the bureaucratic blunder is that the government takes the Eastern tribes and dumps them onto the local tribe's lands because they don't want them east of the Mississippi.

It's like taking a bunch of out of region badgers and dumping them into the middle of a prairie dog town. The prairie dogs naturally will be upset, but the local badgers will be mad as hell, too!

A.P. said, "Take Mad Buffalo and his band just south of here. He's riled because of the Cherokee horse raids this winter, and Major Bradford at Fort Smith hasn't done anything about it. I tell you, Joe, that chief is going to do something about it soon, and I hope that there aren't any scalps hanging on the lances and lodge poles because of it.

"Speaking thereof. I know you and the family were planning to leave about the end of February, first of March! Maybe you, Annie, Ray, Robert P., and I should pay a visit to Mad Buffalo and pour some oil on the water. Maybe take some of the tension out of the situation!"

Joe replied, "A.P., I leave it to your discretion. You've walked that ground. I'll follow your steps, and let's see what we can do!"

So the party got together, and at Annie's request, Sparrow and Granny Anita were included. Joe was concerned, but Annie explained the spirit of the bear jaw medicine being present with Sparrow, her mother, and grandmother would reinforce the power thereof and it's long effect through the generations!

The party, in two canoes, left Salina and arrived at Mad Buffalo's camp within a day. Presents were given, and a pipe parley was held. Mad Buffalo explained the grievances he had with the Western Cherokee and the army's lack of response.

Joe and A.P. listened, and Joe said he would carry Mad Buffalo's message to Major Bradford when the Beeler party departed at the end of the month.

Mad Buffalo was happy that someone would listen and carry his message to the authorities, especially when that someone was the family of the spirit of the bear jaw knife medicine.

He ordered a feast to celebrate the visit of the family. He gave his pipe to Joe to be carried to Major Bradford to signify the seriousness of his message, and the pipe would also provide safe passage for the family through Osage lands.

So at the end of February, the family was packed and ready for departure from Salina. Joe was able to procure a twenty-five-foot Northern canoe, which fit the bill of requirements for the trip since Adam would be staying with the Williams family.

While discussing the upcoming company board meeting in July with A.P., Joe said he would stop at Mad Buffalo's village and ask if one of his warriors would accompany the family to Fort Smith to return with Major Bradford's reply to Mad Buffalo's request for assistance against the Cherokee raiding and kidnapping that had occurred the past year. A.P. agreed that it would close the loop relative to what the family was doing for Mad Buffalo, and he would provide a letter of introduction to Major Bradford for the Beelers.

The stop at Mad Buffalo's village went off without a hitch. With the warrior aboard, the approximately 150-mile trip was made in about six days. The rivers were high with spring melt, and the rainy weather had added to the flow.

The family arrived at Bella Point (Fort Smith) at the confluence of the Arkansas and Poteau Rivers on March 5, 1821. Annie remarked that it was hard to believe that it was a year since the family had left St. Louis. Joe's reply was that in the upcoming year much had to be done in getting the family set up at Sylamore.

Fort Smith 1820

Joe asked to speak to Major Bradford about Mad Buffalo's request for intervention because of the past winter's raids and horse thefts from the Cherokee. Joe was informed by a Lieutenant Martin Scott that Major Bradford was away trying to raise recruits to fill vacancies in the company, which presently was down to forty men.

The lieutenant was polite and listened to what Joe had to say. He was sympathetic and said he would pass the request with the pipe along to the major, but couldn't give anything definitive to the Osage warrior to take back to Mad Buffalo.

After considering what the lieutenant had to say about the army's problems, Joe told him that it didn't mitigate the mission of why the army was in Osage country. Controlling his impatience that he had with government bungling, he informed the lieutenant that if the army didn't respond to Mad Buffalo's request properly there would be a force of angry Osage on their doorstep in Fort Smith to deal with.

The lieutenant stated that he understood the import of Mad Buffalo's message, and he would pass it on to Major Bradford when he returned.

The lieutenant said that the post commissary was open to the family to replenish any supplies they needed to continue their trip. Joe managed to purchase a good horse from one of the traders at Fort Smith which he then gave to the Osage warrior so he could return to Mad Buffalo with results of the parley Joe had with the army in his behalf.

The family set up their camp outside the post walls for the night. During their nightly meal, they talked about the events of the day, and each voiced their opinion thereof. Mother Anita said it wouldn't take a wise old owl to figure out that in a short time Fort Smith would be the scene of ruckus. Joe said the family wouldn't see it because in the morning, before sunrise, they would be on the river heading for Illinois Bayou to see Chief John Jolly about acquiring the 100 acres of land at Sylamore.

On April 9, 1821, Mad Buffalo showed up with 350 warriors and threatened to overrun the post. Lieutenant Martin Scott ran out two cannon and gun crews and prepared for action. Mad Buffalo rethought the situation, crossed the river, threatened a white settler and her children, scalped three Quapaw, stole all the horses they could find, and skedaddled for home.

Annie said, "Husband dearest, today when you and Ray were about your business with the army and traders, Mother, Linda, and I were getting acquainted with our Cherokee neighbors who are here for trade. We met Sara and her husband John Ridge, a Cherokee couple from Spadra Creek (present-day Clarksville). I invited them to supper so you and Ray may meet them."

During supper, the Ridges introduced themselves and made known their plans on returning home in the morning and invited the Beeler family to join them.

Getting on the river before sunup, the two families, with the rapid flow of spring runoff, easily reached Spadra Creek within a day. The Beelers accepted an invitation by the Ridges to overstay a day or so.

Right up front Annie told Joe she never realized the extent of the Ridge's holdings. They presented themselves as ordinary simple folk, unpretentious, warm and genuine, not overbearing.

They had about 500 acres of mixed bottomland and wood on the ridges north of the river. The main house was a sprawling structure that rivaled A.P.'s at Salina. The barns, outbuildings, gristmill, and blacksmith shop were adequate to support the cattle, horses, and sheep that were part of their holdings. John told Joe that they had arrived in Arkansas in 1805 and were part of the earliest migration of the Western Cherokee. The hard work and patience were starting to pay off for Sara and him. Furthermore, he was very concerned about the unrest between the Osage and the Cherokee as well as the army's lack of intervention.

Joe and Ray talked with John about their meeting with Mad Buffalo and A.P., the carrying of the message and pipe to the army, but not being able to get a definitive answer to carry back to Mad Buffalo because Major Bradford was away on a recruiting mission.

John said that one of his ongoing problems was the young Cherokee warriors that worked for him. He said, "Joe, you know the Indian culture. The youngsters need to prove their warrior status with scalps, horses raids, and kidnapping of women and kids. I try to keep them on a leash, but that's like predicting the weather. It's hit and miss. Our Chief John Jolly just tells me to hang in there, because they all grow up at some time. And I agree with you, Joe. There's going to be a ruckus with Mad Buffalo soon, and I hope there won't be any scalps hanging on the lodge poles.

"Sara tells me about your Annie and Linda and the spirit of the bear jaw medicine. I've heard of the bear jaw medicine from some of the northern lakes tribes through the years. Sara and I are honored to have the women of the bear jaw medicine as our guests!" Over the next few days Joe and Ray outlined with John the families' plans to settle at Sylamore and the need to negotiate a deal with Chief John Jolly for 100 acres. John said he would accompany the family to Illinois Bayou to throw his influence and weight into the negotiations with Chief John Jolly. He told his wife, Sara, that what he saw of the Beelers made him feel comfortable with them.

Winking at John, Joe said, "Where would we be without our women folk! Without the blanket talk that gives us the inside track on their women talk, we would be much poorer simple excuses of manhood. Right, Ray?"

Departing the Ridge's farm, the Beelers headed downriver toward Illinois Bayou accompanied by John Ridge and one of his young warriors.

Weber Post/Dwight Mission Illinois Bayou Arkansas Terr. 1820

Arriving at trader Walt Webber's post, John inquired the whereabouts of Chief John Jolly. Mr. Webber told them that Chief John Jolly had returned a couple of days ago from one of his many trips and was in residence at his home.

Upon reaching Chief John Jolly's farm, John introduced the Beelers and were invited to stay for supper. Chief Jolly said he and his wife were honored to have the women of the bear jaw medicine as guests in their home.

After supper, Joe and Chief John Jolly got to the business at hand. First, Joe presented the customary gifts (i.e., trade gun, powder, shot, knife, tomahawk, and blankets). Joe laid out the plans that Chouteau and Company had for trade on the White River with a location of a post at Sylamore. After some time, Chief Jolly consulting with John Ridge was told the proposal would benefit the Cherokees and other tribes located on the White River, and more so the post would be managed by the Beeler family who had an exemplary reputation in the fur trade for being even-handed and honest. Chief John Jolly agreed to sell 100 acres to the Beeler family for the price of $3.25 an acre. Payment was to be in trade goods delivered to Illinois Bayou by keelboat to be distributed by Chief John Jolly to the tribesmen.

A bill of sale was drafted, signed, and witnessed by Joe, Ray, Chief John Jolly, and John Ridge. Joe then recorded the bill of sale at the Federal Land Office in Ole Davidsonville.

Later that night in the blankets, Annie said, "Husband dearest, you haven't lost your touch!"

"My sweet wife, we haven't lost our touch!"

"I agree husband dearest. And you are a good husband!"

"Annie, I am a mere mortal man—nothing more, nothing less!" which got him a quick clip upside his head as usual upon uttering those words to his sweet bride!

Joe brought the family together and laid out the schedule for getting established at Sylamore. He expressed his hope that it would all come together by the end of the year. All the family agreed that it might be doable if all pulled together for that goal and the Great Spirit was in favor of them doing it.

Leaving Illinois Bayou on March 18, the family made good travel time as all were in one canoe, and the spring runoff gave a good current on the river.

Cadron Creek Tavern/Blockhouse

Stopping overnight at John McElmurry's Tavern Blockhouse at Cadron Creek settlement, Joe and Ray caught up on the local news and stuff over a tankard of ale. Getting back to the camp, they told the women nothing new, mainly the rumors of a possible ruckus between the Cherokee and Osage. Also, Major Bradford of Fort Smith had been trolling the area for new recruits with little success.

Joe mentioned that there were no rumors on the Beeler family yet, and he wanted to set a quick pace on getting out of the area. Joe wanted to bypass Crystal Hill and Little Rock and try to make Arkansas Post in five to six days. Despite a day or two of rainy weather, the family made the trip in five days.

Upon arriving in town, Annie, Mother Anita, and Linda made a beeline to Mary John's hostelry for accommodations. Joe sent Ray to look up Mr. Asa McFletch and get the schedule for the next steam packet to St. Louis. Joe looked up Mr. James Scull. Unable to locate him, Joe returned to Mary John's place only to find Mr. Scull in conversation with Annie, Mother Anita, and Linda.

Mr. Scull turned to Joe and said that he would do business with him, as Annie had informed him about the family's plans to locate at Sylamore.

Joe got down to business and asked Mr. Scull if he would be his business agent to help keep on top of the business and political environment in Arkansas Post as well as the impending legislation sponsored by Governor Miller to move the territorial capital to Little Rock.

In the short term, Joe asked him if he would arrange with Asa McFletch to take delivery of a shipment of trade goods from St. Louis and deliver same to Chief John Jolly and John Ridge at Illinois Bayou. The second part was to receive construction supplies and deliver same to Sylamore about mid-summer. To handle the finances of the endeavor, Joe gave Mr. Scull a letter of credit from Chouteau and Company.

Ray came in later with Asa McFletch, and he was briefed on what the impending plans were. Asa accepted the job offer and said that knowing James Scull from previous business dealings, he had no problem working with him to complete the tasks as required by the Beeler family.

By March 30, the family was on the Maid of Orleans and arrived back in St. Louis by April 5. They had been gone a little over a year. Efforts were immediately made to get the relocation project in motion.

Ray and Linda spent a couple of days with George, Caroline, and the Brandseys getting acquainted with the kids. Mathew Shannon was a boy of three and expanding his horizons. Little Shana Marie was two, and what can be said about rambunctious two-year-olds? The good health of the two kids was testament to the care they received from their great-grandparents and the Brandseys, that is Caroline and Charlene.

They then went to St. Charles to set up for the Arkansas move.

In the year the Beelers were gone, change in the form of economics and politics had swept through St. Louis. Missouri had become a state through the contentious Missouri Compromise in Congress of 1820, finally being admitted into the Union on August 10, 1821, as a free state, and the Arkansas Territory was to remain a slave territory.

William Clark lost out to Alexander McNair in the state's first gubernatorial election. But President Monroe appointed him superintendent of Indian affairs, basically putting him in charge of all Indian tribes west of the Mississippi (i.e., issuing trading licenses, confiscating illegal alcohol, removing unauthorized persons from Indian territory, etc.). He extended patronage to fur traders, artists, and explorers who, in turn, assisted him in his mission by establishing friendly relations with the numerous tribes. For the most part it worked because of William

Clark's engaging forthright personality and established integrity in dealing with the tribes.

And, he maintained his investment in Chouteau and Company as a director on the board.

Thomas Hart Benton, lawyer, editor, and owner of the St. Louis Enquirer (established in 1818), and newly elected senator of Missouri, was also a current member of the Chouteau and Company board.

Half-brothers Auguste (Rene) and Pierre (father of A.P. and Cadet Chouteau) were also current board members.

After sending Annie and Mother Anita on to St. Charles to start organizing for the Arkansas move, Joe met with the Chouteau board and laid out his plans and what he had learned over the previous year.

In short, he estimated with A.P.'s figures in the mix, that with an expenditure of 15,000 to 18,000 dollars for the move and setup at Sylamore, the company could see a return on investment approximately of ten to twelve percent with a breakeven after three years. The biggest commodity being bear products (i.e., hides, tallow, and oil), relative to observation and conversations with the indigenous people encountered during the yearlong trip.

After a day of haggling back and forth with the pros and cons of Joe's proposal, the board passed and approved it, with the only nay vote coming from ole Rene, the banker. He was concerned about the recent Panic of 1819, the stiff competition of Upper Missouri outfitters, and the cost and return on investment of young Cadet's expedition to Wyoming. Most board members said, "Gotta spend to get a return." Joe and Annie Beeler's management of the St. Charles operation for the last ten years stood on its own merits, and the company had done well because of them.

CHAPTER NINE
RELOCATION TO SYLAMORE ARKANSAS TERRITORY

Returning to St. Charles, Joe joined with Annie and Mother Anita in getting everything organized for the Arkansas move.

Anne discussed the board meeting with Joe and asked him if he had any concerns for a negative vote on the matter. Joe remarked that with A.P.'s figures and approval vote mixed in the details along with his and Annie's performance at St. Charles, he knew the aye votes would prevail. And he understood Rene's position too. Being seventy years old, in the banking industry for the past twenty-five years, and being one of the founders of St. Louis with his stepfather Pierre Laclède, it was natural for him to have a conservative viewpoint on money matters. But speaking for the other board members each, in their own times of life, had made and lost fortunes and knew that nothing is certain in life except maybe death and taxes.

Joined by Ray, Linda, and the kids, they all got busy with what was required to make the move in a timely manner. Joe wanted to be set up at Sylamore by late September or early October for the fall and winter trading trapping season.

To everyone's surprise, Mr. Dupasquier showed up about the middle of April. He told the family that A.P. and he figured that his help was needed to make the move happen in their timeframe. Joe was delighted and Annie welcomed Robert to the family fold. Joe remarked on the sly to Robert, "Just get used to saying, 'Yes Annie,' and you will do just fine!"

The first order of activity was getting the shipment of trade goods together for shipment to James Scull at Arkansas Post for delivery to Chief John Jolly and John Ridge at Illinois Bayou. Annie already had the goods and manifest ready when Joe arrived back at St. Charles. She had arranged for pick-up at St. Charles by the river steamer, The Washington.

The Washington, with owner and operator Captain Henry Shreve, had overwintered at Franklin, Missouri, and was making the first run of the season to New Orleans with stops along the way.

The pick-up was made at St. Charles on April 18 by The Washington and was on its way for final delivery by Asa McFletch to Chief John Jolly and John Ridge.

The second phase was the planning of getting the materials and goods to Sylamore for building the post buildings required for trade and living purposes. After looking at the manifest of the materials to be shipped, it was decided to utilize the keelboat over river steamer because the keelboat, while slower, had a greater cargo carrying capacity.

Robert called in his connections in the St. Louis region and found a keelboat owner/operator. Mr. John Stallings, who had operated on the White River since 1816 and was a contemporary of Asa McFletch, had two of his boats and one of Asa's on lease in St. Louis.

The timing was right, and a contract was negotiated for delivery of the cargo to Sylamore, with conditions allowing, as soon as possible.

The third phase was planning the overland trip to get the family from St. Charles to Sylamore. The party makeup was five adults and two kids with the trail ramrod and five drovers for the pack animals. Joe, Ray, and Robert D. figured ten animals would cover the immediate family's needs, with another twelve for drovers and required essentials for setting up the post at Sylamore.

Typical keelboat 1821

Joe first asked Mr. Larry Layne, the resident blacksmith-miller, who had worked for the Beelers at St. Charles for three to four years, and he quickly accepted.

Mr. Larry Layne

The five drovers were procured by Robert D. Joe told Annie during their blanket time that he could relax in that he knew they had reliable help. Because at that time (1821), the St. Louis Riverfront was filled with manpower, but most of it was gutter scum and unreliable to say the least!

The next two weeks were chaotic because of Joe's tight schedule to be on the trail by the first week of May. Everyone knew what they had to get accomplished, and all problems that cropped up were handed without too much difficulty. Joe's impatience at times had to be tempered by Annie, but as usual, his love for his bride reined him in, and he complied with Annie's suggestions and will. As Annie stated to Joe during their nightly blanket talk, "Joe, my love, you know you are a 'hoss's ass' for fretting so much about nothing. You stood on the wharf on April 30 and watched John Stallings with his three keelboats depart. Did you not?"

"Yes, Annie, my little Magpie. You are right, and I will try to mend my ways!" replied Joe.

"Bull Floppers!" said Annie as she snuggled into his embrace.

The two kids, Matthew Shannon, three years, and Shana Marie, two years, were a handful for the adults. After a year away from them, Linda had a quick acclimation to go through. With Charlene Brandsey and Granny Anita's help, she did alright and soon was on top and ahead of the kids' antics. Also, the kids instinctively learned not to aggravate Grampaw and to stay out of his way when he was stern.

Ray remarked to Joe, on the sly, that it was his opinion that Linda's experience with the Ponca and the making of the bear jaw medicine, gave her a big kick down her road to maturity.

Joe said, "Ray, I believe you know your bride more than you realize!"

By May 2, 1821, the party was ready to depart for points south. George, Caroline, the Brandseys, and the Clarks were there to see them off. With the exception of leaving the grandparents and Brandseys behind, Joe and Annie didn't look back with sadness at St. Louis as they had when they left Devil's Lake Michigan Territory.

Many political and economic changes were happening in St. Louis. The

Missouri Territory became a state that year. The fur trade was heating up with competition between old established companies and new startups (Manuel Lisa had died the previous year, and his Missouri Fur Company was in court trying to fend off its creditors.)

The previous year, The North West Company and The Hudson Bay Company, after forty years of bloodletting competition (i.e., the Red River incident of 1816) joined together under the Hudson Bay logo, and George Simpson, another Scot, was elected general director. He began an austerity program that reduced the number of posts in the field which effectively reduced the number of employees by almost fifty percent. But, the reorganization within two years began to show a profit for the company.

One of the new startups was The Rocky Mountain Fur Company formed by a partnership between Major Andrew Henry (partner of Manuel Lisa) and William Henry Ashley. They advertised for men by placing an ad in the St. Louis Enquirer in February 1821. This venture left a major mark on the fur trade regarding how it was managed and conducted businesswise for the next twenty-five years.

TO
Enterprising Young Men.

THE subscriber wishes to engage ONE HUNDRED MEN, to ascend the river Missouri to its source, there to be employed for one, two or three years.—For particulars, enquire of Major Andrew Henry, near the Lead Mines, in the County of Washington, (who will ascend with, and command the party) or to the subscriber at St. Louis.

Wm. H. Ashley.

February 13 ——98 tf

All in all, St. Louis was shaking and moving. The Beelers were moving on and were anxious to leave it behind.

The party made good time arriving at Ste. Genevieve in four days. A mandatory visit to Francisco Alberti's grave was made. Granny Anita and Annie had some silent time there.

On the trail, everyone fell in the daily routine of traveling by horse caravan. The adults were acclimatized from the previous year's trip to Arkansas. The spring warmup with the accompanying bug problem didn't faze anyone either. The women kept the two kids lathered up with bear oil mixed with dried mullein, which helped somewhat to keep the bugs off the little ones.

With the women taking over the cooking duties and Joe and Ray handling the acquisition of meat, the entire party ate at one common meal. The hired hands had no complaints with this setup because they knew they were getting the best of the deal eats-wise. Plus, they learned that a dose of politeness got them an extra portion from the women.

Also, with the cooperation of the men, everyone kept an eye on the little ones, distracting them from mischief and physical hurt as two- and three-year-olds are prone to do. It was a big help to Linda, Annie, and Granny Anita in staying ahead of the little buggers.

The 200-mile trip to Ole Davidsonville was made without any major incidents in fifteen days.

Joe, Annie, Ray, and Linda headed to the Federal Land Office where Joe recorded the original deed for 100 acres at Sylamore that the family had bought from Chief John Jolly. Ray and Linda filed for 160 acres of bottomland on the east bank of the White River directly across from the Sylamore Creek confluence through the 1812 Bounty Act, which entitled veterans to file on 160 acres of federal land.

There was a letter from Mr. James Scull stating that the price goods for Chief John Jolly and the Cherokee had arrived at Arkansas Post and were en route by keelboat to be delivered by Asa McFletch.

Overnighting in their own camp, the family was on the trail by sunup and made the Spring River Hewitt Ferry crossing by mid-morning. But same as a year ago when the Beelers passed through, the Hewitt, Wayland, and Robertson families insisted that the party lay over a day and visit, not taking no for an answer. So, much to Joe's annoyance, which was tempered by Annie, the party laid over for an extra day.

Major Haynes and his wife, the Lawrence County representative to the territorial ledge from Dogwood Springs ten miles distant, joined the get-together that evening. Joe read to the families the pertinent parts of the letter he received from James Scull regarding the political on-goings at Arkansas Post.

Governor Miller didn't care to involve himself in the political intrigue but concerned himself more to the bureaucratic part of his job. This left a wide open field for Robert Crittenden, secretary of the territory, to work the political intrigue game to his advantage. One of the projects that he was spending time on was putting together a cabal of businessmen and politicians to support getting a bill passed and signed into law to move the capital from Arkansas Post to Little Rock. The secret was, which everyone knew, the cabal owned land at Little Rock and were speculating on personal gain if the bill was passed.

The families were grateful to the Beeler party for the current news, which directly and indirectly affected their lives and livelihood. All wished the Beelers well in their settlement at Sylamore.

At sunrise, the Beelers were on the trail for Polk Bayou and reached it within five days. The weather even cooperated, and the bug damage was easily handled by Granny Anita and Annie.

A short note on the town of Columbia located on the south branch of the Strawberry River. The Beelers camped in the same sycamore grove as they had done the previous year. Because of the large size of the party, some of the town folk came out to rubberneck on what was afoot. Most left in a short time, but two families remained after introducing themselves as the families of the two boys that had sneaked out the previous year to see the homely squaws. Needless to say, they got an immediate invite to supper, and the boys reemphasized that Indian squaws were not homely or ugly!At Polk Bayou, Mr. Robert Dupasquieradvised Joe to lay over for a couple of days for the men to check the stock, repair stuff (tack, shoes, feed stock, etc.) and replenish supplies as needed at Sylamore for the next two months. Mr. Robert Bean and John Reed, proprietors of the trading posts in town, were able to supply most of what was needed.

Departing Polk Bayou, the party was able to reach Lafferty Creek by the second day, and Mrs. Lafferty insisted, and wouldn't take no for an answer, that the family remain an extra day for her to catch up. And as she said the previous year, it wasn't often that she could entertain quality company.

Leaving Lafferty Creek, the party easily reached Sylamore on June 12, 1821, after a twelve-hour trek. Annie, hugging Joe said, "Husband, dearest, it's nice to be home!"With Joe pushing for a "ready for business" date of October 1, everyone fell to their respective tasks. The plans made the previous year were reviewed relative to building and supporting structures' locations.

First designated for construction was the main post store, warehouse, and landing wharf on the river. Enough tools and building necessities had been brought by pack mules and horses to keep construction moving along until the three keelboats of Asa McFletch and John Stallings arrived.

While at Polk Bayou, Joe received a letter by horse-backed messenger from James Scull that the Stalling keelboats had safely arrived at the post and were starting up the White River. Barring any mishaps or inclement weather, they should arrive about the third week of July.

Unfortunately, on July 18 two of John Stalling's crewmen arrived by canoe with the news that one of the keelboats had struck a snag and sunk at Bloch Island, just above present-day Oil Trough. The good news was that it happened in fairly shallow water, and all cargo except for the milling stones was salvaged.

Mr. Bob told Joe that he would go back with one of the crewmen to oversee the recovery operation and help get the two boats to Sylamore as quickly as possible.

Joe, Annie, and Ray discussed the matter after Mr. Bob had left, and though they figured it was costly to lose the stones and whatever water damage had occurred to the rest of the cargo, it wouldn't set back their schedule to be open for business by the first week in October. Fortunately, there was no loss of life, other than some bruises and skinned knuckles for the crewmen involved.

Finally, on August 1, Annie's birthday, the two keelboats pulled into the Beeler Wharf at Sylamore with two events to celebrate. And celebrate they did, with Joe even breaking out two kegs of high wine uncut for the occasion.

The work continued getting the post set up for the coming fall fur season. The main post store and warehouse were completed and stocked. It turned out that the boat that sunk contained, in addition to the mill stones, kegs containing molasses, flour, and the crew's personal stuff. This was all salvaged, and water damage was minimal. Through 's various connections he told Joe he knew of an extra set of stones over at Columbia that could probably be bought at a decent price. Joe told Bob to put that on his to-do list and see what he could do. Even though the stones were an economical loss, it was not a high priority this year to get the gristmill into operation.

That fall on Mr. Bob's return to St. Louis, he completed the purchase of a set of mill stones at Columbia and arranged for Asa McFletch to ship them from Columbia to Sylamore in the spring of 1822, high water time on the Strawberry, Black, and White Rivers.

Mr. Layne had gotten the forge set up immediately upon arriving at Sylamore and was kept busy fabricating fittings, nails, shoes, hinges, and other essentials that can only be done by a smithy. His skills became irreplaceable as the needs for the construction of the post continued toward completion.

Two dogtrot cabins were constructed for the two families and dogtrot style bunkhouse for the hired help. The combined gristmill blacksmith shop with the water wheel for Mr. Layne, corrals for the livestock, and sheds for livestock feed storage were also completed.

At the spring, a small palisade and spring house were built, like at St. Charles, with water piped to the cabins, bunkhouse, post store, and a center trough for livestock. The privies were built downstream twenty rods or so from the main wharf on the river, and Mother Nature did the rest.

Joe and Ray followed the north branch of Sylamore Creek back about fifteen miles and found Blanchard Springs at its headwaters. The outflow was one-fourth more than their spring at Sylamore. Joe told Ray that they would have to watch the coming years' seasons and track the outflow of the spring and adjust their usage accordingly. Plus, he was of the opinion formed on the 1820 visit that the flow would be adequate to drive the machinery of the gristmill. Ray agreed and said, "We'll have to watch our women because they will start to depend on the convenience the spring will provide them." But after further thought, Ray said, "No, Joe. I'm getting behind myself again. Our brides and Granny Anita are seasoned, lovely women, and we are fortunate to have them, right!"

Joe remarked, "Ray, my little Magpie couldn't have said it any better herself. And she would add that you are a good son-in-law for her Sparrow!"

By October 15, most of the structures at Beeler Post had been completed and were being utilized. The families were ensconced in their respective cabins with running water from the spring. And the privy facilities were working just as designed with all waste being taken care of by the river. Ray and a couple of the work crew had constructed a rude raft for ferry use across the river and had harvested bottomland grass and sedges for livestock feed for the cold months ahead.

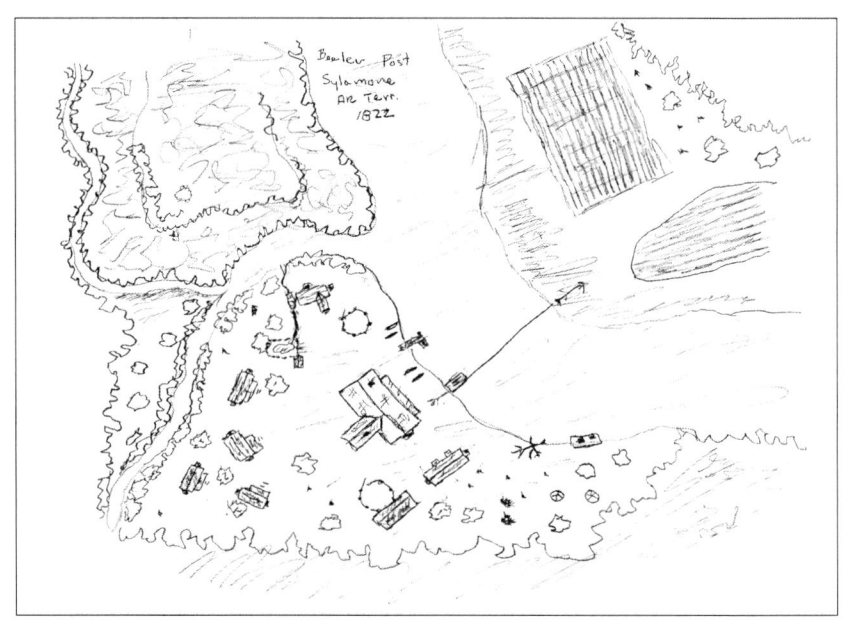

Beeler Post Sylamore Arkansas Terr. 1822

There had been a steady flow of Shawnee, Delaware, and Kickapoo tribesmen in and out of the post store and warehouse since September bringing bear, buffalo, and deer hides along with tallow and bear oil.

It was a good start to the season, and the Beelers expected the trade to increase after the first of the New Year, when the quality fur of beaver, mink, otter, and bobcat started to come in.

Trading in the Post Store

Word of Beeler Post at Sylamore spread to the white hunters and their families, and they started drifting in too for essentials for the year.

Joe and Annie rigidly enforced their one rule that no "liquor was to be involved in the trade. There was some grumbling at first, but when the grumblers saw that they were getting fair prices for their wares and were not being cheated in the process by being "liquored " up by the traders, the grumbling faded into the background.

As is the case with human behavior, there were always a few cases of people getting a little too deep into their cups after the trading was done. But the cure was, like at St. Charles, the culprit was grabbed by a couple of the workforce or Joe and Ray and manhandled, not too gently, down to the wharf and tossed in the river. The water was swift and deep at the end of the wharf.

In September, Mr. Bob made preparations for the return to St. Louis to hook up with A.P. for the coming season. He was to make a stop at Columbia to buy the mill stones that were for sale.

Mr. Larry Layne approached Joe for a short leave of absence to travel to Gallipolis, Ohio, to retrieve his childhood sweetheart, Rita, also known as Scooter, and make her his bride. Joe pretended that he couldn't be without his services for that length of time, but Joe knew that if he said no, the women would be all over him like dew on a chigger. Besides, when it came to affairs of the heart, there was no compromising with the womenfolk.

Joe said okay, but asked if upon their return (Larry and Scooter), they would stop at Columbia in the spring and oversee the shipment of the mill stones to Sylamore. Joe said he would make arrangements with James Scull to have Asa McFletch to be at Columbia with a keelboat to ship same to Sylamore. Larry said not a problem and would make it so!

Larry made it with Mr. Bob to St. Louis and caught a steam packet to Cincinnati. He bought a horse and followed the trails east up the river and arrived at Gallipolis toward the end of October. He proposed to his sweetheart, Scooter, who accepted with the remark, "Mr. Layne, I was getting tired of waiting for you, and it was only my folk's firm resolve that kept me from coming to look for you!" They were married in her folk's cabin by the local Presbyterian preacher. Two days later they were on the river in a Northern canoe heading for St. Louis with a letter of introduction from Joe and Annie to George Beeler and Ed Brandsey.

The Laynes Rita/Scooter

Their 1821 trip down the Ohio River is a story in itself, but suffice to say the Laynes handled it well.

The Beelers and Brandseys welcomed the Laynes and said that they were guests to overwinter with them. Larry, the blacksmith, had a busy winter with George and Ed, the gunsmith and blade maker! Scooter folded in with Caroline and Charlene. Her winter was busy with her new husband, home, and the social circles of St. Louis in which Caroline and Charlene were involved!

In late March, the Laynes departed St. Louis with the A.P. pack train and at Smithville, Arkansas Territory left the pack train and headed south to Columbia to await the McFletch keelboat. Asa arrived about the first of April, loaded the stones and, due to the high water, made good time down the Strawberry and Black Rivers to the White River (future location of Jacksonport). Then, it was a backbreaking pole upstream on the White River to Sylamore which was made in fifteen to eighteen days, arriving about the first of May.

The Laynes were welcomed and, to their surprise, found a dogtrot cabin waiting for them. Annie took Scooter aside and said, "My mother and I worked on Joe, and he made it happen!"

Joe eavesdropped on their women talk and said out loud so that they could hear, "What one must do to keep good help!" which promptly got him a slap upside the head! And Scooter was folded into the Beeler women's circle!

The Mill Stones

The construction of the gristmill/blacksmith shop was completed that spring, which started a trail of business that fall for the milling of corn, rice, and other grains the tribes and white settlers grew and harvested.

Larry Layne, back in his shop, made some improvements to the machinery, mostly in the installation of a trip hammer brought by keelboat with the stones and powered by the waterwheel. As time passed, Ray and Larry found themselves working and collaborating on the repair and fabrication of firearms. As Larry remarked to Joe and Ray, "The winter spent with your dad and Ed Brandsey is paying off!"

Grist Mill/Blacksmith Shop

Trip Hammer Gristmill

The kids had put another season on their little bodies and were growing into a couple of wild Indian kids. The good part was the entire workforce helped keep tabs on them, somewhat relieving the job that was normally handled by the women.

When Annie and Granny Anita were preparing the families' meals, they found themselves continuously catering to a line of men following the aroma of the cooking and asking, "Madams, what's on the spit, and might I have a wee bite?" So Annie approached Joe and asked if a cook and eatery place could be set up in the warehouse, like at St. Charles, and make some income off the effort! With Joe's go-ahead, in record time the workforce had an addition to the warehouse completed, and the eatery was opened for business.

The women asked that an iron box approximately four feet by three feet be constructed and integrated into the stone chimney flue for the purpose of cooking and baking. Mr. Layne and Ray, under the instructions of the women, fabricated the box with an internal oven box and fire box with a separate flue out of sheet iron.

The box was mudded into place with the stone chimney, and doors were added to the oven box and fire box with adjustable louvers to control the heat. This gave a top three feet by four feet surface to cook on and heat other things that needed warming. The two feet by two feet oven box gave adequate space for baking needs. This cook oven was supplemented by the typical open hearth of the fireplace, and in time the women found themselves doing most of the cooking on the oven stove.

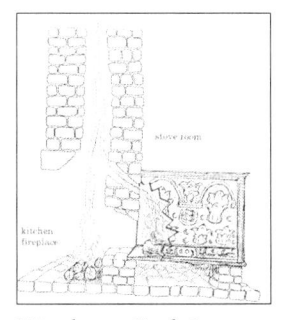

Warehouse Cook Stove

Another improvement made that summer was construction of a smokehouse adjacent to the spring house. Joe took control of this and soon had a supply of smoked meats, jerky, and sausage laid up for the cold season.

With Scooter Layne joining Annie and Granny Anita as part of the cook force, the work was spread around. In the end, the families and workforce messes were combined into two meals a day. The business coming in the door off the river was taken care off during the balance of the day. In addition, Joe had two of his workforce busy hunting to provide meat for the pots.

As the year continued forward, Mr. Bob brought the latest and greatest news from St. Louis on his way back to Salina on the Neosho River. The big event of the spring was the departure of the Ashley-Henry party in two keelboats and 100 men up the Missouri, destined for the Yellowstone River in Montana.

The newly reorganized Hudson Bay Company was starting to flex its competitive muscles and was recognized as a business force to be reckoned with in the Upper Missouri River trade.

The economy was picking up again after the Panic of 1819. Fur prices were holding steady, and the fall season was expected to be similar to the 1818 season. American Fur had gained control of the fur territory and market around the Great Lakes like Astor/Crooks had planned, but were holding off in competing in the Upper Missouri trade. (This didn't happen until 1827.) And more steamboats were docking at St. Louis.

Since Mexico had won its independence from Spain in 1820, the new Mexican government had encouraged open trade with the United States. St. Louis and Franklin, Missouri, became the trailhead of the new trade trail established by William Becknell with Santa Fe/Taos being the destination.

Joe received correspondence from James Scull regarding the political scene at the post.

 The capital had been moved to Little Rock. Governor Miller had resigned claiming health reasons. George Izard was appointed territorial governor by President Monroe over Robert Crittenden, much to his chagrin. He found out that his influence and political connections didn't carry much weight outside the territory. And, he had much spade work in the political arena ahead of him in the coming years to improve his situation.

In September, the family was overjoyed and surprised by a visit from John and Sara Ridge along with Chief John Jolly and his wife, Elizabeth. The Ridges and Jollys had just completed a visit to the new capital of Little Rock to see Governor Izard about white encroachment on

Cherokee treaty lands. Chief John Jolly carried weight regarding these discussions because he was one of the two chiefs that had signed the Turkey Town Treaty of 1817 negotiated by General Andrew Jackson. He said the pattern never changes relative to white settlement. The tribes get shanghaied into a treaty that invariably leads to their getting removed further west of the big river to accommodate further white encroachment. He remarked, "That's life in the Indian track, and one must continue to do what one must until one gives their last breath to the Great Spirit. If only the whites had the principles and character of the Beeler Family!" John Ridge said the need for some firearm repairs and rejuvenation of same brought them to Sylamore. Word traveled to their country of the excellent quality of workmanship of the two gunsmiths at Sylamore. John needed to have his .54-caliber Plainsman re-bored, and Chief John Jolly wanted his .40-caliber Lemans stock and lock assembly repaired and fine-tuned. He was also looking for a good 20-gauge trade gun.

Joe said no problem. Mr. Layne and Mr. Dearmon would take care of their needs, and he had just the trade gun on the shelf for Chief John Jolly. At Annie's insistence, the visitors would extend their visit for as long as it took to fill their needs. She also made it known to the men that some quality visit time would be made amongst the womenfolk—end of discussion. Joe remarked to the men. "That's my Annie!"

Joe inquired of John and Chief John Jolly what route they took from Little Rock to Sylamore. John said, "Fairly easy, Joe. We followed the Southwest Trail to a small settlement of Quitman and then headed northeast up the Cadron Creek flowage until we struck the Little Red River. We followed that to Devil's Fork and followed the east branch north until we struck the White River and followed that to here. I will show you the route on a map for your future use."

Of historical note, Chief John Jolly was the uncle of Tiana Rogers, Cherokee wife of Sam Houston, and she was a looker. Chief John Jolly was a half-brother to Jennie Due, mother of Tiana. Elizabeth Due, who married the old Scot trader John Rogers was the mother of Jennie, John Jolly, and James, his full brother. Chief John Jolly had taken in young Sam Houston as his adopted son back in Tennessee in 1807. When Sam came back to the Cherokee in 1827, he then married Tiana Rogers, his sweetheart.

The rest of 1822 passed uneventfully for the family and business at Sylamore. The end of the season's returns were close to what was expected, but Joe, in discussing it with Annie during nightly blanket time said he was surprised that the major commodity was not furs, but bear oil and hides. Annie remarked that the tip they had been given by the Ridges and Jollys had been good, because the resultant trip to Oil Trough ten miles below Polk Bayou to secure deals with the hunters was paying off! Plus, having Asa McFletch acting as agent and shipper of the product greatly saved on transportation costs.

As 1823 came upon the scene, the family found themselves in reasonably good health other than the occasional cold. Other maladies were minimized by the sanitation procedures put in place, such as the outhouses downstream and the isolation of the spring from two- and four-legged critter soil. Only a bout of malaria flared up now and then but was kept in check by Granny Anita's supply of Jesuit medicine.

Annie quietly remarked to Joe that Granny Anita wasn't as spry as she was the previous two years. Even Scooter and Larry Layne had learned not to bring the subject up to Granny. But everyone was watching out for her. Granny was fifty-nine years old.

The trade was steady off the river, and every group of people going up or downriver could not pass by the aroma coming out of the eatery in the warehouse.

The cycle of business that developed, mostly on its own accord, was one of the major factors they located at Sylamore. In the spring, all the shippable commodities, (i.e., graded fur packs, deer and elk hides, bear hides, tallow and oil) were shipped by keelboat to Arkansas Post. Mr. James Scull, Joe's agent, would oversee the transfer to steam packet for shipment of the same to St. Louis. Mr. Scull also sent the manifest of the needed supplies to restock for the coming season. These shipments of restock would return to Sylamore via steamboat and keelboat overseen by James Scull and Asa McFletch.

The big advantage of this system was savings in shipment costs gained by handling more volume/tonnage less often than if the same supplies were sent by pack train. These savings translated down to lower prices to the customers, the tribes, and white settlers. Everyone in the supply chain got ahead by better profits for the year.

Joe remarked to Anne during their blanket talk, "Annie my sweet, it's capitalism at its best!"

News filtered in from St. Louis that the Ashley-Henry party, in the process of resupplying the company post Fort Henry built on the Yellowstone the previous year, had been mauled by the Arickaree in June, with fifteen men killed and many wounded. A punitive expedition by Colonel Henry Leavenworth, Sixth Infantry out of Fort Atkinson, which included Ashley-Henry trappers, Missouri Fur Company traders, and 600 Teton Sioux went after the Arickaree. But they escaped upriver to the Mandan village, and the expedition burned the empty village. The Sioux left disgusted because of the lack of scalps and plunder. Leavenworth returned to Fort Atkinson blowing his horn, claiming a victory over the Indians. The fur companies were left holding the collective bag of hollow victory and military politics plus having to deal with a bunch of riled Indians for the next five years or more.

As Joe remarked, "It was a simple replay of history all over again. The French did it to the Huron and Iroquois two centuries previously. And the episode with the Arikaree followed similar lines." The Arickaree were the middlemen in the trade on the Upper Missouri between the white man and the isolated tribes further west. So when the Americans tried to bypass them and go directly into the field to trap and not rely on them for furs, it lit a match of opposition that lingered for more than a dozen years, costing many trappers and traders their lives and livelihood. This was the main bone of contention that set the Blackfoot tribes against the Americans for more than sixty years. Ray asked why the North West Company had mostly good success with the Piegan, Bloods, and Blackfeet.Annie answered, "Because we never threaten their middleman position as traders. We built our trade posts amongst them and never took their beaver on our own. Fair, straight and honest trade is what carried the day for us. And no liquor Period. That philosophy came from Father George and Mother Caroline, bless them!"

Word came via A.P. and R. Dupasquier that Cadet had returned, and his expedition up the Platte to Wyoming was barely a breakeven proposition. The area was being steadily blanketed by ole North West men, now Bay men. The first year 1821–'22 was fair in that Crow, Cheyenne, and Arapaho came in, but most wished to trade buffalo robes over beaver. With the exception of the Crow, all tribes demanded whiskey upfront before the start of trade. The corruption was well on its way. What reality must one deal with to complete a trade. Cadet was clamoring for the Chouteau board to partner with Cabanne Company and Pratte & Company, subsidiaries of Astor since 1816. They had used American Fur for their trade goods, and Astor New York had marketed their furs. Cadet was saying Chouteau needed this muscle to buck the Bay men out on the plains and mountains. He said this was the biggest threat to the fur business in St. Louis. Plus, they were damn Britishers!

After listening to Cadet, Rene started quietly and got louder with each word spoken. He stated that for fifteen years he had worked to keep that upstart Deutschland freebooter's fingers out of St. Louis, and he wasn't about to start now with an unholy alliance with the man and his cohorts Crooks and Stuart. Besides, speaking of Britishers, some of the board members around the table still had strong connections back to the northwesterners, Joe and Annie Beeler, for example, and they were some of the best assets of the company.

Cadet lost this round, but before five years were up, Chouteau, Cabanne, and Pratte would be partners or subsidiaries of the Western Division of American Fur.

Cadet sent a letter to the Beelers outlining what he knew about their family members. Stone Hawk, Fox, Jim, and Sara had clerked for him at the post setup on the South Platte, about twenty miles south of the north and south juncture of the Platte River. After the second year, some of the family members of Fox's band of Cheyenne had come in to trade. After a joyous reunion, all had decided to join and return with the band to their home range northwest of the post about 300 miles in the Medicine Bow Mountains. That was the last word he had of them.

While conversing with Joe during blanket time, Annie remarked, "Joe dearest, I worry all the time for Jim, Sara, Stone Hawk, and Fox, what with all the turmoil and trouble on the plains with the tribes in the last year or so!"

Joe said, "Annie, my sweet, I do so, too. But I know we have raised our son well. Stone Hawk is a good man and seasoned well in the ways of the land and men, red and white. Fox and Sara are daughters of the plains and mountains and all have good spirits, and this is all in their favor! I know the Great Spirit watches over them. Plus, the power of the bear jaw medicine is with them. I trust more in the efficiency of the moccasin telegraph over the horse telegraph. They are doing well!"

The year 1823 flowed into 1824 and 1825 following the seasonal cycles of Mother Nature and man-managed business. The family prospered, and the reputation of the Beeler Chouteau Post at Sylamore spread up and down the White River and points south to the capital at Little Rock. The tribes came to depend on Sylamore for yearly returns on their efforts of procuring fur and hides. The white settlers appreciated that Sylamore provided the essentials needed for daily living without having to travel the extra distance to points further downriver.

Down at the capital, the secretary of the territory, Crittenden, was feuding with Governor George Izard. Henry Conway was reelected territorial delegate. White settlements were continuing to encroach upriver upon Cherokee lands.

In the early spring of 1825, a white settler from upriver at Calico Rock came to Sylamore to settle his account from the previous year. He was short of cash, but he approached Joe asking if he could settle up with his slaves that he owned. Joe's moral shutters went up immediately, but Annie intervened and asked Joe if she could discuss the matter with him. She had found out through women talk that the slaves were a family of parents and two children, a boy and a girl. She told Joe that the family was intact, and the cost could be absorbed by the company with no loss to the bottom line. Joe and Annie's moral opposition to slavery wouldn't be compromised.

The settler's account was paid in full, and the Joshua and Lisa Ashe family became part of the workforce at Sylamore. Anne and Joe took the bill of sale and wrote up the writ of freedom documents for the Ashe family. Joe and Joshua took a canoe to Polk Bayou and got Judge Richard Searcy, with Mr. Richard Bean witnessing, to notarize the documents and record the same.

On the way back to Sylamore, Joe told Joshua the next job that he and Lisa had ahead of them was to learn how to read, write, and cipher. The entire Beeler family would be their teachers. Joshua asked Joe how could he ever repay his debt to him? Joe said, "Joshua, it's not in the realm of the Great Spirit that one man must be subservient to another man, but to be true to oneself and one's family. If a person has this as the foundation of one's core principals and deals with his fellow man in the same manner, the Great Spirit will look favorably upon you. This is the faith that I and my bride have lived by, and we have never been poor because of it! Besides, the idea of a man not being able to do anything without a by-your-leave from another man just grinds my innards and leaves me more unsettled than I want to be!"

CHAPTER TEN
LOSS OF GRANDPARENTS

In the spring of 1826, bad news came in from St. Louis! It's a part of our humanity that we get settled into our daily routines of living our lives. When a tragic event upsets that routine, we are knocked off our psychological feet. The true test of one's grit is if one has the inner strength and faith to get back on one's feet, face the tragedy, deal with it, and move on!

A bad bout of influenza had swept through St. Louis that February, and the family lost George, Caroline, and Ed and Charlene's youngest daughter, Kathy. Details of the event were sparse, but Joe and Annie made preparations to depart for St. Louis immediately. They left the operation of Sylamore Post in the hands of the Dearmons and Laynes. Granny Anita wished to accompany Joe and Annie but, not being as spry as she used to be, which she knew to be true, accepted Annie and Joe's reasoning that she would be more of an asset in the care of the kids at Sylamore.

Joe and Annie set a fast pace by horseback and made St. Louis in less than ten days. They avoided the settlements except to pick up needed essentials. They were on the trail before sunup and were on it until well after sunset.

The burial of the Beelers had occurred five days before their arrival, and their final internment was in the Protestant cemetery located on

Fourth Street. Time was spent with the Brandseys in the telling of the events. Ed and Charlene said the influenza had reared its ugly head briefly in the fall and then subsided only to reappear after the first of the year. They figured the family had been affected by the steady stream of customers in and out of the business. They had all been affected. Ed, Charlene, and Michelle had been slow to recover. Being sick and still taking care of the sicker ones took its toll.

George was 67, Caroline was 65, and Kathy was 12.

Joe and Annie spent the next ten days with the family and met with the principals of the Chouteau and Company board, Rene, Jean Pierre, and Governor Clark. Many topics were up for discussion, including the Ashley-Henry rendezvous system of supply to keep their trappers in the mountains all year. Andrew Henry had retired, and General Ashley had sold their company to Davy Jackson, William Sublette, and Jedediah Smith who became their sole supplier. The American Fur Company was moving to expand to the Upper Missouri and was looking at establishing a post somewhere around the confluence of the Yellowstone and the Missouri. (Fort Union). The Hudson Bay Company in the Northwest Columbian River basin out of Fort Vancouver expanded the business by sending their trapping brigades into the Snake River and Green River countries utilizing a trap and eradicate policy to counter the competing American trapping brigades. The military had moved their operations from Fort Smith to a new post called Camp Gibson located at the confluence of the Grand, Neosho, and Arkansas Rivers in 1824 to better mitigate problems between the Osage, Cherokee, and other tribes being relocated into Oklahoma, known as the new Indian territory.

Joe was able to show the directors that the balance sheet of the Sylamore operation was showing a good return supported primarily by the bear oil and hides trade. The fur and deer hides part of the trade was steady. The milling and gunsmithing operations played a large part in pulling in customers old and new.

Bruce and Mary Beth Loudenhagen asked Annie and Joe if they could accompany them on their return trip back as far as Ste. Genevieve. Bruce was troubled by his relationship with his son Adam and wanted Annie and Joe to fill in the blanks between Adam's abrupt departure from home and the receipt of Joe's letter later explaining Adam's situation, plus fill in the silence that had ensued for the last five years since that letter. The Beelers tried and did provide some insight into Adam's desires for his life's direction and the paths he was traveling to achieve this. Also, Bruce and Mary Beth were delighted to know that they were grandparents of two little boys ages four and two. Joe suggested that Bruce write his son a letter, and he would see that it was delivered to Adam.

After spending quiet time at Francisco Alberti's gravesite, the Beelers booked passage on the southbound steam packet to Arkansas Post, while the Loudenhagens returned to St. Louis by horseback!

Arriving at the post, Annie and Joe checked in with Mr. Scull to get the latest on the business and political situation. James briefed them on the Sylamore resupplying manifest that he had received from Ray. He was making arrangements to send it to Chouteau and Company on the next northbound steam packet and already had made shipping arrangements with Asa McFletch on the same. He had a letter for the Beelers from Chief John Jolly requesting, at their convenience, that they pay him a visit to discuss a private matter.

Annie and Joe caught up on the latest social and political doings of the post and Little Rock while overnighting at Mary John's hostelry for a couple of days until the steam packet departed upriver to Little Rock and Fort Smith, river conditions permitting.

Little Rock was now a small town containing sixty-plus structures—seven brick stone, three or four wood frame buildings, and the balance were log cabins.

Governor George Izard was still pressuring the Cherokee to cede land to the state for white settlement and was feuding with Richard Crittenden over recordkeeping matters relative to the office of territorial secretary. Crittenden also had a falling out with Henry Conway over the next year's election (1827) of the territory delegate to Congress. This schism escalated the following year in that Crittenden besmirched Conway, who then demanded satisfaction by challenging Crittenden to a duel. Crittenden killed Conway, and despite Crittenden's desire to be the replacement territorial delegate, the makeup election resulted in the election of Ambrose Sevier as the replacement delegate. Crittenden's political hay ran out in 1829 with his replacement as territorial secretary by President Jackson with William Savin Fulton.

Plus, Governor Izard died in 1828, and President Jackson appointed John Pope as territorial governor. He oversaw the construction of the new State House.

These were events yet to happen in the next two to three years and gives some insight where the Arkansas territory was heading socially and politically.

Joe and Annie, not being political animals, took this news in stride. They were content to let Mr. Scull be their agent and cutting-edge relative to these matters and concentrate on business and social spinoffs that affected them and the family.

The steam packet made it only as far as Little Rock because of a major breakdown with the boiler system. Joe and Annie bought three horses and supplies and followed the trails upriver to Illinois Bayou and Chief John Jolly (Ahuludegi).

Chief John Jolly and his wife, Elizabeth, asked Joe and Annie to be their guests for a couple of days and await the arrival of John and Sara Ridge.

Upon arrival of the Ridges, everyone sat down and discussed the reason for the Beeler's visit.

Chief John Jolly said over the past couple of years that the mounting pressure of the Cherokee presence in Arkansas was increasing due to the encroachments of white settlers and the ongoing conflict with Osage. Two years previously, the military had moved from Fort Smith to the confluence of the Verdigris, Neosho, and Arkansas Rivers and established Camp Gibson to mitigate that problem. Chiefs Tahchee (Dutch) and Diwali (The Bowl) settled on the Red River in Mexican Texas and continued to raid the Osage camps despite any negotiated treaties or truces.

Chief John Jolly's time was spent, through diplomatic efforts, trying to deal with these problems. But, it was his opinion that in a couple of years the Cherokee would be forced to move west again into the area called Lovely's Purchase, Oklahoma.

His request to the Beelers was for his friends, the Ridges. They had been at their farm/ranch since 1805. Chief John Jolly wanted to know if it was possible to get their identity established as white settlers and retain their property despite the upheavals coming in the years ahead.

John Ridge said he had his discharge papers from the U.S. Army for the time he spent with General Jackson during the Creek and New Orleans campaign in the War of 1812. Sara said her father was Henry Reese, a planter from Tennessee.

Chief John Jolly said his adopted son, Ka'lanu (The Raven/Sam Houston) was currently serving his second term in Congress as representative for Tennessee. He offered to provide affidavits verifying John and Sara's citizenship, plus having served with John in the Creek/New Orleans campaigns.

Chief John Jolly asked the Beelers if their lawyer, Mr. James Scull, would represent the Ridge's case in getting the documents recorded and recognized at the state level. In addition, the Cherokee Tribe would be selling the Ridges 500 acres of land, just as they had done for the Beelers five years before.

In the year ahead, this was all accomplished with the documents being brought together and delivered to Mr. Scull who, in a matter of weeks, got the recording of same in Little Rock. The bottom line was the Ridges were recognized as American citizens, and their property was secured with a recorded title as bought from the Cherokee.

Joe asked John Ridge if he would see that Bruce Loudenhagen's letter to his son Adam be delivered to same. John replied, "Consider it done, my friend!"

Joe and Annie set out for Sylamore, taking obscure trails and spending quiet time reflecting on the loss of George and Caroline. In the blankets at night they had subdued conversations about what life had in store for them in the years ahead and reflected on the past thirty years they had been together. Annie said, "Joe, it's hard to come to grips that we are now the old surviving folks, and the kids are now behind us, if you catch my thought." "Yes, I do my love, but past, present, and future are the best because I have you in my arms in blanket time and alongside me in all the things that daily life brings our way," Joe replied.

"Yes, especially our blanket time, husband dearest," said Annie as she snuggled into Joe's embrace.

"My little hussy!" said Joe, which got him the little slap upside his head.

Arriving back at Sylamore, the Beelers were greeted with the news that Scooter Layne had delivered a healthy baby boy with a loud squall and all ten toes and ten fingers. Attended by midwife Granny Anita, everything went well. Mr. Layne greeted Joe and Annie. At Larry's stern insistence, they had to each take a nip of high wine from his jug. Looking proudly and lovingly at his bride and son, Larry replied, "Scooter, my love. Job well done!"Life and business continued normally, as expected in 1826.

In June, a gentleman came riding into Sylamore on the Polk Bayou trail (Batesville). He was looking for the services of the Beeler smithy, Mr. Layne. He had two knives that needed to be sharpened and repaired. He had a drawing of a new knife design, which he asked Larry Layne to fabricate for him. He also had a Lancaster .40-caliber rifle that needed to be re-bored.

Larry said he would handle the cutlery work, and Ray Dearmon would handle the re-bore job. He was informed that the knives repair and re-bore could be done in a week, and the new knife fabrication would be done in six weeks.

That evening over the supper table in the warehouse, the gentleman introduced himself as Mr. Rezin P. Bowie. He had earlier in the year purchased a 1,500-acre plantation off the southern end of Crowley's Ridge near Montgomery's Point at the confluence of the St. Francis and Mississippi Rivers (present-day Helena) with two of his brothers John and James. They had heard of the smithy's reputation with gun work at Beeler Post/Sylamore. In fact, Rezin said it was a conversation with a young river pilot Thomas Todd Tunstall that directed him here.

Mr. Bowie said that he would like, pending approval by the Beelers, domicile at the post until the knife repair and re-bore of the rifle was complete. Annie, rising to the charm of Mr. Bowie and winking at Joe, said it would be no inconvenience to have Mr. Bowie lodge in the crew bunkhouse. Mr. Bowie thanked Annie and Joe and compensated them for room and board.

Rezin Bowie

In the week that Mr. Bowie spent at Sylamore, the family got to know him well. Annie remarked to Joe during nightly blanket time, "Joe, honey, I like that man despite his views on slavery and as a slave owner. His core principles fall in line somewhat similar to ours!"

The Knife

"My little hussy, he's just won you over with his charm!" which got Joe the customary slap on the head.

"But," Annie said, "I think we will be hearing more of him and his family in the future. Now no more of your smearing remarks on my character, husband dearest!" as she snuggled up close to Joe.

Rezin Bowie departed after about a week with his repaired knives and re-bored .44 Lancaster rifle. Plus, he received the "cherry" reamer that Ray used to re-bore the barrel. In the future, if the rifle needed a re-bore again, the current owner would give this cherry to the gunsmith, and upon completion of the re-bore, the owner would receive the new cherry used for the job. This way the owner and gunsmith always had a cherry reamer in their possession. It's a system that worked well in the nineteenth century and, in most cases, never caused a delay in the re-bore job because of the lack of a cherry reamer.

Joe made arrangements with Rezin that when Larry and Ray finished the custom knife, he would get it to Judge Richard Searcy at Polk Bayou. The judge then would send it to Rezin at Montgomery Point via

Asa McFletch, John Stallings, or Thomas Tunstall. Rezin paid Joe an amount in advance considerably above what Joe would charge, despite Joe's protest that it was too much. But Rezin considered the bill paid in full because of the Beeler family's hospitality and the way they had folded him into the family circle.

After Rezin's departure, Joe conferred with Ray and Larry and asked them to double the order. Larry and Ray responded in unison, "Ahead of you, boss. We've got the second blank in the furnace!"

The following year, on September 19, 1827, Rezin's brother James Bowie was involved in an after-duel brawl down at Natchez, Mississippi, on a sandbar. He was severely wounded by some bitter business competitors but prevailed and survived. This brawl gained stature in legend and became known as The Sandbar Fight. The knife he used, which became part of the legend, was given to James by Rezin as a gift.

The next three to fours years passed quickly as time seems to do with each passing season. One good note is that in September 1828, the Laynes added to their family a healthy little girl full of Larry's vigor and Scooter's resolve.

The trend in the business that Annie and Joe had foreseen became reality. The fur and deer hide part of the trade dropped off and were replaced with bear hides, oil, and grease commodities. Joe said, in his opinion, that this was due to the pressure of increased white settlement and the movement of the tribes to territory further west. At the annual Corn Festival at Norfork, Chiefs John Cake of the Delaware and Peter Cornstalk of the Shawnee insisted that they were staying put despite pressures from the white settlers and the government. As Annie told Joe, "The chiefs' resolve is admirable, but only time will tell."

A visit by Chief John Jolly and his wife Lizzy confirmed what he predicted a couple of years earlier. The new Jackson administration was putting extreme pressure on the Eastern and Western Cherokee and on him to relocate to Oklahoma (which happened that year of 1828). John did say that when Sequoyah introduced the Cherokee language alphabet to the tribes, he was instrumental in helping the Western Cherokee adopt a constitution establishing a tripartite government. John said this organization brought order to the governing of the tribe and provided solidarity when dealing with the U.S. Government. Chief John Jolly expressed his gratefulness to the Beelers for their help in securing the assets and property of the Ridges in

1826. There had been some white settlers who inquired into the ownership of the Ridge property. But with the deeded recordings at the Federal Land Office and the court records in Little Rock filed by Mr. James Scull, all inquires were stopped cold in their tracks.

Down at Little Rock with the death of George Izard in 1828, President Jackson had appointed John Pope as the new territorial governor. Richard Crittenden was replaced as territory secretary with William Savin Fulton. As stated previously, Crittenden's political hay was rapidly burning away. He ran against William Fulton for territorial delegate in 1833 and was soundly trounced. Relative to Governor Pope, Crittenden had a difficult time dealing with Arkansas politics. He had a feud with William Woodruff, editor of the Arkansas Gazette over a government print job and another feud with the "Ledge" over expenditures when building the new State House. Finally, in early 1835 President Jackson replaced him with William Fulton as territorial secretary.

Up in St. Louis, the Missouri River fur trade rivalry had intensified. American Fur had established Fort Union under Kenneth McKenzie as its base of operations. William Ashley had sold his and Andrew Henry's company to his field men, Smith, Sublette, and Jackson. Plus, under contract he had become their sole supplier. The company was renamed the Jackson, Sublette, and Smith Fur Company. Joshua Pilcher had a couple of bad years and in 1829 filed bankruptcy proceedings for the old Missouri Fur Company. This company was started by Manuel

Lisa back in 1808. Lisa passed away in 1820. The Hudson Bay was keeping pressure on the competition up in the Snake and Columbia River basins. Chouteau and Company was holding its own primarily by the Osage (Oklahoma) and Arkansas (White River) trade.

At Sylamore, change also occurred with the passing years. Ray and Linda had completed the purchase of 350 acres from the Federal Government directly adjacent to the 160 acres they already owned. The recording of said purchase was at Polk Bayou (Batesville) where the Federal Land Office had been relocated from Ole Davidsonville in 1822. It was found that Joshua Ashe had a talent for farming, picked up in past years from his time as a slave for various planters/farmers. With the ability to read, write, and cipher, his abilities were enhanced. Ray and Linda formed a formal partnership with the Ashe family on the land, duly recorded by Mr. Scull at Little Rock and the land office at Batesville. Joshua eventually ended up full-time on the farm operation, clearing the land and raising wheat, milo, and small lots of Indian corn. These crops were milled and became backup food for the family. The surplus was sold at the post warehouse store, giving Joshua and his family a fair return for his labor.

Change came to the White River Basin with a mighty impact in the form of the steamboat Waverley, captained by Philip Pennywit, piloted by Thomas Todd Tunstall, arriving at Batesville on January 4, 1831. This was followed up with a visit by the steamboat Laurel on February 9, 1831. The lowering of transportation costs of commodities was dramatic. For example, coffee previously priced at fifty-five cents per pound fell to twenty-five cents, and sugar from twenty cents to ten.

Joe and Annie realized the impact of this reduced overhead and immediately reduced their counter prices accordingly. Their customers, the tribesmen and white settlers, reacted to this price reduction by increasing their business with the Beelers.

In 1833, Mr. Thomas Todd Tunstall bought the steamboat William Parsons at New Orleans and brought it to the White and Black Rivers. He owned a section of land with a grist and sawmill on it located near present-day Magness, Arkansas. In 1839, he bought additional land and established the town of Jacksonport at the confluence of the White and Black Rivers. This location was ideal for the steamboat business because the White River from here to Arkansas Post was wide and deep with a sandy bottom. Above Jacksonport, the river was shallow with numerous shoals where water levels had a more negative impact on steamers' travel. This difference was related by defining the river as the upper and lower White. The Black River's course was more like the lower White with the exception that late summer/early fall lower water levels did inhibit travel somewhat.

With every new form of technology that mankind develops, there is always an upside and downside. In the case of steamboat travel, the upsides were faster travel and lower transportation costs due to the large tonnage able to be carried. The downsides were more accidents and casualties due to navigation obstacles and immature designs of the steam propulsion systems. Diseases were spread more rapidly than the speed of a horse or the paddle power of a canoe.

CHAPTER ELEVEN
TRAGEDY STRIKES AND THE DECLINE OF THE BEAVER

Mid-summer of 1831, the small steamer Ottawa paid a visit to Batesville and continued upriver with stops at Laffertys, Beelers, and the corn festival at Norfork as its final destination. The Ottawa normally conducted business on the Black, lower White, and Arkansas Rivers, with occasional runs between Arkansas Post and New Orleans.

As usual, crew and passengers offloaded and piled into the eatery in the warehouse. Chaos reigned for a while until Annie grabbed a hammer and piece of iron, and after raising a racket with it, got the crowd calmed down. She advised them that this was the first time a steamer had stopped at the Sylamore wharf and had overwhelmed them. But, there were beans, ham hocks on the spit backed up with cornbread in the oven, and everyone would be fed if the captain wasn't impatient to be on his way upriver. The Beeler eatery reputation was well known up and down the river for a hundred miles or more, and the captain replied that the boat wouldn't leave until everyone was fed.

Unbeknownst to anyone, a passenger in the beginning stages of cholera had boarded at the little settlement of Oil Trough, ten miles below Polk Bayou on the Oil Trough Bottoms.

After the Ottawa had departed upstream toward Norfork, chaos still prevailed in the eatery part of the warehouse. Due to the large number of people fed, all eatery vessels, including cups, bowls, and utensils, were dumped into tubs and left overnight before the cleaning proceeded the next day. The usual routine was that the eatery vessels and utensils were cleaned the same day because of low customer traffic and the families and workforce ate two meals a day.

That night a couple of the post curs got into the tubs of unclean vessels and scattered them around the yard. Cleaning up the mess the next morning, the workforce missed a couple of cups and bowls. By chance and the fickle finger of fate, a cup and bowl were items used by the cholera-infected man. Plus, it was the little Layne girl and little Ashe boy playing together who found the cup and bowl.

The usual cleanup of utensils and plates was to wash in hot water and lye soap and air dry. This was done to the previous day's vessels and utensils, and nothing more was thought of it!

Four days later the Layne girl and Ashe boy starting showing symptoms of cholera— fever, upset stomachs, and the beginning of diarrhea. Granny Anita immediately diagnosed it as cholera and supervised the care of the kids. She had the kids put in one of the spare cabins to isolate them from the other families and the workforce. The disease quickly ran its course with fever, severe intestinal cramps, diarrhea, and severe dehydration. Despite giving the kids turkey broth, plenty of water, and Jesuit medicine to try and break the fever, they rapidly declined and three days later passed away. Granny Anita, being exposed to the kids and becoming rapidly fatigued because of the severe care schedule, contracted the disease shortly after and five days later passed away. She was 67.

The families were devastated. Unfortunately, some of the other individuals came down with symptoms, but the daily care of keeping water and soup broth in them got them through the run of the disease. Plus, the patient's age and general good health were in their favor of beating the disease. Cholera generally struck down the very young and very old.

The family tried to piece together the puzzle of why and how despite their grief of lost love ones. Finally, they deduced that the infection came from the steamboat and placed a large canvas sign on the wharf, "Cholera, stop at your own risk!" In fact, after ten days, the Ottawa passed by returning downstream toward Polk Bayou and never stopped. The captain was displaying a canvas sign on the side of the boat, "Cholera, come onboard at your own risk!"

The two children were interred in a quiet grove of cedar trees across the river halfway up the hill behind the river. Granny Anita was interred in a hidden rock crypt about two miles up the north branch of Sylamore Creek. Joe and Annie let it be known to the family that they desired this to be their final resting spot also.

Three weeks after the children's death, the disease had dissipated. By this time, Joe told the family and workforce that it hadn't come from the water supply. All items used in the treatment of the patients was deposited in the spare cabin, and all was burned. Plus, Joe had the workforce move the privies fifty yards further downstream with orders that everyone will use them and not some bush close to the buildings. Also, Annie and Joe decided to close the eatery in the warehouse to the general public coming in off the river. It would be utilized by the family and workforce only.

Despite the three families' deep grief over the loss of loved ones, all understood the realities of life in the nineteenth century.

The year 1832 was a shed-fall year for the fur trade industry. Two years before, Jackson, Sublette, and Smith had sold Ashley's outfit to Bridger, Fitzpatrick, Milton Sublette, Henry Fraeb, and Jean Gervais. This new company was called the Rocky Mountain Fur Company. Competition from American Fur's Western Division and Hudson Bay drove this company into bankruptcy by 1834, despite that the principals were better field men, trappers, and traders. All this intense activity drove the search for the beaver into every watershed in the West, resulting in the country becoming a beaver desert.

A rumor, call it a myth, whatever, wafted from The Continent about a French dandy who returned from China wearing a silk top hat. The social fashion fobs all went gaga over it, discarded their beaver felt hats, and demanded silk.

Beaver prices dropped from three dollars down to two dollars, or less. There was no beaver to be found. If found, it wouldn't even pay the cost of harvesting it.

The Herrmeister Jacob Astor had been tracking the trend of the market for some years, and he decided in 1832 it was time for his exit from the fur business. He divided and sold the American Fur Company in two parts. The Great Lakes Division went to Ramsey Crooks, and the name and western division went to Chouteau, Pratte, and Cabanne of St. Louis. Pierre Jr. (Cadet) finally realized what he had been clamoring for ten years previously. American Fur was in St. Louis despite what Rene had said at the time.

Buffalo robes were the commodity starting to come into demand. Squaw tanned robes were commanding as much as fifteen dollars. Green unworked hides were going for five to seven dollars.

Beeler was seeing this demand with the associate pricing at Sylamore. Joe remarked to Annie and the family that the demand for buffalo robes coupled with the traders' use of Montana brew or Platte River whiskey in the trade would be the start of the decline of the buffalo herds and plains Indian culture as they knew it in 1832.

Joe remarked that the brew served to the Indians was so destructive along with being addictive. Some tribes, like the Blackfeet and Comanche, typically thought it beneath their dignity as hunters to trap the lowly beaver. But relative to buffalo hides, which was part of the culture and necessary for the tribes' well-being, there was no loss of dignity or self-pride in procuring the same. But getting hooked on the traders' brew led to the wholesale slaughter of the bison. Animals were killed, stripped of the hides, and the remainder of the carcasses were left to rot on the prairie. True, the white buffalo hunters were guilty of this outlandish practice, but the red man has shared equally in this blame.

The following recipes show how vile the trade whiskey had become:Montana Brew: 1 qt. alcohol, 1 lb. chewing tobacco, 1 bottle Jamaica ginger, 1 handful red pepper, 1 qt. black molasses, Missouri River water as required.

Platte River Brew (Ole Busthead): 1 gal. alcohol, 1 lb. black twist tobacco, 1 lb. black sugar or molasses, 1 handful red Spanish peppers, 10 gal. river water (in flood), 2 rattlesnake heads per barrel.

The Beelers were saddened to see the Western Cherokee relocated from their Arkansas holdings to the Indian territory in Oklahoma four years previously. This event had been predicted to them by their good friend Chief John Jolly when the Ridges' property had been recorded in Batesville and Little Rock.

President Jackson's policy of Indian removal from east of the Mississippi in what was called the Trail of Tears event was in full swing by 1832 and resulted in the relocation of over 4,000 Eastern Cherokee to Oklahoma. This was done by wagon train and steamboat resulting in many deaths by starvation, weather exposure, and disease.

Trail of Tears

The gathering together of the separate factions of the Eastern with the Western Cherokee set the groundwork for the intertribal squabbles and disputes for the next twenty years. Sometimes resolved, but most times not. Every family has its history and drama!

The Black Hawk War was a brief conflict in 1832. The Beeler's old friend Black Hawk and a group of Sauk, Fox, and Kickapoo, known as the British Band, crossed the Mississippi River into the state of Illinois from Iowa Indian Territory in April 1832. Black Hawk's hatred of the disputed 1804 Treaty of St. Louis, negotiated by the wily William Henry Harrison, which ceded tribal land to the United States, gave him reason to believe the tribes could resettle this land.

U.S. officials, convinced that the British Band was hostile, mobilized a frontier militia and opened fire on a delegation from the Native Americans on May 14, 1832. Black Hawk responded by successfully attacking the militia at the Battle of Stillman's Run. He led his band to a secure location in what is now southern Wisconsin and was pursued by U.S. forces. Meanwhile, other Native Americans conducted raids against forts and settlements largely unprotected with the absence of U.S. troops. Some Ho-Chunk and Potawatomi warriors with grievances against American settlers took part in these raids, although most tribe members tried to avoid the conflict. The Menominee and Dakota tribes, already at odds with the Sauk and Fox, supported the U.S.

Commanded by General Henry Atkinson, the U.S. troops tracked the British Band. Militia under Colonel Henry Dodge caught up with the British Band on July 21 and almost defeated them at the Battle of Wisconsin Heights. Black Hawk's band was weakened by hunger, death, and desertion. The survivors retreated towards the Mississippi. On August 2, U.S. soldiers, with the Sioux, attacked the remnants of the British Band at the Battle of Bad Axe, killing many or capturing most of those who remained alive. Black Hawk and other leaders escaped but later surrendered and were imprisoned for a year.

More and more American settlers were coming into the Arkansas Territory following the Southwest trail to the Mexican-Texas Territory. The last terminus before crossing the Red River was the settlement of Old Washington. It was becoming an economic center, like Little Rock, and Batesville (Polk Bayou).

In addition to piling more settlers into both territories, the typical political issues that came with it were morphing into conflicts. In Texas, the settlers were taking issue with the Mexican Government under the "Napoleon of the West" General Santa Anna's heavy hand of governing. Chief John Jolly's son Sam Houston with Jim Bowie, of Sandbar Fight fame, were in the thick of it. The short story is that General Sam Houston defeated Santa Anna at the Battle of San Jacinto April 21, 1836, and Texas was on the way to becoming a republic.

At Little Rock, Governor Pope was having his political tiffs with the local political wannabes. The wannabes had more political connections than Pope in that President Jackson replaced him with William Fulton, the territory secretary.

The political forces were also in the process of applying for statehood for the Arkansas Territory, which happened in 1836. And the political games were on. It's not in the scope of this narrative to get into the details of that arena.

Joe and Annie realized that the heady days of the fur trade of forty years ago were behind them. The days working for the North West Company out on the plains of the Dakotas and Northwoods of the Upper Lakes were all part of their life's memories, good and bad. True, there were still opportunities to earn a viable living in the fur trade, but it would be hard to get ahead, unlike some of the fur barons did in the previous years, like Astor, Crooks, Ashley, and Sublette to name a few.

They decided after twenty-plus years with Chouteau and Company, it was time to retire and separate themselves from the company. When Chouteau became part of the American Fur Western Division, Joe said, "That's it! I didn't want to be part of it when Ramsey Crooks romanced me about it back in the spring of 1817, and I certainly don't want to now! Annie, my sweet, pack your ruck sac. We're heading to St. Louis to haggle with the company board!"

So in the fall of 1832, Joe and Annie once more packed their rucks and set out for St. Louis on horseback with one pack male. Unlike the hard pace trek in 1826 for the folk's funeral, this was steady, and they soaked up all the sights, sounds, and ambiance of the countryside. Call it foresight or intuition, both felt it might be their last trip anywhere together in this manner.

After two weeks of travel, they arrived in St. Louis and were put up with the Brandseys. Joe contacted the board principals of Chouteau, Pratte, and Cabanne Company and started with William Clark, who sponsored him, with introductions to the new board members who were added with the consolidation of Chouteau, Pratte, and Cabanne.

Joe then worked his way through the conversations on his request for retirement and to be adequately compensated for his company shares.

Within a week, a board meeting was scheduled with the request that Annie accompany her husband to the meeting.

Annie spent a day in the ladies mercantiles with Charlene Brandsey picking an outfit that would be appropriate for the boardroom. On the day of the meeting, when Annie came into the Brandsey's parlor she caused the menfolk to scramble to their feet and stammer words of, "Gosh, Wow! Who's this gorgeous lady!"

Annie said, "Gentlemen, please put your tongues back in your mouths before you bite them. And Joe, my handsome husband in his broadcloth suit, what have you to say?"

Joe remarked, "Anita, my little Magpie, you are more delightful to my heart than the day at Grand Portage when you refused to let me fill your dance card. You're like fine wine, only getting more beautiful with passing time!"

As he swept her into his arms, she whispered in his ear, "I'd rather have my moccasins. These store-bought shoes are killing my feet!"

They spent two long days with the board, haggling and negotiating, backed up by the ledgers Joe and Annie had kept through the years at St. Charles and Sylamore. In the end, they got a fair and equitable deal from the board. That is, all the assets and inventory of Sylamore were theirs, plus it was sweetened with an additional cash outlay of 5,000 dollars. The Beelers took a contract for three years in that Chouteau, Pratte, and Cabanne would be their

Annie Ready for the Boardroom

outfitters and marketers of their furs, hides, and bear commodities.

Celebrating later at the Brandsey's residence, with Governor Clark in attendance, he remarked, "Annie, you know why I got the board to request your attendance at the meeting?"

"Of course, William, my dear friend. A pretty woman in the midst of these ole curmudgeons sets them on their best manners, and from a feminine standpoint, it creates a subtle distraction!"

"Plus!" said Joe, "a woman that knows the business and the numbers to support it! A toast to my bride, Annie!" Glasses clinked all around in a toast to her.

Feeling better about their future outlook, Joe and Annie departed St. Louis on the weekly southbound steam packet, which compared to ten years previously, now offered luxuries unheard of then. Plus, the schedule could almost be depended upon.

Arriving at the post, they looked up their attorney James Scull. They sat down with him and discussed wills and estate planning. Yes! Even in 1832, those who had extensive assets and property found it an advantage to have a will and a plan for disposal of assets and property and pay off the creditors who had bills against the deceased estate. Bottomline, it streamlined the probate process, and the family got the estate of the deceased like the deceased intended. Mr. Scull said he would handle the matter and get all recordings done that the law required, and the family wouldn't be exposed. The four families—the Dearmons, the Laynes, the Ashes, and Jim and Sara—would be covered when Joe and Annie passed on.

Mr. Scull gave the Beelers a letter he had received from John Ridge. In the letter John requested that Joe and Annie come visit Chief John Jolly and Lizzie at their earliest convenience. Chief John Jolly was ailing and wasn't well. John Ridge said, "You can fill in the blanks on what the chief was trying to say to his dear friends."

Chief John Jolly and his Cherokee had been relocated from Illinois Bayou four years previously and were now living at Webbers Falls, forty miles above Fort Smith in Oklahoma territory.

Joe and Annie were put up at Mary John's hostelry to wait for the steam packet Reindeer, Captained by R. Miller, to arrive from New Orleans and continue its run up the Arkansas River to Fort Smith. It was described as a fast running vessel of some 130 tons with a passenger capacity of about seventy-five.

Boarding the Reindeer, it was an uneventful run to Little Rock, but about five miles upriver from Cadron Creek settlement, about two in the morning, the vessel ran aground on a sandbar. After a twenty-four hour effort off-loading passengers and cargo, the boat was finally refloated, reloaded, and continued on its way.

They departed the vessel at Ridge's landing and were ushered into the Ridge's lodging. They asked the Beelers about the convenience of steam packet travel, to which Annie replied, "I think there are still some snags in the system that need to be resolved yet. I much prefer my horse or mule. But like Joe says, the greater tonnage of cargo carried at lower costs sure helps our counter prices!"

Joe remarked, "That's my businesswoman, bride Annie!" which got him the expected peck on his cheek!

Joe and Annie agreed that they would accompany the Ridges to see Chief John Jolly. Annie composed a letter to the kids at Sylamore outlining their plans which might involve an overwinter at Webbers Falls. John Ridge had this letter delivered to Sylamore by one of his Cherokee sons. Packing necessities for the trail, the two couples departed by horseback for Webbers Falls by the November 10, 1832.

The party was forced by an early season storm to overstay a day or so at Fort Smith. The town was a wide-open settlement since the military had departed in 1824 for Camp Gibson eighty miles further upriver.

Upon departure by the army, local settler and land speculator John Rogers had bought large tracts of government land and had expanded the town. With steamboat travel now established, intermittently as it was, coupled with the government Indian removal program, it had brought many new people to the area. The downside of this population increase was the high influx of undesirables, gamblers, prostitutes, and other types that operated outside the law, what little there was!

Perusing the settlement briefly, the Beelers and John and Sara Ridges decided to pitch camp in a secluded grove about five miles outside of town, wait out the storm, and continue on to Webbers Falls.

Maintaining a secure watch during the encampment, no problems with two-legged critters occurred. As soon as the storm started to abate, the party broke camp and were on their way. It took two more days of travel to reach Chief John Jolly's residence at Webbers Falls where they were greeted warmly.

Settling in to a good visit with old friends, Chief John Jolly said that he was craving the company of good friends. It had been four years since the government under President Jackson had finally forced the issue with the Western Cherokee and got them to relocate to Indian Territory. The country wasn't all that different from Illinois Bayou, but after a lifetime of haggling and negotiating with government agencies, the end result was the Indian was always pushed further west toward the setting sun. He was tired and lately hadn't been feeling the spring in his step, even under the tender care of his wife, Lizzie. He was asking the Ridges and Beelers to stay a while and help him recapture in a small way the ambiance of the old days. They replied, "Our pleasure!"

Annie told Chief John and Lizzie that she and Joe had sent a letter to the kids that they would be overwintering until spring with the Jollys. Chief John Jolly looked at Joe and asked, "How does she do that?"

Lizzie hugged the chief and whispered in his ear, "It's women's ways, my dear! Not for menfolk to know and understand!"

Joe laughing heartily said, "Chief John, we are mere mortal men—nothing more, nothing less!"

The Jollys offered the two couples lodging under their roof during their overwinter visit. Annie asked Chief John and Lizzie if they would be offended if she and Joe domiciled in a Cheyenne lodge that they would construct on the back area of the Jolly's farm. "It would be our pleasure if you did!" replied the Jollys. Annie went on to explain that they would also like to experience and recapture, like Chief John Jolly, in a small way some of the ambiance of the days living up on the Dakota prairies and Upper Great Lakes country while they still could.

Over the next ten days, with the help of the villagers of the Cherokee town, Joe and Annie constructed a sixteen-foot diameter Cheyenne lodge in the manner that Fox That Purrs had taught Annie. It contained all the necessities of daily living and enough space to entertain any guests or visitors that dropped in. The Cherokee of the town couldn't do enough for the woman of the bear jaw knife medicine and her man. Plus, they were the honored guests of their beloved Chief John Jolly.

During blanket time, Annie whispered to Joe, "Husband dearest, I am so thankful that the Great Spirit has given us this time together with our dear friends, somewhat in the manner of our younger days. Joe, I don't comprehend the fast changing ways of the world around us anymore. I fear for our children in what the years ahead have to offer them. And I especially fear for Jim, Sara, Stone Hawk, and Fox. Other than what little Cadet had to offer, it's been thirteen years since we have had any news of them. Joe, dearest, I only tell you this, but my intuition tells me that our time in this existence is limited! I don't know why or how, but it causes me great concern!"

"Annie, my dear, I wish I could ease your concerns. I too share your bewilderment about the fast changes each year brings. That's why I wanted to answer Chief John Jolly's request for a visit, because I think he and Lizzie feel the same pressures we do. Regarding Jim, Sara, Stone Hawk, and Fox, I too think a lot about their safety and well-being. I pray often to the Great Spirit for them. And if my manly instinct is right, I think we will hear something in the near future about them!"

"Joe dearest, you know I love you and everything you are, and I trust you in all that you are!" whispered Annie as she snuggled into his embrace.

The three months of the winter season of 1832–1833 passed quickly but was enjoyed by Annie and Joe. True, the seasonal ice and snowstorms broke up the monotony of daily frontier living at times, but the daily stream of visitors to the Beeler's lodge and their time spent with the Jollys and Ridges is what really counted in the "life's good memories bucket."A.P. Chouteau, with a small delegation of Osage headmen, came to see Chief John Jolly about the occasional raids by the young warriors on both sides that seem to never diminish into the background. He and Mr. Bob were delighted to see the Beelers, and time was spent on discussion of current business and politics, including the separation of Astor from the fur business; the intrusion of the silk hat in the marketplace; the increased competition from The Bay Company; the success and failures of the Old Ashley, now the Rocky Mountain Fur Company, and their rendezvous system of supply; the ins and outs of Chouteau and Company now being part of American Fur Western Division; and the Beeler's decision to separate themselves from this entity.

The unrest that was developing in the Mexican-Texas Territory with the high influx of American settlers and the Indians that were the casualties of these events. This was one of the major factors contributing to the downturn in the fur industry.

CHAPTER TWELVE
REJOINING OF THE FAMILY AND THE FINAL YEARS

In late February or early March, Joe and Annie decided to make a side trip to Fort Gibson forty miles upriver from Webbers Falls to the settler's store to stock up for the trip back to Sylamore in a week or more. Arriving on the second day after leaving the falls, the Beelers made their customary camp outside the post's perimeter. Joe and Annie were in the store the last day before their departure when a lean trail-worn man in trader's/Cheyenne garb approached them and said, "Hello, Mother! Hello, Father! It's good to see you are well!" Annie turned slowly and looked the man over in shock and disbelief with recognition pouring over her and suddenly leaped into his arms with such force that she bowled them both over to the floor. She hugged and kissed him while mumbling endearments laced with scolding about an undutiful son not telling his mother for years about where he was, what was he doing, and keeping his family away from their wonderful grandparents! Joe picked his bride and son up off the floor, disentangled Annie from her son's grasp, hugged Jim in a huge bear hug and whispered, "It's good to see you too, Son!"

Annie spun around and shouted, "Where's Sara, that beautiful daughter of mine?" Close by the store's main entrance she spied a strikingly good-looking Cheyenne garbed squaw with a nine-year-old boy and seven-year-old girl clutching her skirts with scared looks on their faces. Running to Sara, Annie embraced her like her son with the same litany of scolding and endearments except she didn't bowl her over to the floor.

Fort Gibson 1832

The two children defiantly glared at Annie and said in unison, "Don't hurt our mommy!" This brought Annie up short for a moment, and then she burst out with, "Yes, these are our grandkids, Joe!"

Sara stepped in, hugged the kids, and pushed them into Annie's embrace saying, "Kids, this is your granny, your daddy's mom!"

Annie closing her embrace, kissed them and whispered to them, "Oh, how I have missed you both and your mom and dad!"

After the noisy reunion, the family retired to the Beeler's camp to start the reacquaintance process. Entering the camp, Sara looked around and said to Jim, "Jim, this is home as I remember it," with tears filling her eyes. Annie embracing her, whispered, "Yes, dear, you are home now!"

Over the next day, Joe and Annie were filled in on the kids' last thirteen years of their lives out on the plains and high country of "The Shining Mountains."

Those thirteen years are a complete narrative of their own, but a short version will be told.

After arriving on the South Platte and building Cadet Post, Stone Hawk, Fox, Jim and Sara, had worked the settler's store for two years. In the fall of 1823, a thirty-member band of Cheyenne came in for trade. The Fox recognized one of the warriors as her cousin. After introductions, she met two more cousins. Also, the band was only one-third the size in people as when she married her northwest man back in 1802.

Cadet Trade Post South Platte River 1821

When the band returned to their home ground in the Medicine Bow Mountains west of the Laramie River, Stone Hawk, The Fox, Jim, and Sara joined with them. The next years passed all too quickly but weren't noticed by them because they became totally immersed in the daily ebb and flow of the band's cultural tie to the passing seasons (i.e., the spring move to the high meadows for sheep and goat hunts; the move to the eastern plains, joining with other bands for the annual Sun Dance celebrations; the fall buffalo hunts and back to the foothills for winter camps; plus, occasional raids for horses into Shoshone, Crow and Piegan (Blackfoot) country and the occasional raids on the band proper by enemy tribes. This was down and dirty defense of the homeland in its basic form).

Stone Hawk and Jim quickly gained acclaim in the band due to their expertise and experience with horses. This was achieved by a few successful raids for horses against the Crow, whose reputation as horse thieves on the plains and mountains was second to none.

Jim also participated in the Sun Dance ceremony, achieved warrior status in the Northern Cheyenne tribes hierarchy, and became a member of the Dog Soldier Society of his band.

It was during one of the early spring raids by Piegan raiders in 1826, that the legend story of the warrior from the eastern rising sun came to be told. A war party of about twenty warriors slipped by the band's scouts and attacked the village main. It was led by a warrior who was the holder of the bear jaw medicine bundle and carried the bear jaw knife. It was his misfortune to encounter Jim in the initial rush. Jim quickly dispatched him with his hatchet, seized the bear jaw knife, scalped and disemboweled him. Splitting open the bear jaw bundle, he seized the bear jaws within and jammed them into the warrior's mouth. He then decapitated him and impaled the head on a lance which he stuck in the ground.

This action caused the attack to break and the Piegan fled the scene in fear with Cheyenne warriors in hot pursuit. Not many Piegan lived to escape, and the captured horses were added to the band's herd.

Jim took the scalp, attached it to the bear jaw knife scabbard, and gave it to Sara to wear. "Thank you husband dearest. I will wear it proudly like our Mother Annie!"

Jim/Little Big Head Warrior from the Rising Sun (Dog Soldier)

Sara and Jim had two children, a boy George/Little Possum, born in 1824, and a girl Caroline/Rain That Falls Softly, born in 1826. Little George had his father's stern personality coupled with quiet wit and humor. Caroline, like her mother, was open and carefree, and she saw no danger from any living thing, hence she could cause no harm or hurt to the same.

In 1825, the band started encountering brigades of fur trappers moving through their home range in the Medicine Bows and territory south. Upon inquiry through Jim and Stone Hawk's interpretation, the band learned of the Ashley and Bay companies' competition for the beaver and the rendezvous system of supply that Ashley-Henry had devised to keep their trapping brigades in the mountains year-round. So, in 1827, the entire band forsake the gathering for the annual Sun Dance Celebration. Instead, they traveled across country via the Sweetwater River, Wind River, Tokgoweea Pass, past the Pilot Knobs, through Teton Pass, and on to Bear Lake, Utah, for that year's rendezvous. It was a memorable experience for all, and upon return to home, Stone Hawk, Fox, Sara, and Jim agreed that a return would be rare in the extreme. Some of the young warriors of the band were victims of the traders' brew.

From the perspective of ole Chouteau traders, the outcome was predictable, coupled with the ridiculous mountain prices. All agreed it was a closed-loop system that they didn't want to be part of. Some of the band listened to them, and some didn't. Stone Hawk commented, "Each person has to follow the way their stick floats!"

In the fall of 1829, the band found themselves in the Bayou Salade (South Park near Fairplay, Colorado) for the fall buffalo hunt. Stone Hawk and Jim parleyed with Fox and Sara on the condition that they accompany their husbands and leave the band to conduct a six-week beaver hunt. Leaving the kids with the cousins, they found themselves on a higher country creek flowage with multiple beaver ponds. After camp was set up, they quickly established a routine. Run the traps in the morning, clean and frame the plews (pelts) during the remainder of the day, and repeat same the following day.

Stone Hawk and Fox That Purrs

One day in mid-October, Jim and Sara left early to check the traplines. Stone Hawk and Fox decided to take advantage of the warm, sunny day and found themselves at a secluded beaver pond where they spent quiet time in intimacy with each other.

Even though the couples had maintained good security, driven by

Lawrence Diedrich

years of hard experience, the circumstances of fate were against them this particular October day. A party of seven young Arapaho braves on a raiding foray stumbled across the couple's camp. Stripping the camp of as much as they could carry, they found the trail Fox and Stone Hawk had taken, which led them to the secluded beaver pond. They found the couple laying in each other's arms after a swim. Seven arrows took their toll. Stone Hawk and Fox never realized what happened. Death was instantaneous.

Quickly scalping the couple and ransacking their belongings, the seven braves quickly departed with their plunder and the pack animals.

Late in the day Jim and Sara returned and found the ransacked camp. With dread overcoming them, they quickly pieced together the story of what happened. They followed the trail that led to the beaver pond and found Stone Hawk and Fox. Shattered with grief and flooded with the memories of Jacques, Jim and Sara covered the bodies with a blanket and kept a quiet vigil until dawn of the following day.

Finding a quiet spot along the shore of the beaver pond, they interred Stone Hawk and Fox in an unmarked grave, asking the Great Spirit to guide them on their way to the hereafter.

Jim looked at his grieving wife through tears and said, "Sara, I promise you, we will find those Arapaho culprits, and they will know and suffer the wrath of the bear jaw knife medicine."

Sara and Jim gathered what remained of the plundered camp and returned to the band's main camp. After hearing Jim and Sara's story, an uproar ensued and all available warriors spread out into the surrounding country looking for trail sign of the raiding party. But nothing was found because the Arapaho bucks knew they had kicked open a hornet's nest of repercussions and left the country quickly and covered their back trail well.

At the end of October when the band headed out to their wintering grounds on the Laramie River, Jim, Sara, and the kids decided to leave the band and head south to Taos. Despite the pleading of the cousins and headmen of the band, they were not to be swayed. At the camp council, Jim told them all that his mind was made up, and he anticipated the Arapaho bucks to show up at a trader's establishment sometime in the ensuing years. And he expected that place would be Taos because of the high number of merchants and trappers that traded and overwintered there.

Packing the kids and their gear on three pack horses, Jim and Sara set out for Taos, covering the 300 miles or so in little over a month, fortunately, getting out of the high country before the early snows.

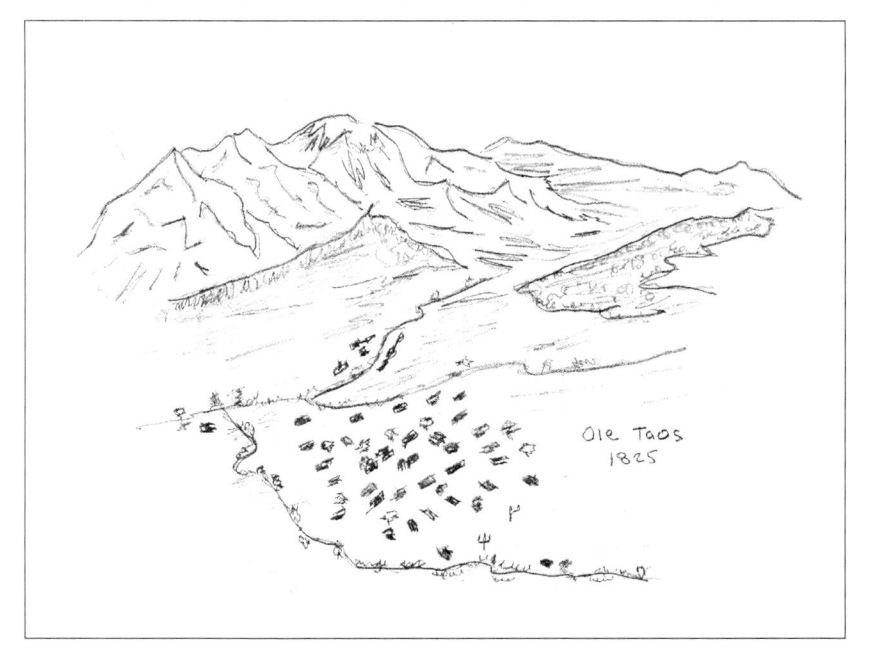

Ole Taos 1825

Once in town, Sara and Jim cleaned themselves and the kids up, purchased Anglo European garb, and went job hunting. Putting forth their best manners, curbing their Cheyenne accents with proper

English, demonstrating their skills in reading, writing and ciphering, they found employment as clerks with the Bent, St. Vrain & Company. Charles, George, Robert, and William Bent partnered in the fur trade with Ceran St. Vrain, also a St. Louis native. They left Missouri about 1826 to explore what is now southern Colorado along the upper Arkansas River to trap for furs and establish a trade business. Within a couple of years, the Bents and St. Vrain had established a trade store in Taos and built two stockades, one on the Huerfano River south of the present town of Pueblo, Colorado, and the other stockade at the mouth of the Purgatoire River on the northern side of the Arkansas River. St. Vrain and the oldest Bent brother, Charles, made the round trips to St. Louis to sell furs and return with supplies.

To set up their trading venture, the brothers used a legacy of their father, Judge Silas Bent. The brothers reinvested the substantial profits of their enterprise to develop their business and primarily focus on trade with the Cheyenne and Arapaho north of the Arkansas River and the Kiowa and Comanche south of the river.

From 1830 to 1832, Jim and Sara kept a vigilant watch on customers that flowed in and out the door. During that time they established themselves as competent employees in dealing with the wide assortment of customers, Anglo, Mexican, and Indian. Their fluency in Cheyenne with excellent sign language skills, coupled with their reading, writing, ciphering, impressed the Bents and St. Vrain, especially Sara. To the male mentality of the times, women shouldn't be able to have those skills plus wear a sacred Blackfoot bear jaw knife with a scalp attached to the scabbard. Sara and Jim were often questioned on the knife, but their stories were always vague and confusing. Finally, their employers just stopped asking, reasoning that it was private business. The impact on the tribal customers was astounding in that they were always on their best behavior when Sara was near and taking care of their needs while in the store.

In the spring of 1832, the company transferred Jim, Sara, and the kids to the post located on the Huerfano River to get a handle on the inventory needed for the fall trade and make up the buyers manifest in time for the Charles Bent and St. Vrain resupply trip to St Louis.

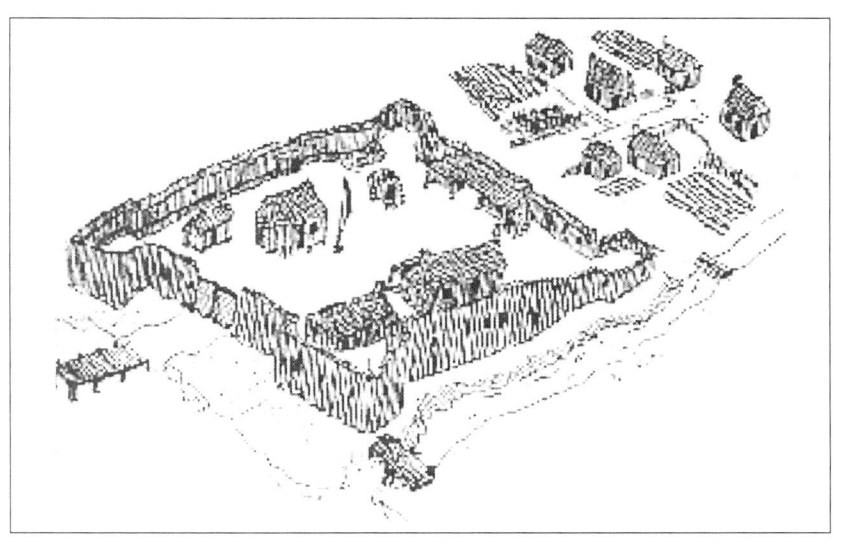

Bent Huerfano River Post

A party of Arapaho came in for trade in late summer or early fall. While taking care of their requests in the settler store, Sara almost lost her composure when she spied a scalp laced with white strands with a small copper broach entwined in it. This scalp was attached to a neck knife scabbard worn by an Arapaho buck. Across the room, Jim spied another buck wearing a knife/scabbard with an attached scalp. Jim also struggled to keep his rage and composure in check. It was Stone Hawk's knife and Fox's broach!Jim looked across to Sara, nodded his head toward the buck, and she likewise nodded in the direction of the other. They both knew these were the ones they had been seeking for the last two years.

Quickly conferring, Jim and Sara realized that they had to get these two culprits separated from their companions. Finalizing the trade transactions with the Arapahos, they gave them two complimentary gallons of trade whiskey and waited for nightfall.

Leaving the kids with their Mexican housekeeper, Jim and Sara found the Arapaho's camp and waited for a couple of hours for the celebrants to drink themselves into the expected stupor. They crept into the camp about one in the morning and found the two culprits. A quick clip alongside of the head with a pistol butt secured their silence. Jim and Sara dragged each to a horse, lashed them on, quietly left the area, and headed for a secluded grove ten miles downriver from the post.

Bearjaw Knife Medicine

Hanging the two culprits with their heads down in a cottonwood, Jim and Sara ripped the knife scabbard and neck knife from them. Taking the two scalps and slapping their faces with them, the two young warriors realized that the couple standing in front of them were the family of the scalps, and vengeance was about to be theirs. Jim took one and Sara the other, and they quickly scalped the two Indians and set a pole in the ground and draped an old bear hide over it. An old stiletto with a bear jaw and the fresh scalps lashed to the handle was stuck into the top of it. Jim then took two bear jaws and stuffed them into the mouths of the Indians, while Sara finished the job by partially disemboweling them.

As the rising sun came over horizon, Jim and Sara left the grove. Jim sternly said, "Let them dwell on their great warrior deeds with what time they have left in this existence!"

With tears flowing from her eyes, Sara whispered, "Jim, dearest, I can only think of Mother and Stone Hawk and that now their spirits can rest in peace!"

When Sara and Jim arrived back at their quarters, they quietly greeted the children and their Mexican housekeeper telling them their business was finished, and soon they would be departing for home and Gramma and Grampa.

Within a day, the moccasin telegraph exploded with the news of the two Arapaho warriors hanging in a cottonwood down the river, done in by the medicine of the bear jaw. No Indian would go within a mile of the grove. Plus, the pretty Métis clerk at the post that wore the Blackfoot bear jaw knife only added to the frenzied beating of the telegraph. Any Indian customer coming to trade at the store was on their best manners and behavior when Sara was there. Powerful medicine, she was, and the red people knew it!Come early January 1833, Jim informed the post factor, George Bent, that they were resigning and planning on returning home to Arkansas. George said he was sad to see them go because they were valued, competent employees, and the company had done well because of them. Jim said they had been gone thirteen years, and it was time to head east for the home hearth. George remarked that after the big ruckus last fall over the bear jaw medicine incident, he privately figured Jim and Sara had finished their real business and would eventually leave. He said he understood unfinished business, especially unfinished family business, and nothing more was said of the matter.

Departing the post the first week of January, the family headed east for the 600-mile trek to Arkansas. Being trail-wise and experienced, the family quickly swung into the routine of nineteenth century travel on the Great Plains in wintertime. That is, keep your eyes on the ridge lines and your nose to the wind. Jim was taking advantage of the fact that the tribes were in winter camps, and any travel away from these camps was only a short distance and local in nature.

Being delayed by a couple of winter storms, detours around two Pawnee camps, and hunting forays for meat, Jim followed the course of the Arkansas River. After seven weeks of travel, the family found themselves at Fort Gibson and encountered Joe and Annie in the settler store.

After a hearty celebration that lasted late into the evening, the family was on the trail before sunrise to Webbers Falls. Annie remarked quietly to Joe that she felt like she had been renewed, like a great weight had been lifted from her. That empty void was now filled knowing Jim, Sara, and those two darling grandkids were back safe in the family fold. Every time she looked their way, the emotion of wanting to hug and squeeze them came bubbling out. Joe told her that he was glad to have been the recipient of that emotion for the last thirty-five years, which promptly got him a light kiss on his cheek! "Ah! My sweet. What a joy you are to me!" replied Joe.

Reaching Chief John Jolly's place at Webbers Falls, introductions were made all around, and the celebrations were renewed again. Upon entering the Beeler's lodge, Sara broke into tears! Annie anxiously asked her what was troubling her. Sara said, "Mother, walking into your lodge, it's so much like Mother Fox and Stone Hawk's. I expected to hear their voices in greeting!"

Annie hugged her and said, "Dear Daughter. In time, all will heal for your heart and mind. You're home with family again!" Even Jim had tears in his eyes when entering the lodge.

His father put his arm around his shoulders and whispered, "In time, Son! In time! All will be well for you, Sara, and the kids!"

Granny Annie couldn't get enough of them or do enough for them, especially Little Caroline. Joe said to Jim, "The Great Spirit help you, Sara, and I if anything harms those little chirps of yours!"

"I know, Dad. That's one of the main reasons that brought us home!" replied Jim.

Little George and Caroline were a bit timid at first, but in a short time were scampering around the lodge and saying, "Mom, Dad, just like Grampaw Stone Hawk and Gramma Fox's place!"

After a week, the family departed with the Ridges for the Ridge's place on Spadra Creek. The lodge wrappings were securely tied to a pack mule. Cutting a wide berth around Fort Smith, the party arrived at Spadra Creek on the third day.

Jim and Sara were mesmerized by the sight of the steamer Reindeer chugging upriver on its run to Fort Smith. They both asked what had happened over the last thirteen years since they left St. Louis. Joe and Annie explained the progress made in travel on the rivers utilizing steamboats. The advantage being shorter travel time, in most cases, and greater tonnage being carried at lower prices. But the downside was navigational hazards on the waterways like snags, sliders, and sandbars due to changing waterways; poor design in the propulsion systems resulting in boiler explosions and fires; and the dangerous spread of disease.

After being gone six months from Sylamore, Joe and Annie were anxious to return there. This return trip, however, was sweetened because Jim and Sara and the grandkids were accompanying them. Joe discussed the aspects of the trip with the family and remarked that he would like to return via horse, thereby avoiding the chance of contracting a disease if traveling by steamboat. Everyone agreed because all were of the same mind that following the trails back to Sylamore would give more time for the family to reconnect with each other. Plus, all were trail-wise and experienced in this mode of travel.

During the last camp before reaching Sylamore, Annie felt frisky and suggested to Joe, Jim, and Sara that she and Joe would ride into home alone. Jim and Sara and the kids would follow a couple of hours later unannounced, thereby giving everyone else the joy of Jim and Sara's return. Everyone agreed and made it so.

Joe and Annie arrived mid-morning and were warmly welcomed by the Dearmons, Laynes, Ashes, the grandkids, and the workforce. They got settled in and were briefed by Ray, Linda, Larry, and Scooter on the state of the business, and they, in turn, were briefed by Joe and Annie on the separation of Sylamore from Chouteau and Company.

During the discussions, Linda noticed her mother's giddiness and all around happiness and remarked, "Mother! Are you alright? I've never seen you like this before. What is wrong with you?"

Annie hugged Linda. " Linda, there is so much to be happy for. Joe and I are home. Everyone is healthy. And the business is on a solid foundation. You, Ray, Larry, and Scooter have done a fine job managing the daily operations. Joshua and Lisa have had a good return on last year's crops. I couldn't be more happy!"

Linda wouldn't let it go. "Mother, I don't know. What is it that you and Paw are not telling me?"

Annie snapped, "Linda! Hush! Stop being suspicious like me! Enjoy the day. It's beautiful." Turning away, she changed the subject back to the business at hand. Joe later quietly remarked to Annie, "My sweet, that daughter of ours is too much like you! Fifty-five percent like you. Like you say to me, 'It's your fault!' And in this case, I'm laying it on you! Remember, I'm just a mere mortal man—nothing more, nothing less!" Around noon when the families and workforce were having dinner in the warehouse eatery, Ray spied a dusty trail-worn Indian family riding into the yard and slowly dismounted. Ray poked Joe and said. "Joe, if my recognition is right, I'd say that Indian family that just rode in is Cheyenne and a bit off their home ground."

Joe's comeback was, "Ray, right on! You haven't lost your touch! Why don't you or Linda go take care of them!"

Ray rose from the table and said, "Come on Sparrow. Let's see what we can do for these Cheyenne."

Ray approached the couple with their two kids and asked how he could help them. The man looked Ray and Linda square in the eye and said, "Sarge, Sparrow, it's good to see you both are well!"

Linda and Ray were dumbfounded for a moment, with Linda finally flinging herself in the man's arms and shouting, "Dear Brother, are you a ghost? No, I feel you! You are real!"

Turning to Sara, she tightly embraced her and whispered, "Sister! Oh how happy it makes me to be able to hug you and know you are home at last!" And the next enveloping hugs were for the kids, who by this time were used to this kind of welcome from Grannies and Aunts.Ray threw a bear hug on Jim and said, "Welcome home, Brother. It's been too long!"

Linda shouted, "Mother, Father! I have a bone to pick with you both!"

After introductions were made all around, everyone retired to the dinner table, and the celebrations commenced for the rest of the day and late into the evening. The tale of the last thirteen years in the Shining Mountains was retold. During blanket time after a day or two of getting settled in, Sara told Jim she appreciated taking up residence in the folk's Cheyenne lodge, but would it be possible to permanently reside in a dogtrot cabin like the folks, Laynes, Dearmons, and Ashe families? Jim said it would be no problem, and after talking it over with Joe, it was made so! Within a month, Sara and Jim and the kids were ensconced in their new dogtrot cabin home.

Life settled down with Sara and Jim being folded into the family and business routine.

Their routine included Jim working with Linda and Sara to take over management of the daily operations of the warehouse and settler's store. This freed up Ray who moved to the smithy's shop with Larry to concentrate on fabrication and repair of firearms.

The yearly inventory supply which in years past had been handled by keelboat was now shipped in by steamer. By getting the yearly resupply manifest to Mr. James Scull by the end of January, he could forward it to St. Louis and have it delivered by the William Parsons steamer owned and captained by Thomas Todd Tunstall. If it was timed right with the spring high water flow in the White River, the inventory could be offloaded right at the Beeler's wharf. Plus, the year's supply of fur, hides, bear robes, grease, and oil could be shipped out on the same trip. The plan worked, for the most part, but the foibles of nature and manmade ways could be counted on to interfere. Therefore plans B and C had to be planned and implemented when required.

Life settled down somewhat relative to the seasonal changes, the economy, and the ongoing politics of business and politics down at Little Rock, up at St. Louis, and far away in Washington D.C.

During blanket time at night with Joe, Annie whispered, "Husband, dearest, the last two passing seasons since Jim and Sara's return have been good to us. The grief over the loss of our loved ones has faded somewhat and is manageable. And I'm content."

"Yes, my sweet, I am too, and you will always be the sweetness in my cornbread." Annie gave Joe a long, deep full kiss that led to other pleasurable intimacies between them.

After regaining her breath, Annie said, "Joe, honey, you're always thinking of your stomach!"

The schooling of the kids became a matter of intense discussions between the adults.

Ray and Linda's Matt and Shana were blossoming into young adults at fifteen and fourteen years old. Their schooling at been handled somewhat by Grandma Caroline, but needed to have the final polish applied.

The Layne boy, the Ashe girl, and Jim and Sara's boy and girl all needed schooling in reading, writing, and ciphering. Plus, Joshua and Lisa expressed a need for more schooling on their ciphering skills.

So, Scooter stepped forward and took over the schooling responsibilities assisted by Granny Annie. Five hours a day were set aside for schooling and no interruptions were tolerated! Annie quietly told Joe that it allowed her to be around her darling grandkids.

The year 1835 passed uneventfully into 1836. May settled into June, and the Arkansas heat and humidity settled in with intensity. In the evenings it was customary for the family, especially the kids, to cool off with a swim in Sylamore Creek. One evening found the Ashe boy, Layne boy and Jim and Sara's boy and girl, watched over by Granny Annie, taking a dip in the deep hole by the spring flow out of the blacksmith shop water wheel. One of the kids screamed, "Snake!" Annie jumped to her feet, looked and saw three water moccasins swimming toward little Caroline!

Seizing a small oak limb, she dove into the creek, placing herself between the snakes and Caroline screaming, "Get help!" and thrashing wildly at the snakes to distance them from Caroline. She was successful in separating Caroline from the snakes, allowing her to gain the bank of the creek and safety.

Water Cottonmouth

Unfortunately, before help arrived, the moccasins bit Annie three times about her neck and face. Jim, Joe, and Larry came on the scene quickly, dispatched the snakes, and pulled Annie from the creek. Hugging her to his chest, Joe broke down, but before Annie lost consciousness, she whispered, "Joe, my love, I will be waiting for you! I'm seeing the face of the young Great Spirit. He tells me all is well! Goodbye, my love."

They moved Annie into their home cabin, and she never regained consciousness. Late in the evening, the poison had done its work. She passed on. Annie was fifty-five years old.

The next day the whole family gathered at the hidden rock crypt and laid Annie to rest next to her mother, Anita.

The family dealt with the grief, each in their own way. Joe was emotionally drained and devastated. He struggled through each day and night. It was the emptiest with the spot alongside him not filled by

Annie as it had been for the last thirty-eight years. He lost the edge to his life.

Fortunately, the organization of the family business coupled with the estate planning done by Annie and Joe with Mr. Scull allowed things to run smoothly with good oversight by Jim, Ray, and Larry Layne.

Joe allowed his health to run down in spite of the continual urging from the family. He lost weight and had trouble fighting off the malarial fevers and numerous allergies that develop living in a hot, humid summer climate in Arkansas.

In the spring of 1838, Joe developed pneumonia after struggling with a bad bout of malarial fever. The women taking care of him called a gathering of the family. Scooter, getting straight to the point, said, "Joe is dying. He has lost the will to live since Annie has passed. All we can do is make him comfortable and pray!"

Joe in his delirium knew he was surrounded by the family. He recognized their voices. "Kids, don't worry for me! The best is ahead where I will be joining your mother and Granny Annie! Take care of each other and love one another and your fellow man. A rich and rewarding life will be yours!"

Joe's vision dimmed and he felt a warm feeling flow over him. He gradually couldn't hear the families' voices anymore. The smiling face of a young man with a beard and piercing hazel eyes came into Joe's vision. He heard the young man say, "Joe, my good servant, a job well done. Now enjoy a well-earned rest with the ones you love. I read your question on who I am, but you know the answer."

"My Lord Jesus, you are The Great Spirit!"

"Well spoken, my good servant. Now, there are some people that have been anxiously waiting for you."

With that, Joe found Annie in his arms whispering, "I told you, dearest, that I was waiting for you, and you've met our good friend, The Great Spirit, Jesus!"

Joe looked around and found himself surround by George, Caroline, Granny Anita, Stone Hawk, Fox, Jacques, Shingabis, Celeste, Francisco Alberti, the Ashe boy and Layne girl, and Kathy Brandsey. And the best was yet to come!

Joe Beeler was interred in the rocky crypt alongside Anita and his bride, Annie.

He was fifty-eight years old.

The Great Spirit Jesus

THE END